CHORAZIN

The Weird of Hali

Novels by John Michael Greer

The Weird of Hali:

Others:

CHORAZIN

The Weird of Hali

Book Three

John Michael Greer

Published in 2023 by
Sphinx Books
London

British Library Cataloguing in Publication Data

A C.I.P. for this book is available from the British Library

ISBN-13: 978-1-91257-393-6

Typeset by Medlar Publishing Solutions Pvt Ltd, India

www.aeonbooks.co.uk/sphinx

The mound was old before the white man came.
The crown of ancient stones upon its crest
Stood long before the first sail ventured west
From Europe's crowded shores. What secret name
It might have had in those far distant years
No legend tells. It stands against the sky
Forgotten, while strange clouds go drifting by
And breezes hint at vanished hopes and fears.
Yet those who dwell beneath it murmur low
That deep within the mound, with vast wings furled,
Some mighty presence from the elder world
Lies bound in sleep. How long? They do not know.
They wait and watch, and chant their ancient lore,
Until the hour the Sleeper sleeps no more.

                            — "The Mound" by Justin Geoffrey

CONTENTS

CHAPTER 1

THE OLD ONE'S TOKEN

The stray glint of mirrored sunlight came from across the valley, where the land swept up from the sinuous silver line of the upper Miskatonic River toward the rounded hills beyond. Owen Merrill paused on the porch of the old school building, raised a hand to screen his eyes from the midday sun. A short beard the same color as his sandy hair made him look older than his thirty-one years, and his flannel shirt and jeans could have been worn by any other man in Dunwich, but the blank look the villagers cultivated as part of their protective camouflage didn't come naturally to him. His eyes narrowed as he strained to see whatever had caught the sun.

For most of a minute he saw nothing but the familiar ragged patchwork of forest and field, broken here and there by the lines of gray fieldstone walls and the gambrel roofs of outlying houses. Then, finally, another glint showed, a little to the right of where the first had been, and he made out the tiny shape of a car picking its way slowly along the road to Dunwich.

Cars were anything but common on that road. Since the state highway had gone in more than half a century before, cutting across the landscape on the far side of those rounded hills, few people remembered the old Aylesbury Pike at all. Fewer still turned left at Deans Corners onto the unmarked and poorly maintained road that led up into the hills from there.

1

These days, a car headed toward Dunwich usually meant one of two things: either some poor soul had gotten hopelessly lost among the backroads of north central Massachusetts, or—

Or the ancient conflict that brought Owen to Dunwich, having first nearly cost him his life and everything that mattered to him into the bargain, was reaching out for him again.

He went down the stairs at a trot, slowed to a brisk walk as he reached the cracked and weathered sidewalk. The houses he passed looked desolate and forbidding, but that was more camouflage. The old families of Dunwich had long since mastered the art of hiding themselves behind a facade of decadence and destitution, and the more recent arrivals had learned the same lesson in an equally harsh school. Other eyes, he knew, had already spotted the approaching car, and other hands would be preparing for trouble, if that was what its arrival meant.

That offered him little comfort. He had a reason to worry about the renewal of the old struggle he hadn't had two months before.

He passed the big barnlike place where Ken and Billie Whateley lived with their six kids. On the other side of it was a little house, scarcely more than a cottage, with the porch in front apparently half fallen in—it wasn't, but the hanging boards looked very convincing—and roses long since gone feral blocking most of the front yard with a barricade of thorns. A sharp turn toward what looked like the densest part of the thicket, and another turn in an unlikely place, got him through the barricade and into the side yard. From there he ducked around to the kitchen door, wiped his feet on the mat, and went inside. "Laura?" he called out. "There's a car coming."

"I know," a familiar voice said from the living room. "Janey Bishop came by about five minutes ago. Everyone's been warned."

He crossed the kitchen, went through the open doorway into the living room. "Glad to hear it. With any luck it's nothing to worry about."

"Oh, I know," said Laura.

She was sitting on an old but serviceable couch in a patch of stray sunlight, brown curling hair cascading down past her shoulders, light brown skin tinged with something between olive and green—the heritage of the Deep Ones, that last— glowing in the light. Skirt and short-sleeved sweater showed curves that had filled out since they'd come to Dunwich, and the main reason for those changes lay nestled in her lap: a bundled shape whose little plump face was closed in on itself in sleep.

Laura patted the couch next to her. "Might as well make yourself comfortable."

"True enough." He settled on the couch, put an arm around her. "How's Asenath?"

"Fine. Annabelle says she's frighteningly well-behaved." She nestled against Owen, and the two of them considered the infant, who just then made a querulous sound in her throat.

A light brown tentacle snaked out from beneath Laura's skirt, hooked something from the end table past the arm of the couch, brought it back: a little stuffed toy octopus covered with brightly colored cloth. A moment later the toy dangled over the infant's face, swung back and forth by slight motions of Laura's tentacle. Asenath made a gurgling noise that sounded pleased, and flailed vaguely at the toy with one small hand.

"Everything's closed up at the school?" Laura asked then.

"Yeah." He shook his head. "I'm still trying to get used to the idea of school shutting down for planting and harvest."

She glanced at him, smiled. "I know. I'm sure I'd have at least as much trouble getting used to things if we were outside."

"Oh, granted." He bent over and kissed her. Just as their lips met, a knock sounded on the back door.

Owen muttered something uncharitable, heaved himself up off the couch, went into the kitchen. "Oh, hi, Emily. What's up?"

Emily Sawyer was one of only four seventh-degree initiates in the town's Starry Wisdom church, a feisty old woman with a taste for loud sweaters. She looked uncharacteristically worried. "You heard about the car, I reckon." Owen indicated that he had, and she went on. "D'you know a Justin Martense? Young man, light blond hair, eyes two different colors?"

"No," said Owen. "Why?"

"He's asking for you, by name. Drove up to the general store, went right in, and asked Jemmy Coles if he knew where to find you."

Owen was silent for a moment, then: "Did he say why?"

"Nope. Said he had some kind o' business with you that wasn't for anyone else's ears." She paused, went on. "I cast the bones this morning, of course, and I think you should meet him. Down at the Standing Stone, maybe? That ought to be safe if anything is."

Owen considered that and nodded. "Okay. I'll be down in fifteen minutes."

* * *

The Standing Stone was the one eatery in Dunwich and also the town's one tavern, a block south of the Starry Wisdom church. Old Mike Whateley had given it that name back in the nineteen-seventies, when a trickle of fans of the horror writer H.P. Lovecraft started finding their way into town, and the old man paid some craftsman in Aylesbury to make a fancy wooden sign for it, with the name in some ornate font and a stone circle above that. These days, the town rarely saw a Lovecraft fan once in three or four years, but the sign remained. From the street, the name wasn't hard to figure out: Sentinel Mountain loomed up in the middle distance, and the circle of stones that topped it could be seen in most weathers.

Out in front of the Standing Stone sat the car Owen had spotted from the steps of the school, a blue compact better than ten years old, with New York license plates well caked with dust. Owen glanced at it and then at the windows beyond it, saw a lone figure sitting at a table on the restaurant side of the building, a man in his early twenties with hair the pale color of ripe barley, his shoulders slumped forward and his chin down.

The hinges of the glass door squealed in protest as Owen went in. The man at the table glanced up at him with no sign of recognition. He had a brown canvas barn coat on, open in front, and the shirt under it was black, giving his pale skin a bloodless look. His eyes were disconcerting; Emily Sawyer had mentioned that they were two different colors, but she hadn't said that one was pale blue and the other a brown so dark it looked black in the dim light. They reminded Owen of something he'd read, but just then he couldn't remember what it was.

"I hear you're looking for me," Owen said.

"You're Owen Merrill?"

"Yeah."

The man nodded, and then drew in an unsteady breath. "And you don't have any clue who I am. My name's Justin Martense, and somebody told me you might be able to help me, if anyone can."

Owen considered that, then sat down on the other side of the table, facing the younger man. Before he could decide what questions to ask first, Billie Whateley popped out from the kitchen. She was short and stocky and well on the far side of forty, with bits of silver showing in her brown hair and a first few wrinkles on her face, and she wore a worn but clean apron over a plain cotton house dress. "What can I get you?"

"Can I have a bacon cheeseburger and fries?" Justin asked.

"Sure thing, hon. Something to drink?"

Justin gave her a doleful look. "Do you have any beer that's not yellow?"

Billie glanced at Owen, who nodded fractionally. "I can do that," she said then. "Our local brew's pretty dark, though."

"That would be great."

She turned to Owen, got his order—BLT on rye, potato salad, another brown ale—and vanished into the kitchen. Owen watched her go, and then said to Justin, "Dark beer drinker?"

Justin glanced up at him. "Yeah. I've been in Europe for the last four years. I thought I hated beer until someone I met in Ghent talked me into trying a glass of bock. You?"

Owen nodded. "We might just get along."

He'd meant it as a joke, something to dispel some of the tension that stood out in the set of the younger man's shoulders. He hadn't expected the bleak and frightened look that appeared suddenly in his face and just as suddenly vanished. "I hope so," Justin said after a moment.

They talked about nothing in particular while Billie What-eley ferried out the beers—tall glasses full of something dark as molasses, with creamy foam on top—vanished again, then brought out sandwiches and sides. Once she'd returned to the kitchen, Justin said, "If you don't mind, I'm just going to tell you my story. I can't think of any better way to explain why I'm here and what kind of help I need. You're probably going to think I'm crazy, but all of it's true."

Owen allowed a noncommittal nod.

"Okay." He downed some of the beer. "My family's from Lefferts Corners in New York State, up in the Catskills. We've been there since the Dutch settlement. A long time before that, though, one of our ancestors got involved in something really bad, and we have to undo it." With a little uneasy laugh: "The family curse. That's the crazy part."

"No," Owen said. "Those happen."

Justin looked at him for a long moment and then nod-ded, once. "It's like this," he said. "In every generation, one of us—one of my relatives, a Martense, a Hasbrouck, a Typer, a van Kauran, it doesn't matter, so long as they're descended from old Gerrit Martense—gets called. There's a voice you hear in your dreams, begging for help, begging to be set free.

And there's a place just this side of Buffalo, a little town called Chorazin. There's a hill there called Elk Hill. One after another, they go there, and nobody ever sees them again."

"And you're the one in this generation," Owen guessed.

"Yeah." He busied himself with his burger for a while, then took another swallow of the beer. "I started hearing the voice right after I turned twelve. Maybe once every six months or so, but I knew what it meant, and it happened more and more often the older I got. I talked to my Aunt Josephine, who's the family historian, and I talked to some others who knew the stories.

"Sooner or later I have to go to Elk Hill, I know that, but I decided that I was going to find out—well, whatever I needed to find out, so that I knew what I was supposed to do when I got there, to undo whatever it was that our ancestor did. That's why I went to Europe after I left high school; the family has some money, so I could afford it. I read some really strange books, and saw some very weird things, but I couldn't find what I needed to know. And—" He stopped, considered the bottle of beer, downed another swallow. "The call kept getting stronger. It's not just that it comes more often. You can't ignore it, and the more you hear it, the harder it gets to resist. It's especially bad before May Day and Halloween."

Owen nodded. The date was April 24.

"So a week ago I was in Paris. I had a day to kill before I flew back to New York City, and I was sitting on a bench by the Champs Elysées with my head in my hands. I knew that once I got home, I was going to go to Elk Hill whether I wanted to or not, and all of a sudden someone was sitting next to me. I didn't notice him sit down; he was just there."

A cold chill rose up Owen's neck, and he knew exactly what Justin was going to say next.

"He was tall," the younger man said, "taller than anyone else I've ever seen, and he wore a long black coat and a black hat with a wide brim. He had brown skin and a hooked nose— he looked like an Arab or something like that. But he said, in English, 'You hear the call, and you don't have the least idea what to do about it. Am I right?'

"I just stared at him, and he laughed and said, 'I don't need to warn you that you're caught up in something very dangerous. What I can tell you is that there are people who have the knowledge you need. If you're willing, I'll send you to one of them, who can help you do what needs to be done.'

"So I said yes, please and thank you, and he told me to go to the town of Dunwich in Massachusetts—he told me which turn to take off the old Aylesbury Pike—and ask for Owen Merrill. He gave me something to show to you, and then—"

He stopped, considering Owen with his disparate eyes, and then made himself go on. "And then he wasn't there. I don't know what happened. He was gone, and I sat there and tried to figure out if I'd just gone crazy."

"So did I," said Owen.

Justin stared at him for a long moment. "Then you do know him."

"Yeah."

"Okay." He slumped, visibly relieved. "Then I'm not crazy. Or not entirely."

He reached inside his barn coat, then, and pulled something out from an inner pocket. "Here's the thing he gave me," he said. "He seemed to think you would recognize it."

Even though Owen knew what the token had to be, the sight of it jolted him like an electric shock. It was an ornate ring of dark metal set with eight tiny stones the gray-green color of the northern oceans, and around it hovered a faint voorish shimmer on the edge of vision, testimony to the power that once flowed into it from an unhuman hand. Seeing it, Owen knew without a doubt who had given it to Justin Martense.

* * *

"Nyarlathotep," Laura said.

"Yeah." Owen stared at nothing in particular. "It looked just like the ring he gave me when we first got here."

They were sitting on the couch in the living room again. Evening sun glowed red against the curtains, and Laura had two oil lamps lit—the electricity in Dunwich had gotten less and less reliable in recent years, and most of the residents had simply shrugged and dusted off lamps they'd saved from their grandparents' time. Little Asenath had finished nursing, and lay nestled against her father's shoulder as he patted her back and gently bounced her up and down, waiting for the inevitable burp.

"Do you have any idea what he wants you to do?"

"No. That's just it. Martense is looking for something that might tell him what the voice in his dreams and the rest of it is about, and what to do when he goes to Chorazin. I have no idea what might help him. I've got a basic knowledge of the old lore—"

"You've got a lot more than that," Laura interjected.

He made a skeptical noise in his throat. "I could spend fifty years just studying the *Necronomicon* and still have plenty more to learn from it. The thing is, I don't know enough to answer his questions—and I ought to know more than I do. Some of the things he's said ring bells I just can't place. I've even heard of Chorazin before, but damn if I remember where."

"That one I can answer," she said. "Ben Moore, Cassie's husband, is from there. A lot of people from Dunwich went there twenty-some years ago, the last time there was trouble here, and Ben and Cassie go back there for deer season most years."

Owen looked at her, nodded after a moment. "That's right," he said. "I remember now. But there's something else that just won't surface."

He considered the baby in his lap, then closed his eyes and let out a ragged sigh.

"You're going with him," Laura said then.

That brought his gaze back to her, hard and fast. "Now of all times—"

"Owen," she said. "You know that can't matter to the Great Old Ones."

He stared at her a moment longer, then slumped and looked away. "Yeah. I know."

Laura waited for a little while, and then asked, "So what's going on now?"

"Martense is staying in the Dunwich Inn Motel overnight. Emily and Bill Sawyer are feeding him and making sure that he's who and what he says he is. The other initiates will be doing a ritual later on, to find out what they can from the Great Old Ones. That's what I know."

"I can tell you one other thing," she said. "We're having dinner with Dad and Annabelle tonight, and afterwards the other priestesses are going to join us and we're going to put a blessing on you to keep you safe."

He took that in. "You knew."

"As soon as you went down to the Standing Stone."

"You're good," he told her.

"Well, I've got some talent for the priestess work—"

"You've got a lot more than that," Owen interjected, smiling.

She laughed, then, and reached for his hands. "Owen," she said, "we'll just have to do what we can and hope for the best. I know you didn't grow up with all this, but I did. I'll be fine. Asenath and I will stay with Dad and Annabelle while you're gone, and I'll work spells and pray to Father Dagon and Mother Hydra for you, and wait until you come back and I can put my arms around you and give you Asenath to kiss, and everything will be just the way it's been."

That was the way of the Innsmouth folk, he knew that well enough, and she'd done the same thing herself, putting her own life at risk in the service of the Great Old Ones while others waited and hoped. This time, though—

This time the quest was his.

Words seemed superfluous just then. He put his arms around her and drew her to him, twisting at the waist so he didn't disturb Asenath. She clung to him, and the tentacles she had in place of legs wrapped around his ankles in an additional caress.

"I wish I could tell you how much I love you," he said.

Her laugh was muffled by his shoulder. She looked up at him then, still laughing, and said, "I think you manage pretty well."

Asenath started fussing then, and he let go of Laura, straightened up, and found the little octopus toy to dangle above her and calm her.

* * *

That night, after dinner with Laura's father and stepmother and the blessing ceremony with the priestesses of the Esoteric Order of Dagon, after little Asenath was sound asleep and the house was silent, they made love for the first time since Asenath's birth, gently, tasting every nuance of each other's bodies. Afterward, Owen slept hard.

Later, toward dawn, he rose slowly into the land of dreams, and he glimpsed a city in a valley, a snowy peak overlooking the sea, and galleys sailing out of the harbor toward distant regions where the sea met the sky. The images began to draw together into a dream worth remembering, but then dissolved into something else: a hill with steep sides and flattened top, too regular to be natural, seen from a distant height against a dim formless landscape beyond it. Then, so faint he could barely be sure he heard anything at all, came the whispering voice.

Help me, it implored him. *Free me*.

He woke with a start and a sudden wordless cry, and found himself in his bed. Warmth and the soft sound of breathing spoke of Laura's presence next to him. She stirred and managed a questioning sound, and he kissed her cheek and murmured, "It's okay," and felt her roll onto her other side and sink back into sleep. The first hints of daylight had begun to filter in through the curtains, though, and he knew better than to try to follow her. Since his stint in the Army almost a decade back, he'd rarely slept past first light, but this time it was more than that. The whispering voice hovered in his memory, chilling him.

He slid out of bed, pulled on flannel pajamas, slippers, and a threadbare bathrobe, and checked Asenath in her cradle— an elegant piece from Innsmouth that had held Laura and her father in its time, with the slats on the sides shaped like tentacles and the Elder Sign carved for protection at head and foot. She fussed at him while he changed her diaper but settled down quietly afterwards, and he slipped out of the room. Their bedroom was on the same floor as the living room and kitchen, for Laura's sake—stairs were a strain for her to climb—so he closed the door as quietly as he could before going into the living room.

He spent fifteen minutes at his Starry Wisdom meditations, sitting on a bare wooden chair in the living room with his hands resting on his thighs and his eyes shut sensing the voor, the subtle force of life that flowed through all things. Another twenty minutes went to his morning workout: pushups, situps, half a dozen others, to chase the sleep from his muscles and keep from sliding down the slope on the far side of thirty any faster than he had to. That done, he fired up the woodstove so they'd have hot water to wash with, and got a kettle on the fire for the day's first cup of tea. All the while, questions he couldn't answer chased one another in circles through his mind. He didn't have any Dutch ancestors at all, as far as he knew, much less any from the Catskill country of New York, so the whispering voice—if it was more than a stray nightmare—stayed unexplained. For some reason, though, the names of Justin Martense and the others the young man mentioned kept running through Owen's mind, as though he'd heard them before.

The kettle whistled at him, and just then the memory finally surfaced. He laughed, got his tea steeping, and went into the living room, where a bookshelf he'd made from raw lumber held those of their books that didn't need to be hidden away from casual observation: some of them books he'd owned when he lived in Arkham, some from Laura's home in Innsmouth, some they'd collected since. Over on one side of the top shelf was a row of old paperbacks with garish covers and browning pages. He pulled out one and flipped through it, then another and another. It was the fourth book that finally gave him the thing he needed.

He went slowly back into the kitchen, sat at the kitchen table, sipped tea and read while flames flickered in the woodstove's little window and water hissed and gurgled through the piping behind it. Outside, the morning unfolded, and the first sunlight caught on the standing stones atop Sentinel Mountain, just visible through one window. The book had nothing to say about whispering voices pleading for freedom, but it told him something that might be more important. He began to nod slowly to himself as the first pieces of the puzzle fell into place.

* * *

Sure of his course, then, he slipped out the door into the cool morning to call on John Whateley, the senior elder of the Starry Wisdom church, to find out what they'd learned from the Great Old Ones in the ceremonial the night before, and then crossed the street to talk to Emily Sawyer, to hear her impressions of Justin Martense. Finally, he went back home, woke Laura, sat on the bed and discussed the whole thing with her. That wasn't simply a matter of affection or courtesy; Laura was an initiate of both the Starry Wisdom church and the Esoteric Order of Dagon, a priestess of the Great Old Ones well versed in the old lore.

Afterward, he walked down to the Dunwich Inn Motel, a bleak and unnerving two-story cinderblock building across a side street from the Starry Wisdom church. Four generations of Dunwich folk had devoted their spare hours to give it an unhallowed and unwelcoming air to scare off uninvited visitors, and they had not labored in vain.

"Oh, yes, I heard all about it yesterday from John," said Sarah Bishop, the plump and grandmotherly manager of the hotel. They stood in the lobby, which featured shabby furniture, peeling paint, and seemingly crude paintings that did an exquisite job of emphasizing all the most forbidding qualities of the local landscape. "I sent word to Ben's folks in Chorazin so they know to expect you, and Cassie found you a highway map." She pulled it out of the big front pocket of her apron, folded it open. "Chorazin Road ain't on it," she said, "but Ben drew it in, right here." She tapped the map. "You take the Emeryville exit. You'll have to keep a close eye out for the turn, though—I don't know as I'd have found it if I was driving there myself."

Owen thanked her. As he finished, one of the doors down the first floor hallway rattled open, and Justin came out, looking haggard.

They said the appropriate things, Owen suggested breakfast, and the two of them left the motel and headed up the main street toward the Standing Stone. "Bad night?" Owen asked.

"Yeah."

"I've found some information that might help," Owen said then. "We can talk about it over food, if you like."

Justin took that in, nodded. "Please."

The door of the Standing Stone gave another cry of protest as Owen pulled it open, waved Justin through. They went to the same table as before, waited for the minute or so before Billie Whateley came bustling out from the kitchen and asked them what they wanted.

"Anything you recommend?" Justin asked Owen.

"The steak and eggs or the biscuits and gravy," Owen replied at once. "You won't regret either one."

He settled on the biscuits and gravy and coffee, and Owen ordered the steak and eggs and black tea. "This is a really strange place," Justin said when she'd gone back into the kitchen.

"The Standing Stone?"

"No, Dunwich." Then: "Most small towns I've seen go out of their way to try to look pleasant, and then you find out they're not so nice after all. This place goes out of its way to look dreadful, but it's actually pretty pleasant."

Owen smiled and said nothing, and after a moment Justin laughed. "Yeah, I know. The voice of the clueless outsider. The couple who fed me dinner last night were as gracious as gracious can be, but I'm pretty sure that the whole time I was there, there were two conversations going on, one I could hear and one I couldn't."

Not as clueless as all that, Owen thought. "Old couples are like that," he said aloud.

Justin gave him a sardonic look. "Sure." Billie came out a moment later with coffee and tea, vanished again. "I saw the sign on the old church," he said after she was gone.

"Do you know what it means?" Owen asked him.

"I've heard some things." He leaned forward, propped his chin on hands and his elbows on the table. "Who was the man in black I met in Paris, the one who sent me here?"

"Nyarlathotep, the Crawling Chaos," said Owen.

Justin stared at him for a time, opened his mouth, and then closed it again.

"Yeah," said Owen. "I know."

"You've met him." When Owen nodded: "How did that happen?"

"I saw something I shouldn't have seen, and he gave me some advice that got me out of a really bad mess." Images pressed up out of memory: the white stone beyond Meadow

Hill, the moon path beyond, the night journey to Innsmouth that followed. "I saw quite a bit of him for a couple of weeks, then he brought me here and went somewhere else. I haven't seen him since."

Justin considered that, then said, "Does he do that kind of thing a lot?"

"Appear and disappear? All the time," said Owen. "For all I know, he might be waiting at Chorazin right now."

Justin nodded after a moment, clearly uncomfortable with the prospect.

The door to the restaurant kitchen swung open, and Billie Whately came out with their orders and set the plates down. She made a little conversation while coffee and tea refilled their cups, then went away again.

They applied themselves to their breakfasts for a few minutes. "You said," Justin said then, "that you'd found some information."

Owen was chewing on a piece of steak just then and so a moment passed before he could answer. "Yeah. You've heard of a horror writer named H.P. Lovecraft."

Justin's face set hard. "Yes. He wrote a really nasty story about my family."

"I know. That's not the thing I wanted to bring up, though. Did you have a relative named Alonzo Typer, who was born in 1855 and disappeared in 1908?"

That got him a startled look from the younger man. "Yes. I'd have to ask Aunt Josephine what exact relation of mine he is, but he's in the family tree somewhere—and I think he's one of the ones who got called. Where did you hear about him?"

"A story Lovecraft helped write," Owen said. "He used to do a lot of revision work for friends and clients, and he worked with a guy named William Lumley on a story called 'The Diary of Alonzo Typer.' The diary was real—Lovecraft mentioned it in a couple of letters he wrote to another friend of his, Robert Blake. It came out of what was left of an abandoned house near

Chorazin, a place that used to belong to a strange old family named van der Heyl. I don't remember how Lumley got it, but he and Lovecraft decided to turn it into a story. Of course they padded it out with the usual clichés and they may have left out some things, but it's got a lot of information in it that I don't think you have."

Justin stared at him. "Do you have a copy?"

"Yes, and we'll get to that. But there's something else. There are people here in Dunwich who've been to Chorazin. It's a town like this one."

"Meaning there's a Starry Wisdom church there?"

"Among other things," said Owen.

"So Nyarlathotep knew what he was doing when he sent me here," Justin said then.

"He always does." In response to the younger man's dubious look: "He's not human, you know. He's the soul and mighty messenger of the Great Old Ones."

Justin concentrated on his breakfast for a while. Owen considered him, wondered what was going through the young man's mind. "There's one other thing," he said finally. "You said you read some strange books in Europe. How thoroughly did you study them?"

"I took some notes," said Justin. "That's about it. I couldn't find anything that I was sure would help me, and a lot of the time I couldn't make any sense of them at all."

Owen nodded. "They don't give up their secrets easily." He leaned forward. "If the story's anything to go by, though, this business at Chorazin has to do with some of the deepest and most dangerous parts of the old lore. It's not surprising that your relatives haven't come back. This isn't the kind of thing you can face with a few notes or scraps of knowledge."

"I have to go anyway," Justin said, staring fixedly at his half-empty plate.

"I know. You need someone to go with you who's familiar with the old lore."

Justin's gaze snapped up to his face, stayed there for a long moment. "Are you offering?"

"Yes. I've discussed it with my wife and the church elders."

The same bleak frightened look Owen had seen earlier showed in his disparate eyes. "I hope you don't regret it—but if you're willing, I'd be grateful for your help." Then, with a slow lopsided smile: "And I could use some company. It's been a lonely road."

CHAPTER 2

THE SHADOW OF TEMPEST MOUNTAIN

"'Writing here grows indistinct,'" Owen read. "'Too late—cannot help self—black paws materialise—am dragged away toward the cellar ...'"

He fell silent. Justin, hands on the steering wheel, said nothing. Outside the windows of the car, the rumpled landscape of the Berkshires had begun to yield to the first rounded summits of the Taconic Mountains. The state highway seemed half deserted, with fewer cars than Owen expected, and the marks of weathering and neglect on the road surface and the railings surprised him. Above, puffy white clouds alternately hid and revealed the sun.

"So that's what Lovecraft and Lumley say we're facing," he said then. "The van der Heyl house, with something hostile in or around it that has black paws; a cellar, with a vault reached by a narrow passage; a door in the vault, and on the other side of the door—something."

"How much of that do you think was Lovecraft's imagination?" Justin asked.

"Good question. I'd expect tentacles rather than paws if he was just making things up."

"He had a thing for those, didn't he?"

Owen laughed. "I suppose so. To be fair, he got that from the old lore. Most of the Great Old Ones take on tentacled forms fairly often, and some of their children have tentacles, too."

He thought of Laura, then, and though it had been only a few hours since they'd kissed and clung to each other, the widening distance between them twisted in him like a knife. Her words stirred in his memory: "You know that can't matter to the Great Old Ones." Of course she was right; being what they were, the lives and happiness of two mortal beings, one human, one half-human, could never be a matter of importance to them.

And if he did not return—

He wrenched his thoughts away from that subject.

"I'm still trying to get my mind around the possibility that they're real," said Justin.

Owen glanced at him. "It's considerably more than a possibility."

"I want to believe you," said Justin. "And the thing is, I've seen some weird things. I met this strange old man in Antwerp who played a game with round pieces of stone, and then told me things about me that I've never mentioned to another person. I went to a ritual in France, at a place called Ximes, where the priestess drank a potion, and her body flowed like water and turned into something that wasn't human any more. I went to an old stone temple in Malta and made an offering there—and I saw what came and took it.

"And there was Nyarlathotep, who appeared out of nowhere and knew why I was in Europe, and that wasn't something I told anyone there, either. So I don't know why it's so big a jump to go from there and accept that the rest of it's true—but it is."

"You've been taught all your life that things like that can't happen," Owen said. "So even when they do, yeah, it's a jump."

Justin nodded. "Yeah. And I've read a fair amount about the others—Cthulhu, Tsathoggua, Shub-Niggurath—"

"Shub-Ne'hurrath," Owen corrected him. When Justin gave him a questioning look: "That's her proper name. Lovecraft changed it, for an ugly reason."

"Now surprise me," Justin said in a tone of disgust.

The highway bent to the left in a great sweeping curve, and a couple of cars went by the other direction, the first two they'd seen in maybe a quarter hour. They crested the rise and started down the far side.

"So Lefferts Corners first," Owen said.

"Yeah. We can find a lunch place between Albany and Kingston. Once we head out of Kingston we'll be on back roads. We can stay the night with my Aunt Josephine, she loves company, and there's something I want you to see, something she keeps at her place. Tomorrow we can drive the rest of the way to Chorazin." He laughed, though there wasn't any amusement in the sound. "And those black paws."

* * *

They got lunch at a burger place in an old factory town on the Hudson River, piled back into Justin's car and headed south. By then they'd finished talking over what lay ahead and silence settled in, or as close to silence as you get in a cheap compact going seventy over a badly maintained freeway. After a while, Justin said, "Mind if we have some music?"

"Not at all," Owen told him. "What do you have in mind?"

Justin answered by pulling a battered CD case from a bin between the two front seats and handing it to him. It was a Folkways recording, *Silver John Plays Songs of the Mountains*, with cover art that screamed 1960s folk revival; he turned it over, found that it had been released on vinyl in 1967 and remastered on CD thirty years later. Owen recognized the names of familiar tunes on the playlist, and said, "This looks pretty good."

That got him a smile. "There's something further on that you'll want to hear, too," Justin said. "You'll know it when it plays."

Owen got the CD into the player and hit the button, and a moment later "Pretty Saro" began playing. Owen didn't recall hearing the musician before, but the man was good; he had a pleasant voice with a Carolina accent to round off all the hard edges, and fingers that knew every bit of the fretboard of a guitar. The tracks that followed were more classic old-time folk pieces, "Old Joe Clark," "The Desrick on Yandro," "Barbry Allen"—that was how it was spelled on the track list, and that was how Silver John sang it. Owen leaned back and closed his eyes, let the music wash over him.

The next track was "The Sleeper in the Hill." Owen didn't recognize the title, or the haunting minor chords that opened it, but by the time the first verse was finished he gave Justin a startled look. Justin smiled and kept on driving.

When the last haunting chords of "The Sleeper in the Hill" faded to silence, Owen pushed the pause button and said, "I want to hear that again."

"Go right ahead," said Justin.

Owen tapped the button that took the player back one track. The eerie opening chords sounded, and then Silver John's voice began singing:

> It's a long lonely road to the hill by Lake Erie,
> Back home my old mama is cryin' her fill,
> Her poor wayward son's goin' down to damnation,
> He's called by the sleeper inside of the hill.

> Look away to the west where the thunder is breedin',
> Look away to the east where the wind has gone still,
> Look away to the south where the road leads me onward,
> I'm called by the sleeper inside of the hill.

The Lord alone knows why the call comes in dreamin'
When April comes warm and October blows chill,
And there's always a soul who must answer the callin'
And go to the sleeper inside of the hill.

Oh, Mama, forgive me, there ain't no way homeward,
The road that I ride, it'll end where it will,
And a dark door of stone's gonna open before me
When I go to the sleeper inside of the hill.

It's a long lonely road to the hill by Lake Erie,
Back home my old mother is cryin' her fill,
Her poor wayward son's goin' down to damnation:
He's called by the sleeper inside of the hill.

Owen tapped the pause button again. "Where the hell did you find that?"

"I bought the CD for three bucks at a used book store in Poughkeepsie," said Justin. "When that track played the first time, I just about fell out of my chair."

"I bet." Then: "Did you look up the musician?"

"Yeah. Appalachian folk singer, recorded a couple of albums in the 1960s, died about the time I was born. I couldn't find anything about that song—and it wasn't for lack of trying." Justin shook his head, and changed lanes to get around a semi.

By then they were most of the way to Kingston. An exit a few miles further on took them onto a state highway, a right turn off the state highway put them on a two-lane road up into the Catskills, and a left turn sent them up the kind of winding, poorly surfaced back road that had been a cow path in Colonial times and still showed its ancestry. Mountains wrapped in forest and touched with the first hints of spring greenery rose up to either side, with here and there a weathered cliff of pale rock breaking out from among the trees. Where the valley widened, houses clustered around a church, an abandoned gas station, or a little rundown store offering bait for fishermen and trinkets for tourists. Elsewhere, signs of human presence were scarce.

Justin's mood brightened visibly as the road and the afternoon wound on. Owen watched him for a while, and then asked, "Home?"

"Yeah." His lopsided smile showed. "When I was a kid, I used to think it was the most boring place on Earth, and when Mom and Dad moved to Florida I thought they were smart. Now? If I could, I'd settle down in Lefferts Corners and never go anywhere else again."

"We'll see what happens," said Owen. "Once this is over, maybe you will."

Justin said nothing, but his shoulders hunched as he drove.

Finally, toward sunset, the road snaked its way up and over a narrow saddle between two rounded heights, and then descended into a wide valley beyond it. On the far side, a gently sloping peak rose well above the surrounding crests. Clouds had begun to pile up over it.

"Tempest Mountain," Justin said then, gesturing at the peak with one hand. "The old Martense place is up on top of it."

"The one Lovecraft wrote about," said Owen.

"Yeah." He made a little choked noise in his throat, perhaps a laugh, perhaps not. "That mountain casts a very long shadow."

Ten minutes later the woodland gave way to fields and pasture, with barns a century old scattered here and there among them. Five minutes after that, the road crossed a state highway and passed the first houses of Lefferts Corners. Half of them were abandoned and the other half looked it, and the little downtown district that loomed up ahead was no better.

"It wasn't this bad when I left for Europe," Justin said. "It really used to be a nice town."

They drove on. Maybe one store front in ten had something in it: a pawnshop, a convenience store, a bar on the corner with neon beer signs blaring against darkness within. The windows above the first floor were all dark, and not all of them still had glass. Most of the people on the streets below, and there weren't many, were old and shabbily dressed.

Six blocks later, past the hollowed shell of a department store, Justin turned, and a block or two later they were driving through a neighborhood where more than half the houses still seemed to be occupied. Tempest Mountain loomed ahead, stark against thickening clouds.

Another turn took them onto a road lined here and there with scattered houses. A mile or so and Justin turned the wheel, guiding the car into the driveway in front of a big farmhouse with rose bushes framing the doorway.

"Well, that's not good," Justin said. "Her car's gone. Wait here a bit." He got out of the car and went around back to the kitchen door, while Owen looked at the house, the huge oaks that rose up behind it, and the great sweeping slopes of Tempest Mountain half visible beyond. After a minute or so, Justin came back, climbed into the driver's seat again.

"She left a note," he explained. "She had to go visit one of my cousins who's got a baby on the way, and won't be back until after dark. She said we should go ahead and make ourselves at home, but it's going to be hours yet." He glanced at Owen, then suddenly grinned. "Care to see the closest thing Ulster County has to the stuff we've been talking about?"

"Sure," said Owen, guessing what the younger man had in mind.

* * *

He was not mistaken. Most of ten miles south on the state highway, a sign in need of fresh paint yelled SLATER'S MUSEUM OF MYSTERIES NEXT RIGHT against a backdrop of tangled willows. Another sign half a mile on promised two-headed calves, shrunken heads, petrified people, sinister relics of

Dutch colonial days, and much more. A half mile after that came another sign, and another a quarter mile further on, then a big gravel parking lot, and finally the thing itself: a sprawling single-story building of cinderblock. The paint on the walls, once bright red, was halfway to brown, and flagpoles flanking the entrance carried red pennons with SLATER'S MUSEUM on them in a faded but still acid yellow. A lone car sat in the parking lot. As Justin slowed to turn, a family of four left through a door marked GIFT SHOP, over to one side of the entrance, and went straight to the car and got in.

Justin parked, opened his door, and turned in his seat. "Welcome to the biggest tourist attraction for, oh, maybe twenty whole miles in any direction." He hauled himself out of the driver's seat. Owen got out, and they walked to the entrance as the car with the family drove off.

A sputtering neon sign above the main door said OPEN. Inside, the lobby bristled with yellowed newspaper clippings in glass-covered frames, documenting the exploits of the museum's founder, one Emerson Slater. The ticket window was on one side, below a big black and white photo of Slater, a round-faced man with a toothy smile and a porkpie hat. Behind the window, a woman with graying hair and thick glasses looked up from a newspaper crossword puzzle. "Can I help you?" she asked, then: "Oh, good heavens—Justin! It's been a while."

"Hi, Annie. Yes, it has."

"Back for good, I hope?"

Justin made a face. "Just for a little while, for now. How's business?"

"Oh, not bad, not bad." The tone of her voice contradicted the words.

"Good to hear," Justin said. "Can I have two tickets?"

"Sure thing." Bills changed hands, and so did the tickets. "Head right on in," the woman said, and pushed a button on the wall next to her. "Straight through the turnstile." The turnstile buzzed until Justin and Owen were on the other side of it, and then lapsed into silence.

Owen had been to plenty of places like it in his youth—it was the kind of cheap entertainment his foster families could afford on summer vacation—and knew what to expect. He admired the murals of colored thumbtacks and postage stamps from exotic countries; he viewed photos of Emerson Slater shaking the hands of bearded ladies, three-toed sloths, and Otto the Octopus Man; he got pleasantly dizzy in the room full of optical illusions, and pondered the Skull of Mystery in its glass case, wondering if it was as fake as it looked.

The doorway just past the Skull of Mystery had a gaudy sign over it announcing THE PETRIFIED PEOPLE!!! Owen knew about the Cardiff Giant hoax, and expected something of the same sort, a crude stone statue or two that couldn't have passed for human in pitch darkness. What he saw, though, made him stop in his tracks and then go closer, with one hand straying up to cup his bearded chin.

Four stone figures—two men, a woman, and a dog—formed a tableau, behind a chest-high glass barrier meant to keep visitors at a distance. The three human figures were naked except for four strips of cloth placed to satisfy local notions of decency, while the dog had a sign hanging from its neck saying, with epic inevitability, "Petri-Fido." One of the men was sprawled on his side as though he'd fallen, and the face was twisted into an expression half frightened and half bitter. The other man sat in an old wooden chair with his head thrown back, and his old gaunt face had the imprint of stark terror on it. The woman, who was young and pretty, lay flat on her back nearby, with her right arm outflung above her head and an oddly satisfied look on her face. The dog stood next to her, and it simply looked puzzled and scared.

Whoever carved them, Owen thought, could have made plenty of money producing something besides sideshow fakes. The human figures were exquisitely rendered, down to every last wrinkle and hair, and they weren't the kind of generic nudes he'd expected—each one could have been a portrait. The dog, a German shepherd, was no less exactly portrayed. He shook his head, impressed.

"Something, aren't they?" Justin said then. "There's a story that goes with them, too."

The story filled a placard on the wall, headed THE LEG-END OF MAD DAN MORRIS. According to the story, the old man was a wizard from the northern Adirondacks, the woman was his wife, and the younger man was an artist who'd stayed with them, quarrying stone for sculptures. From there the story unfolded predictably, with love, jealousy, and murder the well-marked stops along the line. There were only two variations from the usual script. The first was that Mad Dan, to carry out his revenge, chose a magic potion that turned flesh to stone, and tested it first on the dog. The second was that his wife turned the tables on him, and made him swallow a dose of his own potion before killing herself by drinking what was left.

Next to the placard was another framed newspaper clipping about Emerson Slater's nonstop drive to the little Adirondack village of Mountain Top in 1930, when that was still a difficult journey by car. He'd done it, according to the article, to buy the Petrified People before Robert Ripley could get there and snap them up for one of his Believe It Or Not! Odditoriums. Owen considered that, and took another long look at the stone images.

They left the Petrified People and went on to the two-headed calves and three-legged chickens, the Native American artifacts, and the relics of the Dutch settlement of the Catskills, very few of which had anything even remotely sinister about them. Finally they reached the museum exit and the gift shop beyond it. The same woman who'd sold them tickets popped through a door and perched behind the cash register. She looked so hopeful that Owen took the time to look over the faded merchandise on the shelves, and spotted a staplebound booklet that had EMERSON SLATER AND THE PETRIFIED PEOPLE in loud letters on the cover. The title sounded like the name of a Sixties rock band, he thought, but he picked up the booklet, glanced at the price, and then pulled out his wallet.

As they walked out to the car, Justin said, "The Petrified People used to be pretty famous, and not just around here." With a glance at Owen: "I knew people who used to know Emerson Slater when they were kids, and they all say he insisted that those aren't fakes."

* * *

They got back to Aunt Josephine's house as the sun touched the top of the mountains to the west. Her driveway was still empty. Justin considered that, then turned to Owen. "Since we've got a little while to wait yet," he said, "there's something else I'd like to show you."

"Sure," said Owen, and climbed out of the car.

Mutterings of thunder blended with the hum of the distant highway as they walked up the road and then down a narrow, half-overgrown lane that led off to the left, between ancient trees. "This way," Justin said, veering off from the lane to the left along a mostly disused path. They picked their way between two massive oaks and came out again into the fading light. Ahead, gray cracked shapes of local stone sprawled in uneven rows.

"The Old East Church burying ground," said Justin, stopping at the cemetery's edge. "The church used to be over there, before it burned down in 1916." He pointed off to the left. "It started out Dutch Reformed, and a lot of the old local families belonged to the church and had their people buried here— Martenses, Hasbroucks, Suydams, Sleghts, Typers, and van Kaurans."

"You said it started out Dutch Reformed," Owen said. "Did it turn into something else?"

Justin laughed, though there was no humor in the sound. "You know what? You can ask everybody in this town that question, and you won't get a single straight answer."

He started walking again, further into the cemetery, and Owen followed.

Toward the middle of the burying ground, a little apart from anything else, lay a flat slab recognizably newer than most of the other burials. A concrete bench in Art Deco style rose up out of the grass in front of it. Justin waved Owen to a seat, stood there irresolute for a long while, looking at the tomb. Owen glanced at him, then at the writing on the slab:

JACOB A. MARTENSE
1846–1921

"We talked about H.P. Lovecraft this morning," Justin said. "And I mentioned the story he wrote about my family, the one where he turned us into a bunch of cannibal apes." Owen nodded, and he went on. "Here's the other side of it.

"On the night of November 8, 1921, an Ulster County sheriff's deputy who happened to be on patrol up Tempest Mountain near the old Martense place heard a gunshot." He recited the words as though they were a litany, repeated until they'd burned their way into memory. "He drew his gun and went to look. That's how Thomas Francis Malone of Pascoag, Rhode Island, was arrested for murder, and poor Jake Martense became the last person buried in this cemetery.

"When they searched the old Martense place for clues, they found three shallow graves, with three more bodies in them. They turned out to be reporters who'd been in this part of the Catskills—George Bennet, William Tobey, and Arthur Munroe. All of them had been shot dead, and the bullets were from Malone's gun. They confronted Malone with that, and he started raving about how the Martenses were evil cannibal apes who killed and ate Bennet, Tobey, and Munroe. It turned out that he'd been involved in some kind of trouble like that in New York City a while before, though there wasn't enough evidence to get him locked up. This time the judge sent him to a state institution for the criminally insane, where he died eleven years later.

"And here's the thing. Jake Martense lived right at the foot of Tempest Mountain, half a mile or so from here. His servants said that he'd heard a car drive up toward the old Martense place, and decided to go make sure whoever it was hadn't gotten into some kind of trouble. So it was an act of kindness that cost him his life."

"Ouch," said Owen.

Justin went on as though he hadn't heard. "Malone was a friend of H.P. Lovecraft's; they were both into the amateur-journalism thing, I think. So Lovecraft got Malone's side of the story and wrote it up as fiction, the way he wrote up Alonzo Typer's diary, and he didn't even bother to change our last name. That was probably good marketing—there was a lot of press around the case, especially when it went to trial—but if you were wondering why the whole Martense family hates Lovecraft's guts, well, now you know."

"I think I do," said Owen. "My wife's from Innsmouth."

Justin turned toward him. "No kidding." Then: "The froggy-fishy stuff ..."

Owen shook his head. "I have no idea where Lovecraft got that. Laura's got tentacles instead of legs, but there's a different reason for that."

Justin pondered that. "Does she get around okay?"

"Yeah. She'll probably have to use a wheelchair by the time she's fifty—that's the way that usually works out—but we've talked about that, and we'll cope."

"I get that," Justin said. "God in heaven, I get that." He sat on the other end of the bench. "You haven't asked where Malone and Lovecraft got the cannibal ape business: 'a filthy whitish gorilla thing with sharp yellow fangs and matted fur.'" He spat the words.

"He didn't just make that up?" Owen asked.

"Nope. It's the family illness: porphyria—our particular version's got a fancy name I'd have to look up online, but that'll do. We inherit a really rare form of it. I've dodged the bullet so far, though Dr. van Kauran says I'll start to show symptoms before I hit my fifties. Do you know anything about it?"

"Not worth mentioning," Owen admitted.

"I'll spare you the biochemistry. The people who have it bad can't stand sunlight—it blisters them—and they get hair all over, including the face. We also get rheumatoid arthritis pretty often, though that might not be related. But that's just it. Old Jake Martense had it bad. He couldn't stand sunlight at all, he had white hair all over him, his teeth weren't pretty, and he had arthritis in his spine so he couldn't stand up straight. So there's your gorilla thing."

Owen clenched his eyes shut. "Ouch," he said again.

"Yeah," said Justin. "And I might just look like that when I'm seventy-five."

They sat there for a while in silence, facing the tomb, as the thunder growled above Tempest Mountain. "The thing I just don't get," Justin said finally, "is the hate. Lovecraft couldn't let it be an old guy who's hairy and walks bent over. He couldn't even let it be a gorilla that eats people. It had to be 'a nameless, shapeless abomination which no mind could fully grasp and no pen even partly describe.' Why the nastiness toward people he never even met?"

"Well, it was more than that," said Owen. "Lovecraft had a thing about the unnamable, the indescribable. He thought that that's what makes something really scary—that it doesn't fit any of our mental categories and can't be described in words."

Justin considered that. "That's just silly," he said at last, shaking his head. "Even in the story, the creature wasn't indescribable—it's got white fur, it looks like a gorilla, its teeth are yellow, it's got the Martense eyes. And of course if Malone had stopped to talk instead of just pulling the trigger, he would have found out that the gorilla thing was named Jacob Martense, a kind old man with a hereditary disease who just wanted to help."

"Granted," Owen said. "But Lovecraft actually has a point." He looked around, gestured toward a massive willow that had overgrown most of the old cracked slab of a Colonial-era grave. "We can talk about that in words—'willow,' 'slab,' 'stone,' 'grave.' We wave around those labels and we think we've captured the things they label, but we haven't. That—" He indicated the tree again. "—isn't 'willow.' That's something you have to experience to know in any real sense, and if you're obsessed with trying to shove the world into categories that have neat verbal labels, yeah, that can scare the stuffing out of you."

"But the labels help," Justin replied at once. "You learn the word 'willow,' you learn what willows look like, and if you're like my cousin Pauline, that means you can gather willow bark to take care of fevers and achy muscles."

"They help," Owen agreed, "but they also get in the way." He considered Justin, decided to take a risk. "Do you know about Nug and Yeb?"

Justin turned to face him. The younger man was barely visible in the last guttering light of the day. "Yeah," he said after a moment. "Though not much more than the names. I read a little about them in Europe."

"Hsan the Greater called them the two principles of being," said Owen. "Yeb of the Whispering Mists is the world as we know it. Nug of the Silent Stars is the world as it actually is. They can't be separated, not by human beings, but they're never the same. Words come from Yeb's vague whispers, but things as they really are reflect the stars of Nug."

"I get that," said Justin. "But why the hate and the fear? Okay, you see something you can't fit into a nice neat category. It doesn't quite fit your definition of human or your definition of ape—or your definition of fishy-froggy-whatever, let's say. If that happened to me, I'd think, 'wow, that's interesting,' and leave it at that. Lovecraft couldn't leave it at that."

"We're talking," said Owen, "about a man who was afraid of salad."

That stopped Justin cold. "Seriously?"

"Seriously."

Justin laughed, and shook his head.

As he fell silent, a loud creak sounded in the middle distance: the sound of old hinges turning. Justin got up from the bench and faced the black mass of Aunt Josephine's house. A cold wind was rising, setting the grass astir and hissing through the leaves of the willows and oaks. After a moment, faint movement coalesced into an uncertain shape moving toward them.

Lightning flashed over Tempest Mountain, suddenly illuminating the stones of the old burial ground. By its light the moving shape stood out stark against the trees: bent and awkward, with a stick in one hand, its face seemed to be covered with pallid fur and its eyes were blank disks of light. It looked for that brief moment, before the night closed in again, like some creature of an older world, come to haunt the dreams of the living.

"Aunt Josephine!" Justin called out.

Thunder rattled in the distance, and the shape drew closer. "Justin? Yes, I thought I'd find you here, when I saw your car out front." The voice was thin with age. "And this is?"

"Owen Merrill," Justin said, "from Dunwich, Massachusetts."

"Dunwich," the old voice repeated, as though startled. "Well, well." The shape came close. "Pleased to meet you, Mr. Merrill."

"Likewise," Owen said. He offered his hand, and the old woman took it; hers was covered in coarse hair.

Lightning flashed again, and for another instant Owen could see the old woman facing him, smiling, with white hair covering her face and hands and round eyeglasses catching the light. The eyes behind the glasses were the same as Justin's, one brown, one blue. "You ought to come in with me," she said. "A quarter hour from now that storm's going to come this way and if you're still outside you'll get soaked to the skin." She motioned with her walking stick toward the dark shape of the house, and started walking, and Justin and Owen followed.

CHAPTER 3

THE VOYAGE OF JAN MAERTENS

"Yes, I thought you would have to go there soon," said Miss Hasbrouck to her nephew. "More tea?"

"No thanks," Justin said, but Owen accepted gratefully. The old woman topped up his cup, set the teapot on the table and got a blue-checked tea cozy settled over it. All around, the comfortable clutter of a rural kitchen caught the glow of old-fashioned light bulbs, while the scent of roasting chicken seeped out of the oven and rain hammered on the windows.

The change from blue-white lightning to yellow lamplight had done nothing to make Justin's aunt look any less strange. The white hair that covered her face was coarse and straight, and so thick that Owen guessed she had to trim it regularly to keep it out of her eyes and mouth. Hair covered the backs of her hands and her fingers, though not her palms. A white sweater, baby-blue slacks, and brown slip-on shoes added an odd note of normality.

"You're being very polite, Mr. Merrill," she said, as though she'd read his thoughts. "I'm used to people taking one look at me and being flustered for the next hour or two."

Owen sipped his tea and smiled also, thinking of the shoggoths, Deep Ones, voormis, and other far-from-human beings he'd encountered since the world he thought he'd lived in had shattered around him. "I don't fluster easily," he said.

"Sensible of you." She sipped again. "Did Justin tell you what he and his cousins call me?" When Owen shook his head: "Aunt Beast."

"It's actually a compliment," Justin said, visibly embarrassed. "There's a children's book with a character who's called that, and she's an absolute sweetheart."

"I read the same book," Owen said with a smile.

"Well, there you are," said Aunt Beast. "But the porphyria—Justin told you about that? Good—that's supposed to be more than ordinary genetics. Call it a family legend, if you like, but it's supposed to be the curse of Jan Maertens."

"That's why I brought Owen here," Justin said after a moment. "I want him to know about that before we go to Chorazin."

"I'll get the manuscript out once we've had dinner. Speaking of which—" She got up and went to the stove, where water in a stock pot had just started to boil. Peeled potatoes went into it, one after another. While they boiled, she busied herself setting the table and tending other pots, and waved aside offers of help from Justin and Owen.

"Heavens, don't worry about it," she said. "It does a body good to cook for someone else once in a while. This house used to be full of people, Mr. Merrill—when Justin and the others were young, why, they'd be over here as often as at home, and no one was happier about that than me. Now they've all grown up and gone off to find work, and most of their parents have gone too. Until some of the young ones have some babies for me to spoil rotten—" She poked Justin in the ribs with the butt end of a wooden spoon, and he made a choking sound that passed for a laugh. "—I don't have guests anything like as often as I'd like."

Dinner was roast chicken, mashed potatoes, gravy, green beans and mushrooms, and apple pie with crumb topping. Between the sheer volume of food and a running conversation in which Miss Hasbrouck took the lead, it took most of an hour to eat. By the time it was over, Owen knew a great deal about the doings of the old Dutch families in that corner of the Catskills, but none of it seemed to bear on the journey ahead or the desperate resolve in Justin's eyes.

Finally Aunt Beast made another pot of tea and they trooped into the living room, where two bookshelves, a big cabinet stereo in the corner, and overstuffed chairs facing a sofa long enough for a tall man's bed made the furnishings, and cross-stitched pictures in wooden frames provided most of the decor. "Make yourselves comfortable," she said. "I'll get the manuscript out of the safe." In response to Owen's questioning look: "Yes, I keep it locked up. It's irreplaceable, and some thief could get a good bit of money for it." She waved them to chairs, and vanished through a doorway; her footsteps descended a creaking stair.

"I'll leave you to read it," Justin said then. "I promised my folks I'd call them before I went to Chorazin." He stopped. "You want to call home and let them know you're here?"

Owen shook his head. "We don't do that. There are—reasons."

Justin nodded, headed up the stair.

Aunt Beast clumped back up the stairs, then, and came into the living room. She had a box of yellowing pasteboard in her hands. "Here you go, Mr. Merrill," she said, handing it to Owen. "Be very gentle—it's more than five hundred years old."

Owen took the lid off the box and set it aside, then lifted out a thin book bound in leather. It looked, to his trained eye, like a late eighteenth-century binding, but when he opened it, what was inside was something like three centuries older than that. The lamplight showed parchment covered in crabbed handwriting, well faded with age. He struggled with the words on the top of the first page: as near as he could tell, they read *Narratio Johannes filius Henricis Martinensis*.

He glanced up at her. "I'm afraid my Latin isn't very good."

A broad smile creased her furred face. "I'm impressed," she said. "I don't know too many people who can recognize Latin at a glance. You might find this helpful." She handed him a thin sheaf of paper with a half-rusted staple piercing one corner and the slightly smudged black print of old photocopying on it. It was in English, and the first line read:

```
THE ACCOUNT OF JAN HENDRIKSZOON MAERTENS
```

"My mother translated it," she said. "She had a first-rate education—Papa always said she was the real scholar of the family, and he had an M.A. from Columbia."

Owen nodded, paged through the manuscript, and then returned it to the box and handed it back to Aunt Beast. He picked up the photocopy, then, and started to read.

He got to the end of the second page, and looked up at her. "This is astonishing."

"Isn't it? You just keep reading."

He did, and his eyes slowly widened.

* * *

Later, by the yellow light of a single electric lamp, Owen read through the translation again. The little bedroom he'd been given for the night was comfortable enough, and the bed looked inviting, but the story of Jan Maertens' voyage kept him awake for another hour. Aunt Beast had chased down another copy of the translation and given it to him, saying, "Heavens, there are plenty of copies—Mama got a big stack of them made so she'd be able to give them to all the cousins—and if you're going with Justin to Chorazin, you might need one."

```
I was twenty-six years of age when I took
ship in the free city of Lübeck as a man-
at-arms on the cog Mary of Bremen, on the
feast of the apostles Philip and James, it
being the eleventh day of May in the year
of grace 1456. He who hired me bade me
```

```
ask no questions about him or the voyage.
I agreed, for he paid in good gold coin,
and I had reason to travel far from my home
in Ghent, for I had fought in the late war
against Duke Philip and could not expect a
welcome anywhere in his dominions.
```

That was the beginning, and the tale went on from there, simply and artlessly told. The *Mary of Bremen* met up with three other ships at Copenhagen, rounded the northern tip of Denmark and the southern shores of Norway, and then set a course west by northwest past the Orkney Islands into the heart of the North Atlantic. The seas were rough but the wind blew steadily, and the great square sail of the cog strained at the ropes and yards, drawing her on. Icebergs, whales, and the lives and pastimes of the men-at-arms as they sat on deck in good weather, or huddled below the sterncastle in bad—all these found a place in the narrative.

Twice the little fleet weathered storms, and when the second storm finally blew itself out, one cog had gone down with all hands and the others were much the worse for wear. Thirteen weeks after sailing from Lübeck, though, the *Mary of Bremen* and the two other cogs remaining made harbor in Iceland, where those aboard heard Mass in the church at Reykjavik, and got the ships ready for the next leg of the journey.

```
Three days out of Iceland, the master who
had hired us called all the men-at-arms to
the sterncastle. Ahead, he told us, lay the
country the Portuguese call the Land of
Codfish, Terra de Bacalhau in their tongue,
of which I learned a little later on. We
would stay there through the winter, which
was exceeding harsh, though some few fish-
ers wintered over in that place. Thereafter
some of us would sail west and south to
```

another land, where our master and certain
men with him had business. Returning to the
Land of Codfish, we would stay a second winter, and then the cogs, which had business
in Greenland, would return us to our homes
and we would have the rest of our pay.

By the time the little fleet reached the Land of Codfish—Owen
guessed that this was Newfoundland—the weather had turned
harsh, and Jan Maertens was glad to get solid ground under
his feet. He and the others settled into the low sod-roofed huts
of the nameless village there and made friends among the
Portuguese fishermen who were overwintering with them.

Months passed, and spring finally came. The master of the little fleet hired a smaller craft called a balinger from newly arrived
fishermen to take him to another land further west. The cogs
sailed away, and the next day, the balinger set out with Maertens
and eleven other men-at-arms, six fishermen to sail the boat, and
four others, the master and three learned men who spoke Latin
to one another and regarded the landscape with cold eyes.

We sailed north and west along the shore
of the Land of Codfish and passed through
a strait, then kept the land to our right
hand and sailed west. The wind was with us
and blew strong and free, and three days
after we sailed we sighted land to the
south. We sailed on, and passed west by
southwest along a great inlet of the sea,
the water whereof became fresher as we went
on. The people in that land dwelt in fair
villages. They were not Christian folk, but
the fishers knew their tongue, and our master had gifts for their chieftains, so they
permitted us to pass.

The inlet narrowed to a river, and at the river mouth the balinger and all but one of the fishermen left the party and sailed back to the Land of Codfish. From there the party went on foot, the men-at-arms shouldering heavy burdens, the learned men walking alongside them, observing everything and saying nothing. The fisherman knew the language of the native people, and that and more gifts got them safely up the river to the shore of a lake so great the far side could not be seen. Finally they left the lake and followed a river and then a smaller stream to a place Jan Maertens would not describe, where the journey reached its goal:

> And what was done there no Christian tongue ought to utter nor Christian heart conceive, nor shall I confess it until the hour of my death. A curse lies upon me on account of what happened there, and may my lord Jesus and his holy mother Mary have mercy on me and may all the blessed saints beseech God for my salvation that I had even so small a part in it as I did. Here I will write only that seventeen men went to that place and eight came from it alive, all men-at-arms, for the master, the learned men, the fisher, and the other men-at-arms were handed over unto uttermost perdition. We who lived fled down the stream, and when we came to the shore of the lake and our dread was somewhat lessened, we resolved to go to the place where the balinger left us, for there the fishers were to return in the fall of the year.

The return took months, though the journey there had taken weeks, and three men-at-arms died along the way from causes

Maertens would not describe. He and his four surviving companions came to the place where the river flowed into the long inlet. They had learned enough of the native language by then to speak to the people of the nearby villages, and cut up their breastplates and helmets into arrowheads to barter for corn, squash, beans, and venison. With that, they settled down to wait for the balinger to return for them.

It never came.

They spent the winter in one of the villages. One of the men died there of some illness, and another married a woman of the village and told the others that they were fools to leave. When spring arrived, Maertens and the two others traded what was left of their steel for a canoe and provisions, and set out for the Land of Codfish. Five weeks passed before they saw the shore of the Land of Codfish rising out of the mists, and then a storm came howling in and forced them to make for land, even though the nameless village was still far to the southeast. Ten days later, starving and sick, they rounded a curve of the shore and cried out in joy, for the harbor before them was full of ships, with the sign of the Cross painted in red upon their great square sails.

```
The fishers greeted us with amazement, as
though we had risen from the dead. We heard
from them that the Mary of Bremen came
from Greenland while we waited at the river
mouth. The captain thereof told them that
we all had been slain and no balinger should
go to meet us, and the cog then sailed away
again. We were much perplexed by this, and
asked many questions, but the fishers knew
no more. They being good Christian folk
gave us food and shelter. When our strength
returned to us Pieter Slaader and I joined
in their labors, Gottlob Brücker being too
```

ill to work, and he died before the summer was over. We said prayers for him, but
there was no priest to hear his confession
and bless him in his last hour. Before he
died, he gave me what gold he had and begged
me to pay for masses for his soul's sake,
for he felt as I did that a curse was upon
us all. I promised him that if I came alive
again to Christian lands I would do it.

Toward autumn, when the ships from Portugal had nearly
filled their holds with salted cod, a balinger went north to
Greenland to trade for provisions for the voyage back across the
sea. Maertens sailed with it, for he hoped that some misunder-
standing accounted for the false news from the *Mary of Bremen*,
and he had in mind the rest of the pay he had been promised
for the voyage. Neither Maertens nor the fishermen were prepared for what they found once they reached Greenland:

We came then to shore, where we found farm-
steads and a fair stone church but not one
living soul. Two strong men who went into
the first house we found came forth pale
with dread, and told us that within were
dead men only; and this I saw with my own
eyes in three other houses, where all who
dwelt there, man, woman, and child, had
been put to the sword. We sailed further up
the coast, but found the like wherever we
landed. If any Christian folk still lived
in Greenland we did not find them. I thought
then of the business our master said the
cogs had in Greenland, and my heart was
troubled, but I said nothing about this to
the others.

They returned to the Land of Codfish, and Maertens and Pieter Slaader each sailed on one of the Portuguese ships. What happened to Slaader, Maertens did not know, but the ship he took, the caravel *Infante de Sagres*, made a swift passage back across the Atlantic to Oporto, and he had learned enough of sailing by then to earn a seaman's pay. He paid for masses for Gottlob Brücker's soul at a church in Oporto, and then set out for home. His route took him through Portugal, Spain, and France, in each of which he had no shortage of colorful adventures.

```
I had a great desire then to dwell in Ghent
where I was born. Therefore I went at once
to Duke Philip at Douai, and knelt before
him and begged his mercy that I had taken
up arms against him in the late war. They
who call him Philip the Good do not lie,
for he not only forgave me but took me into
his service, and I served him as a man-at-
arms for twenty and six years faithfully. I
did not speak to him or any other of what I
had witnessed across the sea, and when my
service was at an end and I came to dwell
in my son's house, I thought never to speak
or write of it again. I have lately heard,
though, that a captain of Genoa in the ser-
vice of the Spanish king has crossed the
sea and returned; and I wish my son's chil-
dren, and such children as God may choose
to give them in their turn, to know that
terrible things dwell in that land. I feel
sure that a dread fate awaits any of my line
who venture there. Let them remain safe in
their homes in Ghent, and with God's grace
it may be that they will be spared.
```

Owen finished reading the translation, and sat there at the little desk for a long while. If the narrative was a forgery, he thought, it was a very skillful one, and if it was not—

He shook his head, got undressed, settled under the quilts and almost at once slipped into a dream. He seemed to be on a ship that moved silently across dark waters. The green shore to starboard was scattered with ruined houses and bleached bones. Justin Martense was aboard with him, and so was Aunt Beast, but all the others who sailed in that boat were silent hooded figures that had no faces. Then all at once the ship was gone, and he stood in a place he did not know, looking up a steep slope toward a hilltop that was crowned with a ring of standing stones.

Help me. It was the same voice as before, whispering, and he felt sure that the whisper came from the heart of the hill. *Free me.*

* * *

Clatter of dishes came wafting up the stair as Owen descended early the next morning. He'd slept hard, his morning meditations and exercises had gone well, and just at the moment he felt ready to face whatever the Great Old Ones chose to throw at him.

"Good morning!" said Aunt Beast as he came into the kitchen. "You're an early riser, Mr. Merrill. Coffee or tea?"

He gratefully accepted a cup of black tea, sat at the table, answered the usual questions about how he'd slept. Then, once the tea cleared the last cobwebs of sleep from his mind, he said, "That was quite a tale—the Jan Maertens story."

"Isn't it, though?"

"I almost hate to ask whether it's true or not," said Owen.

"You sound like my mother," Aunt Beast said with a smile. "She told me more than once that she started researching the thing to try to prove that it was a forgery, but the more she studied the more details checked out. The *Mary of Bremen*, for example—there really was a ship of that name in the 1450s and 1460s, and it was a cog, just like the manuscript says."

"I'm not sure what that is," Owen admitted.

"The common freighter of the time," said Aunt Beast. "In the Baltic and the North Sea, at least. A big tubby flat-bottomed thing seventy or eighty feet long, with one mast and one big square sail. Cogs sailed from Europe to Iceland and back all through those years, with side trips to Greenland now and then, so Newfoundland isn't out of the question at all."

"The Land of Codfish."

"Exactly. The Grand Banks are off Newfoundland, and those used to be full of cod before they caught them all." She shook her head. "Historians are pretty sure there were Portuguese fishermen on the Grand Banks before 1450, maybe before 1400. The Norse colony in Greenland is supposed to have died out between 1450 and 1500, so that checks out too."

"Died out," said Owen. "Do they know why?"

"No," said Aunt Beast. "There are theories, but …" She shrugged.

"The thing I wonder most," said Owen, "is what happened at the end of the journey."

"I won't argue," the old woman answered. "Mom spent I don't know how much time trying to find something about that—especially after Tom went away."

"He was called," Owen guessed.

"Yes. I see Justin's told you about the other part of the family curse." She got a stoneware bowl out of a cupboard, started measuring flour into it. "Tom was my oldest brother," she said then. "He started hearing the call when he was thirteen, and about a week after his nineteenth birthday we got up in the morning and he and his car were gone. We never saw him again."

"I'm sorry," Owen said.

"Oh, we knew it was going to happen." Milk that had been scalding on the stove went into the bowl, along with salt and oil and yeast, and she stirred with a big wooden spoon. "Mom cried her eyes out when she found out he'd been called, but after that—well, you deal."

She put on a pair of rubber gloves, then turned the bread dough out onto a floured board for kneading. In response to Owen's raised eyebrow: "The gloves? Heavens, I wouldn't want to get any stray hairs in the bread, now would I?" She laughed, and Owen laughed with her.

The old woman kneaded for a time, while Owen sipped his tea. Finally, she plopped the mass of dough back in the stoneware bowl, covered it with a cotton dish towel she'd wrung out in hot water, and poured herself another cup of tea.

"Mom never did figure out what happened at Elk Hill in 1457," she said then. "It wasn't for want of trying. She went to universities all over the state, met with I don't know how many archeologists and historians, visited the Indian reservations at Cattaraugus and Tonawanda to talk to the elders there— everything you can think of. She had a whole filing cabinet full of notes she'd taken and typed up, copies she'd made, and she kept it locked up tight."

"Did she ever go to Chorazin?" Owen asked.

"Not while my father was alive." She pulled out a chair, sat facing him across the kitchen table. "He died in the spring of '89, and after the estate was settled, she told the family that she was going there. I won't say any of us was happy about that, but she wasn't the kind of woman who listened to arguments once she got her mind made up. So she drove away, and I don't think any of us expected to see her again.

"But a week later, toward sunset, back she came. She wouldn't say anything about what she saw, and that night she took everything out of that filing cabinet and burned it to ashes in the fireplace. She never would talk about it afterwards, not even when she was dying."

Owen nodded, let a silence slip past. "What do you think happened in 1457?"

The old woman looked away. "I couldn't say."

"When Justin said that I'm from Dunwich," Owen pressed, "you knew the name. I'm guessing that you know more than that."

Aunt Beast said nothing for a long time. "Mr. Merrill," she said finally, "there was trouble here, bad trouble, in my grand-parents' time about—that sort of thing. The Old East Church got burnt to the ground and a bunch of people got taken away: by the police, everyone says, but when I was a good deal younger, I knew people who watched it happen and they never saw a uniform or a badge. So there are things that nobody in Leffert's Corners talks about."

She finished her tea, poured another cup for each of them. Then, leaning forward across the table, she said in a low voice: "But I'll say this much. I think that there's something from the elder world there, down under the hill. They woke it with their spells, and the heirs of Jan Maertens are going to keep on going there to die until they can figure out how to be rid of it."

* * *

Breakfast involved enough pancakes, bacon, eggs, and poached apples to feed a small army, or at least that was Owen's impres-sion. All through it, Aunt Beast kept up a lively chatter, as though Jan Maertens' voyage and her brother's disappearance had never been mentioned. Justin said little. He'd come down-stairs looking haggard. He'd slept well, or so he claimed, but Owen could imagine how the journey to Chorazin must weigh on him.

Once breakfast was over, though, the old woman's stock of amusing stories trickled away into silence. Owen stood up and said, "Miss Hasbrouck, it was a real pleasure meeting you, and I hope I'll see you again sometime soon."

"Likewise and likewise." She got to her feet, not without effort. "If you ever find yourself in this part of the world again, Mr. Merrill, I certainly hope you'll stop by."

He promised he would. Then, to Justin: "I'll be waiting outside."

The morning was cool and crisp. Clouds drifted in from the west, but the air felt washed clean by the thunderstorm of the night before. Owen walked over to Justin's car, and stood there looking past the nearby trees to the slopes of Tempest Mountain.

One silent and terrible November night in distant Arkham, he'd gazed into the eyes and mind of Yog-Sothoth, the Gate and the Guardian of the Gate, and seen all of space and time in a single shattering glimpse. Ever since then, at intervals he couldn't predict, that vision returned to him; sometimes it was space that opened up before him, and sometimes space and time both, but most often it was time alone. As he stared up at the mountain, one of those instants of vision seized him and stretched moments into millennia.

All at once the house beside him was a forest, a pasture, a building site, a newly built home, an abandoned hulk with peeling paint and broken windows, a tumbledown ruin, a forest. The street beside it went through its changes from trail to cow path to dirt road to paved street to broken pavement half overgrown with weeds, and then back to trail again. His vision broadened, and he saw peoples ebb and flow like waves, from the first fur-clad hunters who ventured north across windswept tundra through a dozen forgotten cultures to the Shawnee and the Iroquois, the Dutch, the English, the Americans, and on past them into the far future, when once again fur-clad hunters trailed the herds across the tundra of a future ice age. Then Tempest Mountain's vaster trajectory seized his inner sight, and all in the same moment it surged up from archaic seas to become a soaring glacier-topped peak with dinosaurs roaming its lower slopes, and then dwindled age by age until the waves of another sea rolled over it once again.

A sudden noise brought Owen back to the present moment with a jolt: the kitchen door of Josephine Hasbrouck's house, as it opened and closed. Owen turned, to find Justin coming around the side of the house. His disparate eyes were edged with red, but he wore an expression of forced cheerfulness. "So," he said. "Away we go."

He had a substantial brown paper bag with him. "Lunch," he said, indicating it. "Did I mention that Aunt Josephine likes to cook?"

He got lunch settled in the back seat, and they climbed into the car. The engine grumbled to life. A few minutes later they were weaving their way through the mostly empty shell of Leffert's Corners, and a few minutes after that they turned north onto the state highway and the landscape began to move past at something more than a crawl.

"So what do you think of my Aunt Beast?" Justin asked.

"One very pleasant lady," said Owen.

That got him a glance, and then a smile. "When she said my cousins and me were over at her place as often as we were home, she wasn't kidding," Justin said then. "She never married—she told me once she couldn't bear the thought that one of her children might be called—but you'd always find half a dozen kids there, and somebody older staying with her who was just out of the military or getting over a divorce or what have you, and dogs. She loved dogs, and always had three or four of them around."

"Not any more?"

"No, not since she got arthritis in the knees and she couldn't take 'em for walks any more." He shook his head, started laughing. "When I was seven, I got this plastic Roman helmet for my birthday, and I managed to train two of her German shepherds to be my chariot horses. I'd take their leashes and get on my skateboard, and they'd take off at a run, towing me behind them, down some back road that didn't see a car once a week. That was my Roman triumph."

Owen laughed with him. "That must have been quite a sight," he said.

"Oh, it was. There are pictures; my relatives get them out to embarrass me sometimes." With a sidelong glance: "I'm curious. Do you get that kind of treatment?"

"Not really," Owen said. "I spent most of my childhood in foster families. My folks died in a car crash when I was seven."

Justin said nothing for a time. Then: "That must have been tough."

"You deal," said Owen.

"Yeah," Justin said. "I get that."

A sharp turn got them onto an onramp, and then westbound on State Route 23.

"You've read Jan Maertens' story," Justin said then. "What's your take on it?"

"I've got more questions than answers," Owen admitted, "and one question that matters more than all the others—what happened at Elk Hill in 1457?"

"I wish I knew for sure," said Justin. "But I have a guess."

Owen glanced at him, said nothing.

"I think the point of the expedition was to call something up." Justin stared fixedly at the road ahead. "To summon it—isn't that the way the *Necronomicon* says it? The men who spoke Latin were sorcerers, I figure, and the men-at-arms were there to guard them while they worked."

The highway spun away beneath the car's wheels.

"They called it up," Justin said then. "but they couldn't send it back, and that's why it's still there, and why so many of them ended up dead. That's what I think. It's going to keep on calling Jan Maertens' descendants until somebody figures out how to banish it again—but we don't know how." In a whisper: "And maybe we never will."

CHAPTER 4

THE STONES OF CHORAZIN

By afternoon they were in the hills of western New York. Half-abandoned farm towns full of decaying buildings huddled in the valleys. Forest covered the uplands, stark with winter's browns and grays, waiting for spring. They paused at a rest stop, ate the lunch Aunt Josephine had packed for them—huge roast beef sandwiches on homebaked bread, two thermos containers of hot corn chowder, and molasses crinkle cookies—and then climbed back into the car. Neither spoke much. Pastures, woodlots, and cornfields rolled past to either side beneath broken gray clouds as they headed west on the state highway.

Finally a sign marked the exit for Emeryville. "Here we go," said Owen. Justin nodded, slowed the car, turned onto a long straight road running north.

Owen counted the roads that headed off eastward, moving his finger up the map toward the mark that indicated Chorazin Road. "Next left," he said finally.

There was no next left. There were no left turns at all. The road ran due north over low hills with a few gravel roads veering off to the right, but on the left they passed nothing but a few abandoned driveways that vanished into brush and ragged trees. Ten miles from the highway exit they reached Pine Center, a crossroads with an off-brand gas station, a tavern, three rundown houses and half a dozen mobile homes that weren't in much better shape than the houses. Justin stopped the car, and they looked at each other. Without a word, Justin turned around and went back south, driving more slowly.

That didn't help, and neither did a third drive along the same ten miles of road. If one of the abandoned driveways was Chorazin Road, it apparently hadn't had much traffic on it for a decade or more—and which one? Neither of them could tell.

As the gas station came into sight again, Owen said, "I suppose we can ask somebody."

"I should get gas anyway," said Justin. "Might as well."

Except for a boy walking toward the station along the road to the north and an old woman sitting on her porch across the street, Pine Center could have been deserted. The gas station had two pumps under a rusting awning, and the pay-by-card machine had a handlettered cardboard sign taped over it saying OUT OF ORDER—PAY ATTENDANT. The attendant in question, an old man in jeans and a checked shirt, his flyaway white hair sticking out from under a John Deere cap, came out from the station; he had a card reader, an old model, hanging on his belt. "How much you want?" he asked as the two younger men got out of the car.

"Twenty bucks worth," said Justin, handing over a card.

"Sure thing." The thing on his belt beeped and chittered, and he handed the card back with a receipt. Justin took it and went to the pump.

"How do we get to Chorazin Road from here?" Owen asked the old man.

He got a sharp look in answer. "Why the hell you want to know?"

"I've got friends in Chorazin," Owen told him.

It was apparently the wrong thing to say. The old man gave him a disgusted look, and turned away without another word. The door slammed behind him a moment later.

Owen and Justin looked at each other. Just then, another voice spoke: "Mister?"

They both turned. A boy of maybe twelve was standing there, watching them; Owen realized after a moment that it was the same one he'd seen walking on the road. He had olive skin and straight dark hair, and his clothes had seen many better days. "Yeah?" said Owen.

"Who do you know in Chorazin?" the boy asked. His eyes were a disconcerting dark blue, and he was considering them with a look Owen knew well from Innsmouth and Dunwich, the kind that gives away nothing a moment too soon.

"Walt Moore," said Owen. "Ben and Cassie Moore are friends of mine."

The boy considered that. "You wanna give me a ride," he said, "I'll show you the way."

"You live in Chorazin?" Justin asked.

"Bit under a mile this side."

Justin and Owen looked at each other, and then Justin nodded. "Climb in."

"Sweet," the boy said with a sudden grin. "Thanks."

Justin finished with the pump, and he and Owen got in front as the boy settled in back. "Down Pine Road," he said, motioning the way they had come. "I'll tell you where to turn."

Four miles or so down the road, the boy said, "Okay, here's the turn. Just past the big oak—it's better once you're through the trees."

Justin gave him a dubious look, for the only thing even approximating a road there was the most unkempt of the abandoned driveways they'd passed. Still, he turned, and drove at no more than a walking pace through a ragged woodlot and into the open ground on the far side. From there, a cracked and potholed one-lane road headed west, tracing an unexpectedly straight line across the rolling landscape. Owen considered the notch on the horizon ahead where the road crossed the nearest ridge, nodded slowly.

"Just keep on going and you'll get there," the boy said then. Justin glanced back at him. "Thanks."

"Sure thing. Beats walking," the boy said with another grin.

The landscape along Chorazin Road was in one sense no different from the scenes Owen had watched unfolding all the way through western New York, a hilly countryside with woodland and stretches of open ground, here in pasture, there in corn, the whole dotted with houses and barns. In another sense, he might have crossed into another country. While the farms they'd passed earlier looked like most rural landscapes he'd seen, battered and broken by hard times but still marked with the last fading traces of a vanished prosperity, everything he saw along Chorazin Road spoke of people who'd always been poor and knew how to cope with it. The houses had only one story each, with old metal roofs and few windows, and the barns were not much more than oversized sheds; gardens were ragged and burgeoning; chickens pecked about, and goats munched thoughtfully in the pastures. At one of the farmhouses, a woman in her twenties and a child maybe five years old sat crosslegged on the boards of the porch, a basket between them, busy at some chore Owen didn't recognize. They looked up as the car went past; both had the same dark straight hair and olive skin as the boy who'd guided them.

"Okay," said the boy after they'd gone maybe five miles. "My grandma's place is right up ahead." There in the middle distance, under the shadow of a gray craggy ridge, was a farmhouse like the others they'd passed: small and low, with the first sprouts of early vegetables coming up all over the front yard and a big orange cat stalking through them as though it hoped to grow up to be a tiger someday. There was no driveway, just a wide place in the road, and the old pickup parked next to the house looked as though it had been there for a very long time.

Justin pulled up in front of the door, and the boy got out. "Just keep on straight," he said, "right over the ridge and down, and you're there."

They thanked him, and he grinned. "I'll probably see you in a bit—my mom and dad live in town, but I've got something for Grandma." He closed the car door, waved good-bye and headed toward the house. Justin got the car moving, and drove up and over the ridge.

Below lay a broad crooked valley. A creek ran through the middle of it, glinting here and there with light from the gray clouds where its waters could be seen among the trees, making its way north toward the Tonawanda River and the shores of Lake Ontario. Maybe half a mile ahead, huddled in a fold of the land, the roofs of a small town showed dimly in shadow.

Just west of the clustered roofs, its top lined up perfectly with the road, a hill rose up out of the valley bottom. With its steep sides and flattened top, it looked artificial, a breach in the natural order of things—an impression that was not dispelled by the circle of standing stones that ringed its crest. Over it, visible to Owen's trained senses, a faint shimmering dome of voor hovered in the air. Something seemed amiss with it, though Owen could not tell what.

Justin slowed the car, stopped. Chorazin Road ran straight down the slope ahead, toward the roofs of the town and the stark unnatural mass of the hill.

Owen glanced at him. "Elk Hill?"

"Yes." In a whisper: "I've seen it in my dreams."

So have I, Owen wanted to say, but didn't. "Your call," he said after a moment.

Justin gave him a bleak look. "No. I've got no choice."

He stepped on the gas pedal, and the car headed down the slope toward Chorazin.

* * *

Chorazin wasn't Dunwich. Owen had to remind himself of that more than once, for the same sense of destitution and decadence he knew from the Massachusetts town hung heavy over Chorazin. Thirty rundown houses, a church with a nearly illegible sign, a general store with two disused gas pumps out front, a bar and grill with a handpainted sign saying BAR & GRILL and nothing else, and a motel that looked as though the cockroaches must be holding hands to keep it from falling down: it all seemed achingly familiar to him, and so did the absence of people in sight. The ring of standing stones atop Elk Hill might as well have been a twin to the circle atop Sentinel Mountain, off past the town he'd learned to call home.

The motel had a sign saying ELK HILL MOTOR HOTEL in faded letters. A red neon NO VACANCY sign sputtered irritably just below it. Justin considered both signs as the car dodged potholes up Chorazin's one paved street. He gave Owen a dubious glance, and then turned into the gravel parking lot and eased the car to a halt.

Owen got out of the car without a word, and Justin followed. The glass door to the lobby had a broken step in front of it, and the glass hadn't been washed in a very long time. The lobby inside was no more promising: poorly lit, with two ugly and uncomfortable-looking chairs, bleak faux-wood paneling, and framed photos of the local scenery that managed to make it look dreary and menacing at the same time. Owen looked around the room and nodded, knowing how much effort must have gone into making it so unwelcoming.

The main desk was on one side of the lobby, with a space behind leading back into the manager's quarters. On the desk sat a bell with a little handlettered sign saying RING FOR SERVICE. Justin, who had been looking around the lobby, glanced at Owen and indicated the bell with a motion of his head. Owen shook his head and grinned. Justin shrugged, and waited.

The canonical five minutes passed, and then a door somewhere off behind the desk clicked quietly open and a lean old man came to the desk. He'd had black hair once, though it was a salt-and-pepper mix of dark gray and white now. His skin was olive, his eyes were the same startling dark blue as those of the boy they'd met at Pine Center, and his face had the same unreadable look on it. He considered them for a moment, and then said, "Can I help you?"

"You must be Walt Moore," Owen said at once. "Cassie, Ben, and the kids say hi."

That got a brief smile. "You're Owen Merrill." He reached out his hand. Owen took it in the grip of recognition of the Starry Wisdom, and was relieved to feel the same grip in answer. "Pleased to meet you. And your friend—"

"Justin Martense," said Owen.

"Ah." The old man took that in, and his face tensed visibly. "Welcome to Chorazin, Mr. Martense." They shook hands.

"You'll be in number sixteen and seventeen," the old man said then. "In back, so you can come and go without being seen. There's parking back there, too." He handed them each a key. "Breakfast's between six and ten; go through the door in back that doesn't have a number on it. Some of the locals have breakfast here now and then; don't mind 'em, they're with the church. Lunch and dinner, you're on your own, but I'll tell you that Carla's place across the street is better than it looks. We just have one other person staying with us right now, though of course that could change any time. You need anything at all, you just ask."

"Mr. Moore," Justin said then, "do you know why I'm here?"

That got a stiff nod. "Reckon I do."

"I don't know if there's anything you can tell me, or ..." His voice trailed off.

The old man considered him for a long moment. "No." Then, relenting a little: "If you want to go up Elk Hill and see the stones, I can send for one of Janey Hale's boys to come on down here and show you the way. It can be tricky getting up there."

"Please," said Justin, "and thank you."

"Other'n that—" He gave Justin another long look, went on in a low voice. "Miz Eagle might see you. She knows all about that sort of thing. I'd have to go to her place and see if she's willing to talk to you. But I could do that."

"I'd be grateful," said Justin.

"Done." He glanced at them both. "I'll let you get settled in, and go talk to Janey."

They said the usual things, and Owen and Justin headed back out to the car. "No bill?" Justin asked, once they were outside.

"Not when it's—" Owen fumbled for words. "The people of the Great Old Ones. Did they charge you in Dunwich?"

"Yeah. It was pretty reasonable, though."

They climbed into the car. "They weren't sure of you," Owen said. "If you're part of the—network, I suppose you'd say—you've got a place to stay wherever the Great Old Ones are revered. We all know we might have to hide somewhere else on no notice. Charging money just makes that more difficult, and it could be tracked by the other side—like phone calls, or any electronic media, for that matter."

Justin gave him a startled look. "I didn't know there was another side."

Owen glanced at him, nodded after a moment. "Yeah. With any luck you'll never have to deal with them—but they're out there."

* * *

The motel rooms looked as though they hadn't been redecorated in forty years, but they were clean and comfortable. Owen got his things stowed in the closet and the well-aged bureau, and went back out. On the far side of the gravel parking lot, just past a trio of well-weathered picnic tables, the lower slopes of Elk Hill rose up, covered in brambles that hissed in the steady wind. A line of poetry surfaced from someplace in Owen's memory then—

The mound was old before the white man came ...

—but that was all he could remember of it. He frowned, kept looking up.

The nearest of the stones on the hilltop stood stark against the clouds. The voorish dome still hovered above it, warning of subtle powers and presences within. Looking up at it, Owen frowned, for the voor wasn't right somehow; there was an indefinable wrongness to it that he'd never encountered before. It set his teeth on edge.

Justin came out of his room a little later. "Not half bad. Let's see if our guide's here."

They went back into the lobby. Inside, perched on one of the uncomfortable chairs, was the boy they'd met at Pine Center. He grinned at them, got to his feet. "Hi again."

"Small world," Justin said to him.

Walt Moore was sitting at a chair behind the main desk, busy with paperwork, but he got up as soon as they came in. "Robin," he said to the boy, "these are the fellows who want to go up Elk Hill. Mr. Merrill, Mr. Martense, this here's Robin Hale; he'll show you around."

Hands got shaken and thank-yous said, and then the three of them, Justin, Owen and the boy, were out the back door. "There's trails all over the hill," Robin explained as they crossed the gravel parking lot, "but you gotta watch out for the brambles. They're wicked."

They were, too. Great thick canes lined with hooked barbs an inch long, they coiled and snarled on the hillside. "Are the berries any good?" Owen asked him.

"There ain't any. Never have been—no flowers, neither." He led them past the picnic tables to one end of the parking lot, where a twisted pine huddled against the flank of the hill. Just past the pine, a narrow trail edged with brambles led up the slope.

"We're going up to the stones," Robin said then. Owen wondered why for a moment, since that had been settled already, and then realized that he hadn't been talking to them.

He seemed to be talking instead to the brambles. If they heard, they gave no sign of it, but the boy started up the trail a moment later. Justin and Owen followed.

The trail bent to the right, curving around the great smooth shoulder of Elk Hill. Other trails branched off it at intervals, but all of them seemed to be partly or wholly overgrown. As they climbed, the roofs of Chorazin gradually fell behind, and silence settled on the hill.

As they climbed, something made Owen uneasy, though it took him some minutes to figure out what it was. Only when a hawk high in the air to the north veered suddenly away did he realize that no birds moved or sang anywhere on Elk Hill. Thereafter he looked more carefully as he followed Robin up the trail. It wasn't just birds—no animal, not even an insect, stirred on the hill, nor did anything grow but the brown monotonous brambles.

As they walked on, the creek Owen had seen from the ridge crest came into sight, a thin bright line snaking north, hidden here and there by clusters of trees. Beyond it was another, lower ridge, notched by a road that seemed to line up with the hilltop and Chorazin Road behind it, and off in the middle distance past that, half-hidden by the rumpled landscape, lay the dim shapes of buildings, some of them long and stark.

"What's off that way?" Justin asked, pointing.

"Attica," said the boy. "Where the prison is. You used to be able to walk there pretty easy, but the bridge over Huntey Creek washed out four years ago."

"Huntey Creek's this one right below us?" Owen asked.

"Yep," said Robin. "Runs from up south of here all the way to the Tonawanda."

The trail wove this way and that as it climbed the hill. Finally, though, it led out of the brambles and into an open area where only moss and sparse clumps of grass grew. Just ahead of them, at the summit of the hill, the great stones loomed up stark against the clouds. Above them voor hung heavy in the air, thick with the same sense of wrongness Owen had noticed before.

There were eight stones in a circle maybe thirty feet across, with a ninth, taller than the others, at the center. The boy glanced back at Owen and Justin, as though to be sure they wanted to go on, and then led them to the circle. He ducked his head and murmured something under his breath and then hung back, obviously unwilling to pass within the ring of standing stones.

Owen recalled little from his one undergraduate class in geology, but even that little was enough to tell him that the menhirs weren't made of any ordinary stone. A dirty yellow-ish color in the flat light from the clouds, the standing stones glinted with tiny flakes of dull green, for all the world like scales, when a beam of sunlight broke through to shine on them. When Owen touched one of the stones, it felt cold and clammy despite the warmth of the day.

Justin finished his examination of the stone before Owen did, and walked into the middle of the circle. He was halfway to the tall central monolith when all at once he stopped and stood still, as though listening. Owen came out to join him a few moments later, and noticed the wind. It was keening to itself among the stones, and something more than wind-murmurs seemed to move through the sound: a shrill piping mixed with hissing that almost took the form of words.

"Do you hear it?" Justin asked him in a low voice. "The wind's trying to say something."

They stood there and listened for several minutes, but the voice of the wind never quite made sense. Finally the two of them walked to the central monolith. Owen considered that for a time, then saw that Justin had crossed the stone circle to its far edge and stood outside it, looking down the slope. He crossed to where Justin was standing, asked, "What is it?"

In answer, Justin simply pointed. The hillside below was thick with brambles, broken here and there by trails and clearings, and they flowed out well beyond the foot of the hill, maybe half a mile, maybe more, until the great oaks of the valley floor closed in. A little stream seemed to rise somewhere close to the foot of the hill below them, and flowed eventually into Huntey Creek. Something else stood in the middle of the bramble-covered area. At first Owen thought it was another standing stone, rougher than the ones on the hill and of a different color. Looking more carefully, he recognized it: the ragged remains of a great stone chimney of Colonial age.

"The van der Heyl house," Justin said then.

"Probably. We can find out." He turned, and called across the hilltop: "Robin, can you come around here?"

The boy appeared a moment later, giving the stone circle a wide berth. "Sure," he said, but he looked more nervous than he had before they'd reached the top of the hill.

When he'd joined them, Owen pointed at the old chimney. "What's that down there?"

Robin gave him a dismayed look. "That's the Hell House."

"Haunted?" Owen guessed.

The boy bit his lip, then: "Yeah, but it's not ghosts. They say if you go there something'll get you and you won't never be seen again."

Owen glanced at Justin, who looked away. Just then a sudden flash, like summer lightning come months too soon, lit the clouds to the north of Elk Hill. Almost at once the thunder came, if that was what it was: a single loud detonation, fading into a hiss that, just at the end, broke into a faint rhythm that sounded uncomfortably like laughter.

"We should probably head back down," Owen said. "I wouldn't want to be up here during a thunderstorm."

"Yeah," Justin said. He glanced back at the ruins, then turned sharply away.

They followed Robin around the outside of the stone circle, to the place where the trail left the brambles. The mouth of the trail had vanished. Justin looked around in puzzlement, but the boy walked up to the edge of the brambles and said in an outraged tone, "C'mon, play fair!"

Something rustled off to the right, and Owen turned. About twenty feet away, a clear trail led down into the brambles. He was sure no such trail mouth had been there a moment before.

"Like I said," Robin told them, "you gotta watch out for the brambles. They're wicked."

"I guess," said Owen, impressed.

Justin stared at them both, and followed wordlessly down the slopes of Elk Hill.

* * *

The door to the nameless bar and grill swung open with an unearthly groan. Inside, half a dozen conversations stopped suddenly, leaving the room in silence. Owen led the way in, and crossed the room to a booth over to one side, well away from the bar. The light was dim enough that he could only just see the other patrons, and he made a point of not looking at them. Justin, who had been told what to expect, did the same thing, and sat down facing Owen. After a moment the conversations at the bar started up again, one by one, in lower tones.

A few minutes passed, and then a young woman in a plain brown dress and an apron came out from behind the bar and crossed to the booth. "Menus?" she asked.

"Please," said Owen.

She doubled back to the bar, returned and plopped two menus on the table. Owen took one—a single handwritten sheet—and glanced down it. "What's good?"

She considered him. "Linny in back cooks a heck of a burger. Other'n that, I'd have to say the smothered chicken or the meatloaf platter." They got their orders settled, and she went on. "Anything to drink?"

"What's the local beer like?" Owen asked.

That got him another assessing look. "How dark d'you like it?"

"Road tar's a good start," Owen said at once, and she laughed. "I can do that."

"Make that two," Justin said. She nodded and headed back to the bar.

"I thought everyone in rural America drank yellow beer," Justin said once she was gone.

"You're not in that rural America," Owen replied. In response to Justin's puzzled look: "It's kind of hard to explain." He thought for a moment. "The America you know is like a blanket stretched out over the top of another country. Most people don't know the other country is there, but there are holes in the blanket. If you get to one of the holes, you can drop right through it into the other country."

"Where they make good beer," Justin said. "Do they have a brewery here, or what?"

Owen shook his head. "No, it's brewed at home, the way most people used to brew their beer a hundred years ago. In Dunwich, the people who are really good at brewing take turns making batches for the Standing Stone; I don't know how they do it here." He stopped talking as the waitress came back over with two tall glasses. The beer in them was nearly black, with a little tuft of brown foam on top.

"Now that looks good," Justin told her, and got a faint smile in answer.

She went back to the bar, and Owen went on. "On top of the blanket, the other side I mentioned earlier—they pretty much call the shots. They want everything to follow their idea of order and reason. Every bottle of beer has to taste exactly the same." He sipped his beer; it had the kind of earthy flavor that sang of sun on hop leaves and smoke rising through roasting barley. "And never like this. Never anything that reminds you that every bit of your body used to be dirt in a farmer's field, and is going to turn back into that in due time."

Justin nodded slowly, and then downed some of his beer, blinked, and grinned. "If this is what they brew in the other country, I'm ready to go there."

"You're already in it," Owen said.

Justin took that in. "Dunwich is part of the other country."

"It's one of the holes."

He drank more of the beer. "Innsmouth?"

"Used to be one of the holes. Maybe it'll be one again someday."

"And—Elk Hill."

"That's the thing," said Owen. "The hidden country isn't all good beer. It's all kinds of things that nobody on top of the blanket remembers any more. Some of them are as good as this." He took another swallow of his beer. "Some of them are even better—but then there are other things, and some of them are pretty scary."

Justin nodded after a moment, his expression suddenly gone bleak. "And some people fall through the holes and nobody ever sees them again."

Right then the waitress came back with their meals, a double-decker cheeseburger and fries for Justin, meatloaf and mashed potatoes for Owen. "You want another of those?" she asked Justin, whose beer glass was well on its way to empty.

"Please," Justin told her, and she left.

Once she'd returned with a second full glass, Owen went on. "I fell through one, and a lot of people never saw me again," he said. "It happens that way sometimes. But you're right—there are things in the other country that you don't want to meet. There are powers there that can snuff out a human life the way you and I step on an ant, without even noticing it. And there are things that hunt us." He paused. "There are protections—but now and then they fail."

"Yeah," said Justin. "I get that." He gave Owen a troubled look, and picked up his burger.

* * *

Neither of them said much for a while. On the far side of the room, patrons came and went at the bar, dim shapes in the uncertain light. Owen ate his meatloaf and considered the things they'd seen since their arrival. Justin wolfed his burger, downed the second beer, ordered a third, drank it and ordered a fourth. His lips pressed tight together as he stared at the table.

"If the story's right," he said finally, "the van der Heyl house is where it's going to happen." With a sudden sharp laugh: "The Hell House. That was one smart kid."

"Maybe," Owen replied. "If Lovecraft and Lumley copied the diary accurately, Typer disappeared there, and probably the van der Heyls too. We don't know about the others." He leaned forward. "Tomorrow I'm going to see if I can meet with the elders here—and there's the witch that Walt Moore knows, if she'll talk to us."

Justin blinked in surprise, and after a moment said, "The 'Miz Eagle' he mentioned." When Owen nodded: "How do you know she's a witch?"

A line from an old movie passed through Owen's mind, but he managed to suppress the smile. "The way he talked about her. Depending on what this one knows, we can figure out what the next step's going to be."

Justin nodded, finished his beer, flagged down the waitress and got another. "I'm pretty sure what my next step is," he said, looking down at the table again. "The only question's when."

"We don't know that," said Owen.

"Give me one reason that's not going to happen." His words slurred faintly.

"We've been here four whole hours," Owen reminded him. "I have a lot of questions to ask and a lot of places to look before I'll have any kind of idea of what's going on. I'll say this much, though. Whatever's on or in Elk Hill is alive, and it listens. You saw how the boy talked to it. If we can figure out how to communicate with it there's a real chance we can find out what's behind all this."

Justin said nothing. Owen watched him. The younger man's face, usually bloodless, looked flushed—or was that just a trick of the light?

He sipped the last of his beer, set the glass down. Justin gestured at it: another? Owen shook his head, and as though in answer, Justin picked up his glass and drank most of it down, then waved the waitress over.

"It's your business," Owen said, "but I'd go easy on those. Tomorrow's going to be kind of a long day."

"Look," said Justin, his voice loud and slurred, "I've come here to die—"

He stopped. All the other conversations in the bar had stopped as well, and everyone at the bar had turned to look. He stared back at them for a moment, and then slumped, burying his face in his hands. He mumbled something incoherent, then all at once started to cry.

The waitress, who had been on her way, stopped in the middle of the room but came over as Owen got to his feet. "What do I owe you?" he asked.

"Not a thing," she said. "We heard from Dunwich." Then: "Need any help with him?"

"No, he'll be fine. Thanks."

He stood up, took hold of Justin's arm. "Come on. Let's get you back to the motel." The younger man gave him a blank unfocused look but let himself be hauled to his feet. Owen got the arm settled over his shoulders, and half-hauled him across the room to the door.

Outside night had closed in, and a few stray stars flickered down through gaps in the cloud. Dim lights here and there cast a fitful gleam across Chorazin, vanished without a trace in the vast dark mass of Elk Hill beyond. Owen got Justin's weight settled and started across the street. As he got to the far side, he felt the younger man's body sag and shudder in a way he recognized, and lowered Justin so that he could vomit into the weeds, holding his shoulders so he didn't pitch forward face first into the mess. Once the last of it was over, he lifted the younger man, got the arm over his shoulders again, and hauled him around to the back of the motel.

It took a moment to find the key in Justin's pocket, but that was the only difficulty. Owen half-carried him inside, stripped him to his underwear and got him into bed, thinking of the times he'd done the same thing for somebody back in his Army days, or somebody had done it for him. Lay him on his side so he'd be okay if he vomited again, put the room key and a glass of water on the nightstand and a trash container close by: it made him feel young and brash and scared again for a moment. He shook his head, turned out the light, made sure the door latched tightly.

Wind rustled in the brambles, and seemed for a moment to be calling: *Follow, follow*. Owen glanced over his shoulder at the hill, and said aloud, "No, you don't. Play fair."

The voice dissolved back into empty wind, and Owen went into his room and got ready for bed. Sleep came quickly—he'd managed to keep the Army trick of falling asleep whenever circumstances allowed—and for a time his dreams wandered among scenes from his childhood and memories of Laura. In the darkest part of the night, though, tall stones and a vast black-pawed shape came into his dreaming, and the voice whispered again: *Help me. Free me.*

CHAPTER 5

THE STARRY WISDOM

He was up before dawn as usual and left his room a few minutes after six. Chorazin was still in shadow, though red morning sun on the upper slopes of Elk Hill gilded the brambles and made the standing stones glow like hot coals. First things first, he told himself, and went to the unmarked door Walt Moore had mentioned. It was unlocked, and he let it close behind him and shut out the hill's riddles for a little while.

Inside was a windowless room with an old couch on one side, a long counter topped with steam tables and a coffee maker on another, and a big ramshackle table in the middle surrounded by a random assortment of chairs. Walt Moore was sitting at the table, nursing a cup of coffee, and a sleepy-eyed young woman with short bottle-black hair was half-curled on the couch, her belly showing the early stages of a nine months' process Owen recalled well.

"Morning," Walt said, looking up from his coffee. "Early riser, I see."

Owen grinned. "I could say the same thing."

"Old habit," the older man said. "Got it in the Army."

"Me too." Owen got a cup of tea steeping, found a chair at the table.

Walt watched him for a moment, then: "I'm gonna guess infantry. You see action?"

"Yeah," Owen said, impressed. "I was in Iraq. You?"

"Special Forces, 1966 to '70, mostly over in Laos. I've got friends' names on the big black wall in Washington, and damn if I know why mine isn't there too." A quick shake of his head dismissed the question. "I hope your friend is okay."

"News travels fast," said Owen.

The old man chuckled. "I go over to Carla's for a drink most nights after closing up—but yeah, it's that kind of town."

Owen nodded. "I figure he'll be fine. Too much beer on top of too much stress. You know how that goes."

"Ain't that the truth." He sipped his coffee. "That used to be me way too often." He waved at the steam table. "Food's already there, Help yourself—it's liberty hall."

"Thanks." Owen got his tea dark enough, downed a swallow, got up from his chair. Just then the young woman let out a little whimpering sound. Before the old man could respond, Owen said to her, "If there's anything I can get you, just let me know."

"A little hot water," she said in a small squeaky voice. "Please."

"Sure." He got up, filled a cup half full, gave it to her. "My wife had our first two months ago," he said. "She didn't have a lot of morning sickness, but there were times."

The young woman gave him a grateful look, sipped at the hot water, curled up again. Owen found a plate, checked the contents of the steam tables, spooned out scrambled eggs with peppers and onions, buttermilk biscuits, sausage gravy. Those kept him busy for a good quarter hour. Afterwards, he made another cup of tea, settled in his chair again, and glanced at Walt Moore. "You told Justin you know why he's here. If you don't mind my asking, how often do you get people coming to Chorazin for that reason?"

The old man's face tensed as he considered that. "Once in ten years, maybe. Counting your friend, I've seen five of 'em since I got out of the service. But it was going on long before my time." He shrugged. "How long, I don't know. Like I said, I don't know a lot about this stuff—but there are others that know more."

"You mentioned a Ms. Eagle last night," Owen ventured.

"Yeah. I went to look for her, but couldn't find her. She's that way—you find her when she wants to be found. You deal with witches much?" When Owen nodded: "We got one of the ordinary kind here too—you need bleeding stopped or ill-wishing taken off your animals, Betty Hale's the one to talk to. Old Sallie Eagle, she's not your ordinary kind of anything—she's something else again. But I was thinking of some others besides witches."

He set down his coffee, then, and put three of the fingers of his left hand over his right wrist at a certain odd angle. The moment he was sure Owen had seen it he moved his hands apart again. Owen put three fingers of his right hand at a different angle across his left wrist. Walt caught the gesture instantly, and Owen picked up his teacup again.

Walt nodded. "No rush, but once you're done with breakfast, you got a little while?"

"Sure," he said. "I can leave a note for Justin."

"Might be a good idea." Walt glanced at the couch, where the young woman had finally managed to doze off for a while; the empty teacup sat on the cushion beside her, and her head was slumped down on her chest. He turned back to Owen, then, and in a low voice said, "You saw the church? Good. Go to the back door, give the knock, grip, and password of your degree. Don't worry about the dishes; that's my job."

Owen nodded, got to his feet. "Thanks. Might as well be now."

* * *

From outside, the church looked derelict. Paint that had once been white peeled from the clapboards; the windows were dark; the front stairs angled crazily where they hadn't simply collapsed in on themselves; a padlocked chain held the front doors shut. Sharp-thorned rose bushes ran feral along the sides of the building, discouraging the casual visitor. Owen knew how to read certain signs, though, and ducked through the narrow gap between the rose bushes and one side of the general store.

On the far side of the gap was an alley, and beyond it gardens where the first shoots of corn, beans, and squash had shoved their way through the soil. Owen turned, walked down the alley a few yards, and reached the church's back door, which was covered in sheet metal and pierced with a peephole at eye level. He walked up to it and knocked once, then twice.

A moment passed, and then a heavy deadbolt clicked and the door opened. A lean gray-haired woman in a plain cotton house dress stood inside; she let him take her hand in the second degree grip of the Starry Wisdom, tilted her head so he could whisper the password into her ear, then released his hand and said, "Good morning, Mr. Merrill," in an unexpectedly deep voice.

He said the polite thing, let her close and lock the door behind them and lead him down a flight of stairs. A short dimly lit hallway ended at another metal-covered door, where Owen knocked twice and then once.

Knock, grip, and password weren't the only protections the Starry Wisdom Church used. Owen knew some of the others, though not all—that knowledge would have to wait until he received the higher initiations. Still, a prickling ran up the back of his neck as he stood at the door. Though he knew the three-lobed eye of the Watcher wasn't actually staring at him from the shadows, it always felt that way.

The door finally opened. Inside was a plump and balding man with a ready smile, who took Owen's hand in an ordinary handshake and said, "Mr. Merrill. Thanks for coming over. Can I get you coffee or tea?"

He waved Owen toward one end of a long table in the church's social hall, where another woman sat. It all looked very familiar to Owen. The tables and chairs in the room could easily seat a hundred people, and white plaster walls and a tin ceiling stamped with ornate patterns made the hall look bigger than it was. On one end were two doors, one closed, with a sign saying CHURCH OFFICE, the other open, letting onto a kitchen. On the other end, a stair led to the worship hall above. Old lithographs in fancy frames decorated the walls: here an allegorical print of the seven degrees of the Starry Wisdom; there a picture of the Mother Church in Providence with its tall steeple; next to the stair, an image of the ankh, the looped cross of Egypt, with the emblems of the seven degrees clustered around it and the Shining Trapezohedron in the center of the loop.

Introductions followed. The woman who'd met him at the door was Betty Hale, a fifth degree initiate; Owen noted the name, remembering what Walt Moore had said. The man was Bill Downey, seventh degree and a church elder, and the other woman, whose thin hair was stark white and whose bright eyes regarded him from a face full of wrinkles, was Cicely Moore, seventh degree, the senior initiate of the church. All three of them had the olive skin, the straight hair, and the high-cheekboned faces that Owen had begun to think of as the Chorazin look.

"So," Bill said, once he'd gotten a mug of something hot for everyone. "We got word yesterday from Dunwich, as I'd guess you know already."

Owen nodded. "I heard last night at Carla's."

"There you are. But we're hoping you can give us some idea of what all this is about."

"I'm guessing you know quite a bit more about it than I do," Owen said.

"Maybe," said Cicely Moore. "But maybe not the same things. To have the Crawling Chaos involved in this business—that's not something any of us expected." A quick shake of her head punctuated the words. "Perhaps you can tell us what this Justin Martense is here to do."

"That's just it. He doesn't know." Owen sketched out what Justin had said about the family curse. "He spent years in Europe trying to figure out what he was supposed to do, and couldn't find a thing. Nyarlathotep met him there when he'd run out of options."

"And sent him to you," the old woman said.

A brief silence came and went, and then she glanced at Bill, who nodded fractionally. "Here's the puzzling thing," he said. "You know this happens every so often, right?" Owen nodded, and he went on. "Twice now—around the end of the last century, and again about seventy years before that—we've had people like him who knew exactly what they meant to do, and didn't bother to hide it. Both said there was something evil inside of Elk Hill and they were going to go and banish it. Folks here were concerned, and there was some rash talk from some of our young men, but then they both up and disappeared the way most of 'em do, one night—it's always by night that they go, when that happens."

"That's interesting," Owen said. "What happens to the ones who don't vanish?"

The man's face tensed. "It's not pretty," he said. "Head's half torn off, and not a drop of blood left in the body. But that's just now and then. Usually you just don't ever see 'em again." He shook his head. "But we always figured the others had the same thing in mind as the two I mentioned, and just wouldn't talk about it."

Owen took that in. "I don't imagine any of them got a room at the motel."

That got a sudden laugh from Cicely. "Nope. Nor anything fit to eat at Carla's, nor any help finding their way 'round the place. You two would have gotten the same treatment if the Dunwich elders hadn't recommended you—but you can see why we're good and puzzled."

"If you don't mind my asking," said Owen then, "what's in the hill?"

"Nobody knows," Bill told him.

Another silence, and then Betty Hale spoke. "There used to be songs, Mr. Merrill, 'bout the Sleeper in the Hill. We still know a couple of 'em, but most—" She shook her head. "They were very old, or so I've heard. I've seen one in a book from 1928, but I'm guessing they go back a long ways before that."

Owen considered her, and then the others. "Back as far as 1457?" he asked.

The blank looks he got told him that the date meant nothing to them. "There's something else you should know, then," he said. "I didn't get this from Justin. I learned about it from his aunt; we stayed with her the night before we came out here. It's a story they got from an ancestor of theirs—a man named Jan Maertens." He drew in a breath, began the tale.

* * *

An hour later, maybe, Owen picked his way around the feral rose bushes and crossed the road to the motel. The sun was well above the hills to the east, and he could hear the bleating of goats from pastures somewhere nearby, but the town looked as deserted and dusty as ever. Even so, from the middle distance, he heard children's voices rising in a singsong chant:

> "The King is in Carcosa,
> The Goat is on the hills,
> And there and back the One in Black
> Goes wand'ring where he wills.
> But down below the ocean,

The Dreaming Lord's asleep,
Until the night the stars are right
And call him from the deep.
He waits for one year, two years, three years ..."

It was a rhyme for jumping rope, one Owen had heard many times already in Dunwich. They would count the years until one of the jumpers made a misstep. He slowed, listening, and suddenly thought of little Asenath back in Dunwich. He clenched his hands, missing her, missing Laura, and only when the chant dissolved in laughter—they'd made it to the count of eighteen before that happened—did he cross the street to the motel.

He went around to the back, thought about knocking on Justin's door, and decided against it: too early yet, probably. Instead, he went to the unmarked door and the breakfast room inside, and there Justin was, sitting at the table hunched over a cup of coffee, staring at nothing with a bleak expression on his face. The young woman was gone, and sounds of water splashing from the far side of a half-open door announced Walt Moore's location.

Owen got himself a cup of tea, sat down facing Justin. The younger man glanced up at him, then looked away. Finally: "I hope I didn't say or do anything too stupid last night."

"No," Owen said. "Not particularly."

That got another glance, longer. After another silence: "Walt Moore said you were over at the church."

"Yeah. I got to talk with some of the elders. I can fill you in."

"Please. I'm trying to nerve myself up to breakfast."

"Probably a good idea," Owen said. "We've got a bunch of things to do."

Justin got up, went to the steam tables, served himself eggs and biscuits, considered the sausage gravy and looked vaguely green for a moment. He slumped back into his chair and gave the plate a dubious look, but started eating, a little at a time.

As he ate, Owen recounted the conversation he'd had with the Starry Wisdom elders.

By the time he'd finished, Justin's bleak look had returned. "Okay. Head torn off and blood drained out—if that's what it's going to be, that's what it's going to be."

"We don't know that," Owen cautioned him. "And we do know something else: whatever happens to the people who disappear, it happens at night. That's a clue. Some of the creatures of the elder world are only active in darkness. If one of them's behind this business, there are protections—and we can also make sure you're indoors when the sun's down."

"Protections," Justin said. "What kind of protections?"

"There's a spell I can teach you," said Owen. "It's called the Vach-Viraj incantation, and it will protect you against some creatures. There are some things I can do as an initiate, and we can also ask Ms. Eagle for help if we get the chance to talk to her."

The bleak look on Justin's face began to fade. "Witches do stuff like that?"

"All the time. When I first stumbled into this whole business, a witch named Abigail Price gave me an amulet, and it literally saved my life."

Justin nodded slowly. "Okay."

"And there's another thing," said Owen. "The others who were called—the people here thought they were on the other side, and didn't talk to them at all. You only have a few pieces of the puzzle, but they have a few more, and maybe, if we put them together, that'll be enough."

"Okay," Justin said again, and sat up a little straighter than before. "That's more promising than anything I've heard since I first got called."

"Good." Owen finished his tea. "Because I think we need to do something you're not going to like much. If we're going to get to the bottom of this before—anything happens—we're going to have to check out the van der Heyl house—the place where Alonzo Typer disappeared—and see if there's anything left of the things he wrote in his diary."

"Yeah," said Justin. "I kind of expected that." He drew in a long breath, then: "I think you're right, though."

"When do you think you'll be ready to try that?"

He picked up his coffee cup, regarded the contents, downed them at a gulp. "The sun's up," he said. "Might as well be now."

* * *

Broken pavement and old gravel crunched beneath their shoes as Owen and Justin walked south on the remnants of an old road. Elk Hill rose stark and brown to their right; to their left, the steep eastern slopes of the valley drew close, dotted with oaks and maples. Sunlight streamed down from a clear spring sky, making the valley a little less foreboding.

"Right around 1760," Owen was saying as they approached the narrow place between the hill and the valley's side. "That's what Lovecraft and Lumley's story says."

"That's pretty early for white settlement in this part of the country, isn't it?"

"Very early. We're something like seventy-five miles on the wrong side of the Line of 1763—you might just remember that from history classes." When Justin shook his head: "The British government made a rule that year that settlement couldn't go west of the headwaters of the rivers that flowed down to the Atlantic coast. Here, the line of 1763's not much this side of Elmira. This was Seneca country then, too, so they must have gotten the tribe's permission or they'd have been chased off the land or worse."

"You know a lot about American history," Justin said, impressed.

"I just finished teaching that part of it to a room full of teenagers." In answer to Justin's questioning look: "That's what I do these days—teach the upper classes at the Dunwich

Starry Wisdom parochial school. Literature, composition, and history, mostly."

Justin laughed. "Not the *Necronomicon*?"

"No, there's Sunday school for that." He pointed ahead of them. "Okay, here we go."

On the far side of the narrows, Elk Hill curved away to the west, and the bramble-covered ruins of the van der Heyl house came into sight. At first glance, all Owen could see was a mass of brown, savagely barbed briars, with the distant shape of the old stone chimney rising out of the midst of them. As they walked further down the road, half-overgrown gaps in the briars appeared here and there, as though they had been trails once and might be again.

Remembering the way they'd climbed the hill, Owen turned toward the brambles as they walked, and said aloud, "We're going to the house."

Nothing happened at first. They walked on, and not ten feet further they discovered a gap that wasn't overgrown at all. The trail beyond it seemed to lead in toward the old chimney. Owen and Justin looked at one another. Justin swallowed visibly, and nodded; and without another word, the two of them left the road and started along the path. As they went, a hush seemed to gather, as though something had stopped the spring breeze. An effect of the hill's closeness? Owen doubted it.

The trail went on, never quite straight, for close to a quarter mile before it reached the ruins of the old chimney. There the briars thinned, and Owen could make out irregularities in the ground that spoke of foundations, passages, and cellars, all of them filled in long ago.

"This is really weird," Justin said suddenly: the first words either of them had spoken since they'd left the road. "It's like I've been here before."

"It seems familiar?" Owen asked.

"Really familiar." Justin looked around uneasily. "The story said there was a vault somewhere under the house, didn't it? A vault with a door."

They picked their way around scattered brambles toward Elk Hill. "North of the house proper," Owen said as they walked. "At the end of 'a long, outflung northerly ell'—that's what Typer wrote, according to Lovecraft and Lumley—and that's where the door was."

"So, maybe here." Justin indicated an uneven depression in the ground, two feet or so deep, that stretched away to the north.

"Maybe," Owen agreed. "There's another one over here."

They started working their way back and forth over the ground systematically. The ground sank here and there into shallow swales and depressions that might have been remnants of underground rooms. Scraps of broken tile and fragments of stone with mortar clinging to it hinted at the vanished house but gave no clue about its arrangement.

"I wonder how far these extend," said Owen. "If one goes further than the others ..."

They walked further north over more uneven ground, going most of the way to the foot of Elk Hill before great masses of brambles barred their way. If the vault described in the story went further north than the other ells of the old house, no mark on the ground revealed it.

Justin folded his arms and looked around. "We need a plan of the house—" Then, his face lighting up: "The county records office up in—what's the county seat here again?"

"Emeryville."

"That's the one. They ought to have something."

"The public library might also be worth a try," said Owen.

That got a sudden grin from Justin. "I didn't even think of that, and one of my grandmothers was a librarian. Good. We've got some options, then."

"Do you want to head for Emerysville now?"

Justin shook his head. "Tomorrow, maybe. I think we should give this place a good thorough search first. Let's try working our way back to the house."

Owen nodded and turned. Just then two tiny, simultaneous flashes caught his eye, up on the ridge overlooking the valley to the east. He recognized the sight at once from his army days: the glint of sunlight reflecting off the lenses of binoculars.

He gave the ridge a hard look, but could see nothing else. After a moment, he turned his attention back to the ground and the traces of the van der Heyl house.

* * *

They spent most of three hours going slowly over the entire ruin, or as much of it as they could reach through the brambles. Very little remained. The battered hulk of the old central chimney was the one part of the structure that still rose out of the ground. One corner of it jutted out from the surrounding briars. The thing was made of great rounded stones mortared together, and it looked to Owen's eye as though it could be climbed.

He made sure the stones were still solid, and then turned to Justin. "I might be able to get a better view from up on this thing. Can you give me a boost?" He mimed cupped hands, and Justin nodded, put his hands together, and let Owen get one foot braced in them. A sudden heave upwards, and Owen was hauling himself up onto the ragged shoulder of the chimney. Once he'd gotten himself in a stable position, he looked around.

Most of the landscape looked no different from his new vantage point, but he spotted a peaked roof of modern shape among the trees toward the creek, maybe a mile away. He glanced east to the ridge to see if he could see anyone up there, and then concentrated on the ruins. "Okay," he said aloud. Gesturing: "That way—a little further. Now straight out maybe thirty paces. There's something that looks like brick sticking up from the briars there."

Justin went out, came back. "Got it. Yeah, it's brick. I'm not sure how we managed to miss it earlier."

"I don't think we went that far west." He turned back to the landscape and tried to find any other sign of the missing vault. If there was anything on the surface, the brambles hid it. He happened to glance back west, toward the modern roof, and suddenly scrambled down the chimney and dropped to the ground.

"We've got company," he said. "One person, coming this way from the southwest. I couldn't see him well, but there's a house that way—he might be from there."

Justin gave him a startled look, nodded. "If we get asked questions—"

"Genealogy," Owen told him. "If he knows the local traditions he'll recognize your eyes."

"That ought to work. Let's check out the brick thing before he gets here."

They wound their way through the briars to the mass of brick Owen had spotted from the chimney. It wasn't anything either of them recognized at a glance, just a low uneven shape that might have been a thick wall, the base of a brick fireplace, or something else. They were still examining it when a rustling of brush and a voice announced the newcomer, and Owen glanced back over his shoulder.

There stood an old man in a polo shirt and pressed slacks, with a nondescript hat pressed down on his thin white hair. "I trust you'll excuse me," he said, "but I wanted to make sure you weren't in any trouble. This isn't the safest place to be, you know."

"Oh, hi," Justin said. "No, we're fine. Is this the van der Heyl house?"

The old man gave him a surprised glance. "Why, yes, it is. Not that many people know about the van der Heyls."

"They're distant cousins on my mother's side. I looked them up on a genealogy site last year." Justin wiped his right hand on his slacks, offered it to the old man. "I'm Justin Martense, and this is my friend Owen Merrill."

"Pleased to meet you both," said the old man, shaking hands. "I'm Aubrey Keel. So—a relative of the van der Heyls? There are some very strange stories about them, you know."

Justin should have gone into the theater, Owen decided then; he managed an utterly convincing look of surprise. "Really? No, I didn't know. None of my relatives'll talk about that end of the family, but I figured that meant they partied a lot or something."

Keel looked amused. "A reasonable assumption, but not, as it happens, correct." He glanced at them both and then went on. "May I push the limits of propriety by inviting you to my home for lunch, and perhaps a few beers? I live less than a mile that way—" His head motioned toward the house Owen had seen. "—and I don't have the pleasure of guests anything like as often as I would prefer. Besides, I know a great deal about the folklore of this region, and can fill you in about the notorious van der Heyls."

Justin glanced at Owen, who said, "Sure." "Please," the younger man said to Keel. "If you ever see me turn down a free meal, check my pulse."

The old man laughed. "A very sensible attitude. When I was an aspiring poet in New York City, I assure you I guided my affairs on exactly the same principle."

"You're a poet?" Owen asked.

"In a manner of speaking. It's been a long time since I've written anything serious. One of those things." He gestured toward a winding trail through the briars. "Shall we?"

CHAPTER 6

THE WHISPERING HILL

"I moved here just over half a century ago," Keel said, leading the way up onto the porch of his house. "An inheritance from a distant relative coincided, in a most timely manner, with a growing lack of enthusiasm for living in New York City. While I can't say that life here is without its disadvantages, I've never been tempted to go back."

He unlocked the door, waved them through. Inside, a short entry hall let onto a living room with a cathedral ceiling pierced by skylights. A staircase went up one wall to a loft above, from which big picture windows looked north and east; elsewhere, bookcases and cabinets lined the walls. In the middle, a long sofa and a matching armchair of Scandinavian-modern style sat on two sides of a glass-topped coffee table.

"Make yourselves comfortable," Keel said, gesturing toward the couch. "I'll see to the promised lunch—yes, and the beer. I trust an IPA won't be out of place. Food issues? No? All the better. If you'd like to wash up, there's a bathroom through that door." He waved off their offers of help and vanished into what, from the noises that followed, had to be the kitchen.

By the time they'd both washed and returned to the living room, Keel was ferrying out beer in glasses and sandwiches on plates. "And here we are," said the old man, settling on the chair. He picked up his glass and raised it: "To the van der Heyls." Owen and Justin repeated the gesture and the words, and sipped. The beer was a commercial brew, the kind of thing Owen had liked before he'd come to Dunwich; now it tasted insipid.

"The van der Heyls," Keel repeated. "One of the strangest stories of western New York. It begins with Dirck van der Heyl and his wife Judith, who left Albany in 1746 in a hurry. There were, it's said, rumors of witchcraft, and although that wasn't as heated an issue in New York as in Massachusetts, it was serious enough. You may be interested to know that Judith's maiden name was Corey, and she came from Salem—her father was the notorious Abaddon Corey, who is still quite a figure in Salem legend, I believe.

"They were here by 1753, when they were mentioned in the journal of an officer in an Irish regiment stationed at Fort Niagara. They lived in a simple cabin of the usual frontier type at first, but the house whose ruins you were exploring today was finished in 1761.

"They were wealthy and eccentric, and they kept to themselves, especially after the Revolution, when settlers started to arrive from further east. This valley was theirs—the Indians shunned it as an evil place, and sold it to them for very little—and they wouldn't sell property to the newcomers for any price. But there were settlers of a different sort." He gestured off into the distance toward Chorazin. "Indians, escaped slaves, indentured servants who'd run away from their masters: every sort of stray and renegade from the country all around. For some reason the van der Heyls welcomed them, and their descendants are still here. You came through the town east of the hill, I believe? The people there, and in the uplands to the east, are of that stock.

"And there were rumors." Another gesture, as though to summon them. "Strange noises heard from the house and the hill behind it, especially on May Eve and Hallowe'en. Strange rites practiced by the van der Heyl family and the villagers.

Sudden disappearances, some of them suggesting that old dark rites of human sacrifice were still being practiced. Children of the van der Heyls that weren't quite human. All through the late eighteenth and early nineteenth centuries, stories about the house spread through western New York and provided plenty of fodder for colorful stories around hearth fires from Buffalo to Syracuse. I could show you clippings from the old Buffalo newspapers that would amuse you no end.

"And then all of a sudden, on April 30, 1872, the entire family vanished, along with everyone else who was at the house—all the servants and two house-guests from I forget where. Gone, just like that." Keel snapped his fingers. "To this day no one knows what happened, or why. But the house kept its reputation. People who tried to live there came to bad ends—there were, as I recall, three unexplained deaths, five disappearances, and four cases of sudden insanity. There were plenty of others who tried to sort out the mystery without living in the house, and they had no better luck. It really does seem to have been a cursed place.

"But finally the house blew down. That was on November 12, 1935, in one of the worst storms ever recorded here. After that—well, you've seen what's left. People keep coming to see it, for any number of reasons, and a certain number of them are never seen again. That's why I came out to the ruins when I saw the two of you from my balcony upstairs. I do that whenever I see people in the ruins, as I have no interest in seeing the body count increased."

"Thank you," Justin said, picking up the last bit of his sandwich. "Do you have any idea what happened to the people who disappeared?"

Keel tilted his head, considered that. "A good question. It's been claimed that there were cellars and vaults underneath the house, and I suppose it's possible that there are deep pits full of water hidden under the briars here and there, or some such thing. Of course the locals insist that some sort of evil ghost haunts the ruins." He made a dismissive gesture. "In this day and age, you wouldn't think that people would believe such things, but there it is."

"An evil ghost?" said Owen. "That's wild. Do you know any stories about it?"

"Not to speak of. It's supposed to be really quite large, many times bigger than you or I, and it's always in the ruins but it can't be seen when the sun shines. When clouds block the sun, it can be glimpsed; when night falls, it can be seen; but its power is greatest on a night when stormclouds gather over the hill." The old man shrugged. "That's literally all I've ever heard."

They finished their sandwiches, and Keel took away the plates and brought out another round of beers. He told them more stories about that part of western New York, and then insisted on showing them the collection of pottery fragments he'd discovered over the years. They were laid out, with hand-written labels, in shallow drawers in one of the cabinets. One drawer held bits of china from the van der Heyl house; another had fragments of the delicate handthrown pots the Seneca made. Below it was a drawer of heavier shards painted in striking patterns.

"These are my pride and joy," Keel confessed. "Do you know of the Hopewell culture, the older of the two great mound-building cultures of North America? No? This part of New York State is the northeasternmost region where their sites are found, and I've wondered more than once if the hill is actually a mound of theirs. These shards are classic Hopewell. I have another drawer of them, and something else of theirs, something really remarkable." He closed the drawer when they'd finished admiring the contents, and slid out the one below it. It contained more bits of Hopewell pottery, and a shape of hammered copper, green with verdigris, cut and styled in the half-abstract image of a winged elk with spreading antlers.

"Copper *repoussé* was one of the Hopewell culture's fine arts," said Keel. "There are old copper mines in various parts of the Great Lakes region, where you find copper in nuggets—the Hopewell people never learnt to smelt ore, of course. Chalcolithic, we called that stage of culture back when I was at Dartmouth. I have no idea what they call it now."

Owen nodded. Next to the copper elk was another shard that didn't look like Hopewell pottery at all. It was heavy stoneware with a pale gray glaze, and it curved so little that he guessed it must have come from some very large vessel. "What's that?"

"Ah. You have good eyes." Keel turned toward him. "I found that about a mile upstream, where the creek cuts through glacial till. I'm sorry to say there was only the one shard. That's by far the oldest thing in my collection—it dates from before the last ice age. It's Hyperborean, from the Uzuldaroum period: Uzuldaroum IIIa, I think scholars call pottery of that kind."

He was watching Owen closely while he said those words. Owen, who knew a great deal about Hyperborea, took care to keep his face blank and give a vague nod. After a moment, Keel closed the drawer.

* * *

The old man offered them another round of beers and tried to engage Justin in talk about his family, but the sun was well into the western sky by then and Justin begged off. "We ought to be going," he said. "Our friends are going to pick us up at five, and it's a bit of a walk."

"Well, there you are," Keel said. "I'm glad to hear you didn't leave a car in Chorazin. They're not the most honest people you'll meet. I suppose that's to be expected, but—" He shrugged. "A certain amount of caution is advisable. I don't imagine I'll see you again."

"Oh, we may take another look at the house before we head back home," Justin said. "I promise we'll keep a close eye out for those pits."

"And the evil ghost," Owen added with a grin.

After the briefest of pauses, Keel nodded. "Please do be careful." They said their goodbyes, and Keel walked them to the porch and stood watching as they started east along the narrow dirt road. Neither of them spoke until they were well out of sight of Keel's house.

"An odd old bird," Justin said then.

"I won't argue." Owen considered him. "Has anyone ever told you that you do a very good imitation of a clueless young idiot?"

Justin grinned. "That's my patented Catskill hillbilly routine. Making people think I'm a lot dumber than I am has been a useful skill more than once. You're pretty good at acting dumb yourself, you know." Owen laughed and thanked him.

"So what do you think of him?" Justin went on.

"I don't know. He might just be a really odd old bird—but I was surprised that he knew about Hyperborea. That's not common knowledge at all."

"I've certainly never heard of it," Justin admitted. "Where is it?"

"Was," said Owen. "It's Greenland now, but this was before the ice sheets covered it."

"So a long time ago."

"A really long time ago. Before Atlantis—" He stopped in mid-sentence, seeing odd shapes in the sky off past Justin, close to the western horizon.

Clouds, he thought at first, then wondered if that was what they were. Long serpentine shapes, they writhed and drifted across the sky toward the stones atop Elk Hill. Justin gave him a startled look and then turned and followed his gaze, and the two of them stood there on the crumbling road for some minutes, watching the high dark shapes as they moved closer.

Then one blocked the sun for a moment. All at once Owen saw, or thought he saw, a dim half-transparent shape towering over the ruins of the van der Heyl house. The one thing Owen saw clearly was two dark shapes like paws, reaching out toward the place where he and Justin stood. A sudden gasp from the younger man told Owen that Justin had seen them too.

An instant later the sun came out from behind the cloud, and the shape vanished. "Let's get out of here," Justin said then, his voice unsteady. "Now."

Owen didn't argue. The two of them hurried along the remnants of the old road as quickly as they could, and got to the narrow place where the side of the valley came close to the side of Elk Hill a few minutes later. Above, the serpentine clouds seemed to be caught in an eddy of wind over the hilltop; it looked for all the world as though they were circling the ring of standing stones. Owen gave them an uneasy glance, kept walking.

A glance forward revealed that the two of them were no longer quite alone. On a big rock to one side of the road, half screened by the briars, sat a figure Owen recognized at once.

"Hello, Robin," he called out when they got within speaking range.

The boy got up and came toward them. "Hi. Bobby Downey says he saw you two go to the Hell House this morning. I told him he was full of it."

"Nope," Owen said. "We went there."

Robin's eyes went round as he took that in. "I wouldn't go there for anything. Did anything try to get you?"

"No," said Justin. "But we met an old man who lives about a half mile further on."

Robin scowled. "I know about him. He's not very nice." Then: "But Mr. Moore told me to see if you came back this way, and tell you that you're both invited for dinner at old Mrs. Moore's tonight, and take you there if you don't know her place."

"We don't," said Justin. "Lead the way."

They were halfway through the narrows when the sound of a car's engine came echoing from the road ahead. A few minutes later it came into sight: a new model compact, bright red. Owen and the others moved to one side. As the car rolled past, the driver glanced their way: a blonde woman in her forties, wearing the kind of expensive outdoor clothing Owen had rarely seen outside of catalogs. She looked at them closely, then drove on.

* * *

Dinner was at Cicely Moore's, and a dozen Starry Wisdom initiates had also been invited. While the meal lasted, it could have been a family dinner anywhere in the less affluent parts of the country. Platters and bowls passed from hand to hand; scents of roast pork, gravy, and homemade biscuits filled the air; amiable conversation circled around general topics that left no one feeling excluded. Only after the dishes went off to the kitchen, and everyone settled in the living room, did anyone breathe a word about the reason why Justin was in Chorazin.

"Owen tells me," Bill Downey said, "that we may have had some wrong ideas about the relatives of yours who came here in the past."

"So I hear," Justin replied. "That's not really surprising. We're kind of used to keeping the whole thing quiet—in the family, you know."

"So are we," said old Cicely Moore.

Justin nodded. "I get that."

Bill waited a moment, and then went on. "If you don't mind my asking, do you have a relative by the name of Rowena Slater? Blonde, maybe forty, dresses nice?"

Justin considered that, shook his head. "No. I know some Slaters back home, but they're not related to us, not that I ever heard—and none of them like that."

"We may have seen her driving south to the van der Heyl house," said Owen. "Two, maybe two and a half hours ago, on the way back up here with Robin Hale."

Bill nodded. "That was her. She came into town about two o'clock, said she was studying folklore at some university in New Jersey, wanted to know about local legends. She didn't know any of the signs of recognition, so nobody told her anything, but it occurred to some that there might be a connection."

"Mr. Merrill told us about your ancestor Jan Maertens this morning," Cicely said to Justin then. "We didn't know a thing about any of that before now."

Justin nodded. "And I don't know a thing about what's gone on here since then—except my relatives keep coming here and nobody ever sees them again. People here talk about the Sleeper in the Hill. I don't know who that is, or anything about her."

"You know it's a her," Cicely said.

"I hear her voice in my dreams," Justin told her.

The room went very silent. Owen glanced around the circle of faces, caught quick looks passing between senior initiates, and sensed secrets within secrets hovering in the room.

"That's been known to happen," said Cicely.

"If you don't mind my asking," Owen said, "do the people who hear it always vanish?"

"No," the old woman responded after a moment. "Not always. Sarah and Micah Moore heard it and came here. Red Eagle heard it and brought them here. The van der Heyls, they're all supposed to have heard it, and most of them lived out their lives—and now and then, somebody from outside with eyes like Mr. Martense comes here, stays a while, and then goes away."

"Sarah and Micah Moore," Justin said. "Red Eagle. Who were they?"

"The people who founded Chorazin," Bill Downey said. "Red Eagle was Shawnee; he had a vision that sent him up into the Adirondacks, where he found the Moores and brought them here. They were brother and sister, and they came from a town called Roodsford in Maine."

"I've heard of Roodsford," said Owen. "The town the Puritans destroyed."

"That's the one." Cicely nodded. "The Moores were just about the only people who got out, the way we heard it, and they went west when there wasn't much that way but wilderness—not even many Indian villages, with the smallpox and all."

"And the Sleeper in the Hill called them here," said Justin.

"That's what we believe," Cicely Moore said.

He drew in a breath. "Do you know who the Sleeper is?"

"We don't," the old woman replied. "I wish we did."

"Is she a Great Old One?"

Cicely made an equivocal gesture. "Something from the elder world, surely."

Justin stared at her for a moment. "Okay. Does anyone know?"

All the Chorazin folk in the room looked at each other. "Miz Eagle might," Cicely said. "Sallie Eagle, that is. There isn't much she doesn't know."

For a few moments no one spoke, and then Betty Hale's deep voice broke the silence. "I know this probably doesn't matter a bit to anybody else, Mr. Martense," she said, "but I hear you come from Lefferts Corners in New York." When Justin nodded: "Would you happen to know about an old church there that burnt down in 1916?"

Justin nodded "Yeah—my aunt lives right next to it." He turned to Owen. "The old cemetery we visited night before last—that used to belong to it."

"That was one of ours," said Betty. "A Starry Wisdom church."

That got her a startled look from Justin. "Okay," he said. "That makes sense."

Owen waited for a moment, and then turned to Betty. "Miss Hale," he said, "when we talked earlier, you said that there are songs about the Sleeper that the people here still remember— I wonder if you could share some of those with Justin and me."

She glanced at Cicely Moore, got a fractional nod, and then said, "I can sing you one of 'em, if you like." She turned to one of the younger initiates. "Tim, you got your harp?"

Justin gave her a startled look, apparently expecting the stringed instrument to make an appearance, but the man grinned and pulled something gleaming out of his shirt pocket. "Try catchin' me without it," he said, then cupped his hands around the harmonica and put it to his mouth.

The first long low wailing minor chord told Owen what song he was about to hear, and the one that followed confirmed it. As the young man played a third chord, Betty began to sing "The Sleeper in the Hill." The tune was the same, but the words were a little different:

> It's a long lonely road to the hill in the valley,
> Back home my old mama is cryin' her fill,
> Her poor wayward son's got to answer the callin',
> To go to the sleeper inside of the hill.
>
> Look away to the west where the thunder is breedin',
> Look away to the east where the wind has gone still,
> Look away to the north where the fire's on the hilltop,
> I'm called by the sleeper inside of the hill.
>
> Oh, nobody knows why the call comes in dreamin'
> When May flowers warm and November blows chill,
> And there's always a soul who must answer the callin'
> And go to the sleeper inside of the hill.
>
> Oh, Mama, forgive me, there ain't no way homeward,
> The road that I ride, it'll end where it will,

A door old as time's gonna open before me
It goes to the sleeper inside of the hill.

It's a long lonely road to the hill in the valley,
Back home my old mother is cryin' her fill,
Her poor wayward son's got to answer the callin',
To go to the sleeper inside of the hill.

Betty drew out the last note, and then let the harmonica's low voice finish the song.

"In its own way," Cicely Moore said then, "that song's precious. We've had trouble here from time to time, bad trouble, and some things got lost that shouldn't have. People back in the day knew things that nobody knows any more—things the van der Heyls knew, and the folk knew who came here before their time." She glanced at Justin, and then at Owen. "Now that you've heard it, maybe the two of you can figure out something we've missed."

* * *

Gravel sprayed from beneath the wheels of Justin's car as he turned off Chorazin Road onto the main road north, through Pine Center to Emeryville. The sun hung bright in the eastern sky. Owen sat back in the passenger seat, watched the fields and farmhouses roll past, and tried to put together the scraps of knowledge they'd found so far into a pattern that made sense.

Earlier that morning, when Owen went to the breakfast room, he'd found Justin already there, scooping a substantial breakfast onto his plate. They'd made plans in low voices, used the phone in the motel lobby to get recorded messages from the county records office and the library and find out when they'd open. That left more than two hours, and Owen put most of the time to use teaching Justin the Vach-Viraj incantation and coaching him until he had the words by heart.

"The town in Maine they mentioned last night," Justin said. "You said you knew about it."

Owen took a moment to recall what he'd learned about Roodsford. "It's an ugly story. There were people in colonial Massachusetts who didn't like the way the churches ran everything, and some of them left for places where they could believe what they wanted and live as they chose—Roodsford was one of those. Some families there worshipped the Great Old Ones, and they taught the others about them, so the fields and herds flourished, fish came to the nets, and more people started going to Roodsford, just walking away in the middle of the night so nobody could figure out where they'd gone or why.

"You can imagine what the religious authorities thought about that. So one day in 1693 the Reverend Gideon Godfrey took three hundred armed men to Roodsford, surrounded the town, killed everybody there—men, women, children—and burned it to the ground. I never heard that there were any survivors at all."

"I don't think I ever heard of that," Justin said.

"There's a lot of things in early American history that nobody talks about," Owen said. "Did your history classes in high school cover much of anything before the Revolution? Mine certainly didn't."

"No." Justin slowed down at an intersection, then stepped on the gas. "We got everything before 1776 in one week. I remember the *Mayflower*, the French and Indian War and the Salem witch trials, but that's about it."

"The *Mayflower* landed in 1620," Owen pointed out. "There were European settlements in North America before then, more than a few of them, but we'll let that go for now. Things really started moving toward revolution with the Stamp Act, which was in in 1765. There's a hundred and forty-five years between those dates. It was a hundred and forty-five years between the second inauguration of George Washington and the bombing of Pearl Harbor, and I think a few events happened in between those two."

Justin laughed. "Just a few." Then: "So what happened between 1620 and 1765?"

"Lots of things," said Owen. "One of them is that the worshippers of the Great Old Ones got a foothold established on this side of the Atlantic, and then they got stomped."

"The way Roodsford got stomped."

"Pretty much."

"Okay," said Justin. "By the other side you've mentioned."

"Exactly."

Justin was silent for a while. Then: "So what you're saying is that the hidden country you talked about—it's got its own history, too."

"Yeah." Owen glanced at him. "It goes back a lot further, too."

By then the houses had begun to crowd one another, and not long after that the road turned into one of the main streets of Emeryville. It didn't look much more prosperous than Lefferts Corners, but a dollar store in a strip mall just outside of town was still in business. Owen got out, went inside, came back with two spiral notebooks and a pair of pens.

The big brick county courthouse leaned above the town like a dowager hunched over her cane. That landmark, and a lucky guess that the other county buildings would be nearby, got them to the library, and within sight of an ugly four-story concrete building with the words CAPERNAUM COUNTY in once-modern script near one end.

Justin parked in the library parking lot, turned to Owen. "If you finish and I'm not back yet, come find me—I'll do the same. Anything else?"

Owen shook his head. "Nope. I'm good to go."

That got a grin in response. "Let's see if we can crack this open." The two of them got out, and Owen went to the library while Justin headed for the county records office.

* * *

The library was empty except for a middle-aged man behind the counter and two old women in garish dresses picking romance novels from a carrel. Owen smiled and nodded to the librarian, ducked past the old women, and started looking for the local history collection.

It didn't take him long to find the big double shelf next to the reference books, and before long he had a decent-sized stack of books he hoped might contain lore about Elk Hill, Chorazin, and the vanished van der Heyls—everything from a fat 1958 volume titled *A History of Capernaum County* to a recent glossy-covered paperback from a print-on-demand press, *Ghosts and Legends of Western New York.* He found a table well away from the door, sat in a chair that allowed him to track comings and goings without seeming to watch, and got to work.

Most of what he found confirmed the account they'd gotten from Aubrey Keel, but he copied it down anyway. The book of ghost stories was full of lurid tales about the Hell House—apparently Robin Hale's name for it wasn't original to him, or to the children of Chorazin. Several of the stories made Owen nod slowly. There were accounts of a giant with great black hands that haunted the banks of Huntey Creek, tales of people vanishing without a trace near the van der Heyl house, and an old Seneca legend of a great serpent that came down from the country of the sky people, coiled its body around Elk Hill, and ate anyone who came near it, until He-noh the thunder spirit drove it under the ground with his lightning arrows.

The history books were just as unsettling in their own way He found records of the van der Heyls themselves, the flurry of stories and speculations that followed their disappearance in 1872, accounts of others who went to the van der Heyl house and were never seen again, and some stranger tales. One case in particular stuck in Owen's mind: a man with a French name and an Asian face, who'd turned up near Chorazin in 1903 with a blank mind and bizarre mutilations. The local authorities had finally traced him to what was then French Indochina, and put him on a train for San Francisco after cabling the French consulate there. What had happened to M. Henri d'Ursuras after that, the local histories didn't say.

It took Owen well over an hour to get everything written out. When that was done, he gathered up the books, put them back where they belonged, and then went to the counter where the librarian sat, looking bored. He'd meant to ask about the van der Heyl house, but the eyes that glanced up at him were the same dark blue Owen had seen so many times at Chorazin.

"Can I help you?" the librarian asked.

"I'm not sure," said Owen. "I'm visiting with a friend, and yesterday we took a wrong turn and ended up going through a little town our map program didn't know about, and the people there weren't any ethnic group I recognized. Can you tell me anything about them?"

The librarian glanced around to make sure no one else was in earshot, and then said, "Yeah, you've met the Chorazin people—our local minority. Ever hear of the Melungeons down south, or the Lumbee people out on the Carolina coast?"

"Not to speak of," said Owen.

"They're mixed race, from way back. We've got a study of them from 1928; it's kind of outdated but as far as I know nobody's done anything since. I can get it for you if you like."

"Please," Owen said.

The librarian disappeared through a door, came back a moment later with a hefty book bound in gray library cloth. "It's reference, so you'll have to read it in the library," said the man, and then leaned forward. "And you don't want to talk too much about the Chorazins around here. A lot of people, especially the old folks—they're pretty prejudiced. Just a suggestion."

Owen thanked him for the book and the warning, and returned to his table. The book turned out to be a volume published by the US Ethnographic Survey:

THE CHORAZINS OF CAPERNAUM COUNTY
A Historical and Ethnographic Study

It was riddled with the biases found all through American ethnography in the first half of the twentieth century, and spent something like thirty pages discussing skull measurements, but the historical section was admirably detailed. The authors had copied out scores of early references to Chorazin and its people, and traced some of its early residents—an African slave who escaped from her owner in Albany in 1722, a pair of Irish brothers who were shipped across the Atlantic as boys in 1692 and found their treatment at a Pennsylvania farm intolerable, and so on through a long list. They even speculated about the origins of the Moore family, though apparently nobody had seen fit to mention Roodsford to them.

An appendix included songs, stories, and customs of the Chorazin folk. Owen wasn't surprised to find a version of "The Sleeper in the Hill" there, not too different from the two he'd already heard. The stories were mostly tales of the sort that pop up everywhere on the planet, though the Seneca legend of the serpent and the thunder spirit had found its way into the Chorazin repertoire with few changes. Of the customs listed, the only one that seemed relevant was the habit of building a bonfire atop Elk Hill on May Eve and Halloween. Down at the bottom of the page was a footnote in small print:

> The Chorazins themselves say that a spirit
> dwells within Elk Hill, and that these
> rites protect her from other beings that
> are hostile to her. The only particulars
> that could be learned about this being are
> found in the song "The Sleeper in the Hill"
> (p. 383-4 above). The stupidity and taci-
> turnity of the Chorazins made it impossible

> to determine more than the mere existence of
> this belief, as inquiries into the nature
> of the spirit or her enemies did not elicit
> informative responses.

Stupidity and taciturnity, Owen thought irritably. Or maybe they just didn't trust the Ethnographic Survey as far as they could throw it, and with attitudes like the ones the book demonstrated, it was no wonder. He paused, then, and kept reading. It wasn't simply official attitudes or ordinary prejudices, he knew. There was another factor at work, covert, disciplined, pursuing its own agenda across the centuries—

The Radiance.

You didn't even mention the name casually, not if you were one of the people of the Great Old Ones, part of the hidden country he'd tried to explain to Justin. Sometime soon, he decided, he'd have to tell Justin about the Radiance, the seven temples, the Weird of Hali.

He went through the index to make sure he hadn't missed anything, then took the book back to the librarian, thanked him, and left the library. Outside the day had gone sultry, and high wisps of cloud were streaming out of the west. He started across the parking lot toward the sidewalk and headed for the Capernaum County office building at the far end of the block.

He was maybe ten yards from the big glass doors in front when one of them opened and Justin came out. "Any luck?" he asked when the two of them met.

"Yeah," said Justin. "Quite a bit." He glanced around, made sure there was no one else within earshot. "The property got surveyed by the state after the van der Heyls disappeared," Justin went on. "I got copies. But there's something else." In a low voice: "The clerk said I was the third person to ask about the van der Heyl house this week."

Owen gave him a startled look. "Did you find out anything about the others?"

Justin grinned. "Yeah. I did the clueless and friendly routine, and got the clerk talking. There was an Asian guy two days ago, and a nicely dressed blonde late yesterday afternoon." In response to Owen's glance: "Yeah, that's what I thought too. Rowena Slater."

They started toward the library parking lot. "Did you find anything?" Justin asked.

"Maybe. Quite a few ghost stories and news items of people disappearing, and a lot of history about the van der Heyls—but I'm not sure if any of it will help."

"You never know," said Justin.

They reached Justin's battered blue compact and climbed into the car. "I figure we should probably get some lunch. Then—" He took a sheaf of papers out from inside the front cover of his notebook, handed them to Owen. "I'm pretty sure I know where the door was. If there's anything still there, that might be a clue."

"Sounds like a plan," said Owen. Justin nodded and turned the key.

CHAPTER 7

THE VOICE OF THE THUNDER

They got back to Chorazin around one-thirty, after a
leisurely lunch at Emeryville's one pizza house. More
clouds had rolled in from the west—not the lean writhing shapes they'd seen the evening before, just ordinary pale
sheets that turned the sun into a pearl-colored blur and veiled
the further hills. The clouds had piled up over Elk Hill, and
Justin gave the sky an uneasy look as they got out of the car.
"If this was home," he said, "and that was Tempest Mountain,
I'd expect a nasty storm right around sunset."

"Do you still want to go to the ruins?" Owen asked him.

Justin considered that, and nodded. "Yeah. We should have
three or four hours before the weather starts getting ugly."

Ten minutes later they stood by the crumbling mass of the
chimney. "Okay," Justin said then, consulting one of the sheets
of paper he'd brought with him. "Thirty-two feet to the back
wall of the original house, straight toward the hill."

Owen paced it off, did the same thing three more times as
Justin traced the longest of the house's northerly extensions out
toward its end. The brambles seemed heaped up even higher than
they'd been before, and Owen guessed they'd changed place as
well. Finally, though, he got to the same low shapeless mass of
brick they'd found the previous day. "Okay," Justin said, following behind him. "This pretty much has to be where the door—"

He stopped in midsentence. Owen was already staring. The day before, there had been a low irregular swale in front of the brick mass, no more than a foot deep at most, but something or someone had been digging. The depression was knee-deep now, a great uneven scar in the ground, with loose earth piled up all anyhow on both sides and the near end. Worse, the earth still in the pit didn't look as though shovels had been used on it; a backhoe might have left those widely spaced gouges, but the loose earth around the trench showed no tread or tire marks. It looked unnervingly as though the digging had been done by huge paws.

As they stood there, thunder muttered over the crest of Elk Hill. The clouds above the hill had darkened. "I think we need to get out of here," said Owen.

"Yeah." They turned away from the excavation, tried to make their way back to the road, but every path they took somehow curved insensibly toward the hill instead. Owen tried saying, "We're going to the road," but the brambles ignored him.

Before long they were hurrying along a narrow path surrounded by walls of brown tangled briars. Owen hadn't meant to hurry, and he was pretty sure that Justin hadn't intended it either, but something kept him from slowing, something that clouded his thoughts and drew him along at a breathless pace. He tried to chant the Vach-Viraj incantation for protection, but the words of the ancient spell went spinning away into confusion. The most his mind would manage was a simple stumbling prayer: "*Iâ Shub-Ne'hurrath*—Black Goat of the Woods, be with me." The prayer circled in his mind as the thunder grumbled above them. Justin's face was tense, his mouth compressed to a hard line; Owen wasn't sure what his face looked like but guessed it wasn't much different. It seemed all too likely to him, just then, that he and Justin would shortly become two more of the people who were never seen again.

The path suddenly veered to the left, toward the creek. The clouds darkened to black. As they hurried along, Owen glanced over his left shoulder, and wished he hadn't. The vast half-seen shape they'd glimpsed from the road the previous day loomed up against the lowering sky, reaching out great dark paws toward them. The brambles offered no shelter. The paws spread outwards, taking on more solidity as the light failed, and Owen waited for them to descend.

Instead, lightning blazed above the crest of the hill, and a first spatter of fat raindrops pocked the bare dirt of the trail. The thunder came in hard bursts like blows from a hammer, and there seemed to be words in it, though they weren't words in any language that Owen knew.

All at once another lightning flash cast harsh shadows all around them. A moment later the wind hissed hard in the brambles, and rain came sluicing down from a sky the color of ink. Thunder rolled again, and this time there were two voices in it that chilled Owen's blood. One of them sounded like laughter, except that it couldn't have come from a human throat. The other, high and shrill, was a scream.

The trail seemed to veer from side to side—or was it simply that he and Justin were stumbling and slipping in mud and streaming water, as the rain poured down on them and the thunder roared? Owen did not know. All sense of direction had long since gone spinning away into the unknown. There was only the narrow path between walls of bramble, the black curtain of the rain, the thunder's voice roaring unknown words, and a vague but growing sense that someone or something waited for them at the path's end.

Then a glow that wasn't lightning glinted through the streaming rain in front of them, a little point of pale yellow light. It took Owen minutes of stumbling forward through the rain and murk before he recognized it as the light of an old-fashioned kerosene lantern. The dark shape that rose behind it turned eventually, with the help of a lightning flash, into a low house, little more than a shack, nestled in the midst of a grove of ancient oaks.

The path led there and nowhere else. The two of them clambered through the mud and rain to the house, found themselves on a wide porch that gave some shelter from the storm. The lantern hung by a wire bale from one of the rafters, as though it had been set there to guide them. Nearby was a door, closed, and a small-paned window that let in on perfect blackness.

Owen wiped the rain from his face, pushed his sodden hair back, blinked repeatedly. Justin was doing much the same thing. When they could both see clearly again, they glanced at each other, uncertain.

Just then the door near them rattled and opened. "You'd best both come in," said a voice: old, female, cracked. "The storm won't stop 'til you do."

The two of them gave each other worried looks, but went to the door.

* * *

"You're lucky you found me," the old woman said, glancing back over her shoulder at them; her eyes gleamed in the dim light. "These days, I'm elsewhere far more often than here. Ah, this will do nicely."

She came away from the battered little woodstove in the corner of the room with a mug in each hand, set them on the little round table in front of Owen and Justin, went back to fetch the lantern from over the stove, and hung it on an unseen wire above the table. Owen thanked her. After a moment, Justin did the same.

The room was as small and low-ceilinged as the outside of the house suggested. Big bundles of herbs tied with string hung from the rafters, filling the stuffy air with resinous scents; a few pieces of ancient furniture lined the walls. The blankets she'd thrown around their shoulders were warm but malodorous, and so coarse that Owen wondered briefly if he'd been handed the pelt of some large animal. Still, he and Justin were safe from the storm. The warmth of the blanket was welcome, the mug of hot liquid in front of him smelled of herbs he'd learned to use in Dunwich, and he thought he knew whose house they had so unexpectedly reached.

The old woman pulled a three-legged stool over to the table, perched on it. "Drink up," she told them. "A storm like this one wants a life, but it needn't be either of yours."

She was, Owen thought, quite possibly the ugliest human being he'd ever seen. Her face, framed in long white stringy hair, had long ago collapsed into wrinkles and folds. Her mouth was wide as a frog's, with chinless jaw to match. Her eyebrows were thick, white, and bushy, and they met in the middle of her forehead; beneath them, small rheumy eyes glittered cold. Coarse garments hid all the rest of her but her hands, which had short fingers and crooked yellow nails. Just for a moment, she reminded him of someone, but the memory would not surface. He picked up the cup, sniffed, murmured a traditional blessing, drew in a deep lungful of the vapor, and then sipped at the hot liquid.

"Ah," she said. "You've been to see a proper witch before now."

That confirmed his guess. "Are you Ms. Eagle?"

She smiled, showing discolored teeth; they looked unnervingly sharp. "That I am." Before Owen could speak: "No, you needn't tell me who you are, Owen Merrill, nor you, Justin Martense. I knew that much before you came to Chorazin."

"You heard from the Dunwich folk," Owen ventured.

"Them among others."

He wondered what that meant.

"Then you know why I've come to Elk Hill," Justin said then.

She turned toward him and smiled again, and the jagged teeth caught the lantern light a second time. "I knew that a long time ago." She gestured at the mug. "Drink that up before it cools down—it'll protect you from worse than colds."

Justin gave her a startled look, picked up the mug. Owen had just drawn in another lungful of the vapor before sipping, and Justin imitated him.

"Good," said the witch. "Quick to learn. That might just get you through all of this with a whole skin."

"If there's any help you can give me, I'd be grateful for it," Justin said. "I don't know if there's anything I can do for you in return, but ..." He left the sentence unfinished.

"Maybe, might be," she answered. "If you live, why, then I'll have something to ask of you, you can be sure of that. But help for you—that you'll have. To start with, we should see what the cards say. Have you had those read for you?"

"Not by a proper witch," Justin answered.

That seemed to amuse her greatly. "Well, then." She heaved herself up off her stool, went to a dilapidated chest of drawers, and came back with a little packet wrapped in a frayed silk cloth. "The cards know more than they'll tell, but they might just tell enough."

The cards fluttered in her hands as she shuffled them, dealt out three in a stack, turned them over and fanned them out. They had cheaply printed images on them, faded from long years of use. "The Lilies, the Clouds, the Tower," she said. "That's the past. Lilies and Clouds tell of your family sorrow, the Clouds mean its real nature's hidden from you, the Tower tells of death seen from far off. Nothing there we didn't know already."

She dealt out three more, turned them over and fanned them. "The Birds, the Book, the Broken Mirror. That's the present. There's danger near, but there's something secret at work in all this that might protect you. The Mirror, though, that's bad, that's very bad. Someone is dead, someone you know. There'll be more blood spilled before all this is over, and it'll be spilled in the same manner."

Three more cards fanned out in the yellow light. "The Fox, the Lightning, the Crossroads. That's the future. Someone's laying a trap for you. Be on your guard. You've got hard choices to make, and that'd be difficult enough even if you see the things that count. The picture's in front of you, but you haven't put the pieces together. Someone else might do that for you. Maybe."

Three more cards joined the ones she'd already dealt. "The Swords, the Eye, the Dog. That's the road before you. There's danger, grave danger, and someone is watching you that you can't see, maybe for good, maybe for ill. They'll take a part in this before the end, but on which side? That's the question. You need help—that's the Dog's message. You've got good people to help you, but they can't save you, not by themselves. There's another, though, who might."

A fifth fan of three cards went below the others. "The Mountains, the Rider, the Flame. That's the end. The mountains, those are powerful enemies that stand in your way. They're not here yet, but they're coming. The Rider, that's a traveler from afar who comes to your aid, and how does it end? Maybe good fortune for you, maybe not, but nothing stays as it was." She glanced up at him, her eyes gleaming in the yellow light. "Nothing."

* * *

Something like an hour passed before the storm finally drifted off to the east and the long red rays of the setting sun slanted across the valley. While they waited, the witch brewed them each a second mug of whatever she'd given them, and muttered something over it before bringing it to the table. It was, Owen knew, risky to sample unknown beverages in the house of a witch one didn't know, but it was even more risky to insult a witch by refusing her hospitality, and so he breathed in the vapor and sipped. There were protective herbs in it, he could tell, and others whose purpose he could not begin to guess.

"The Sleeper in the Hill," said the witch, leaning forward; Justin had just asked about that mysterious figure. "Oh, I know a name for her, but it's not a name you'll ever know, not if you lived a thousand years and read lore that's been lost since before Atlantis went under the waves. What you'd call her I've no notion. She's been here beneath Elk Hill for a good long time. Before the van der Heyls, before Mishkwapelethi led Micah and Sarah Moore here with the treasure that's lost, since the men crossed the sea to die here—"

Justin drew in a sudden sharp breath. "You know about them."

That earned another of her sharp-toothed smiles. "Oh, I know a good many things. But it goes back before them, too, to seven temples of the ancient gods, seven rituals of blood and bane, and one prophecy that hasn't yet come to pass." She glanced at Owen then. "One Weird." Owen stared at her wide-eyed, catching the reference, and she smiled again.

She got to her feet, then. "Listen up, now. What help I can give you will come later on, when the time's right. But the storm's about blown by, and once it's gone you both need to get back to Chorazin just as fast as you can. Take the path I'll show you. Don't go back the way you came, or it'll be the death of you both. Once you get to Chorazin, if folk ask, let 'em know where you've been and what I told you. You understand?"

They both said they did, and she nodded. "Good. Time to go outside."

They followed her out onto the porch. Raindrops still pattered down from the leaves above, but the sky to the west was clearing, letting orange sunlight spill over the ridges that framed that side of the valley. The dark mass of Elk Hill rose behind them. Ahead, past the black trunks of the oaks, Huntey Creek splashed and gurgled over rocks not twenty yards away.

"There's your path," the witch said, pointing toward the water. "Alongside the stream, going the way the water goes. When you pass the last of the brambles there'll be an old road back to Chorazin, and that'll be safe. Don't leave the path until you find the road, and don't leave the road no matter what 'til you get to the town."

The rain stopped, and she waved them toward the path. "Now's the time. Go!"

They both thanked her and hurried through the trees toward the creek. When they got there, the sun blazed low and red to the west. Owen glanced back the way they'd come, but he could see no trace of the little shack, the oak grove around it, or the old witch.

The waters of the creek ran brown and turbulent, and Owen guessed they were well above their usual banks. The path the witch had described, though, stood well back from the water's edge, atop a steep bank of heaped stone. He turned to Justin, and found the younger man staring upstream with a blank look on his face. "Justin? We should get going."

Justin blinked, as though waking from a doze. "Yeah." He didn't move, though, until Owen took hold of his arm and pulled him downstream, along the route Sallie Eagle had described to them. Then he blinked again, shook himself, and followed.

There was a force pressing against them. Owen could feel it, like a wind in his face, but he'd learned the disciplines of the Starry Wisdom well enough to keep his mind and will clear despite it. Justin had no such defenses, and Owen had to keep hold of his arm to keep him moving. The slopes of Elk Hill rose stark to their right, reddening with the sunset; the creek rushed past on their left, brown and roiling; the old path curved sinuously between them.

Then the brambles fell away and the big oaks of the valley floor picked up. An old road came around the foot of the hill, cut across the ancient path, and tumbled away in ruin into the creek. On the far bank, Owen could see more fragments of the wrecked bridge Robin had mentioned. His hand still gripping Justin's arm, he turned onto the road.

"We have to go back," Justin said then in a slurred voice.

"No, we don't," Owen told him. "Remember what Ms. Eagle told you."

"Yeah," he said. With an obvious effort: "Somebody's messing with my mind."

"I know. Once we get back to Chorazin, there are ways to put a stop to it."

Justin didn't answer, simply let himself be guided. Once he tensed suddenly, and Owen thought that he was going to try to break away, but the tension trickled away after a moment.

From the sun's motion, Owen guessed that they'd been walking for maybe forty-five minutes when the first ragged roofs of Chorazin came into sight, but it felt as though hours had slipped past. The last five minutes or so were made easier by Justin's sudden blinking recovery. "What the *hell* was that?" he asked Owen, turning toward him with an incredulous look. "It felt like someone was trying to put thoughts into my head."

Owen nodded. "Someone was. I felt it too."

Justin stared at him for a time, and then forced out, "How?"

"Maybe sorcery, maybe something else—the other side has machines that can do that."

That got him a wary look, and Justin seemed about to ask a question, but nodded uncomfortably after a moment and they walked on.

* * *

Another five minutes, maybe, brought them to Chorazin's one street. Well before they got there, Owen began to feel uneasy. For the first time since they'd come to Chorazin, people were out in plain sight, standing on porches or in the street, looking south toward the gap between Elk Hill and the slopes to the east, where the road led to the ruins of the van der Heyl house. That in itself was a sign of trouble; worse, no one spoke. Alone or in groups, they watched and waited.

Owen and Justin threaded their way down the street, followed by low murmurs that only seemed to add to the hush. When they got to the motel, they found Walt Moore standing in the front parking lot, facing the same way as the others. He seemed to sense their approach, and glanced back, then turned full around and gave them both a long hard look before motioning with his head toward the lobby.

They followed him inside. As soon as the door swung shut, he turned to them and said, "Where've you two been?"

"We got caught in the storm in the ruins of the van der Heyl house," said Owen. "We ran for shelter and—I don't know how this happened, but we ended up at Sallie Eagle's house."

That startled the old man. After a moment: "Where was it?"

"West of the hill, near Huntey Creek."

He turned suddenly to Justin. "What happened when you were there?"

"She gave us something to drink, we talked for a while, and then she read cards for me."

"What kind of cards?"

"I don't know," Justin admitted. "I've never seen cards like those before. They weren't playing cards or Tarot—there was a dog, a rider, a tower, a broken mirror."

Walt considered them for another moment, and then nodded. "Fair enough."

"Something's happened," said Owen.

"Yeah."

He motioned with his head again, and they went back out to the parking lot. The Chorazin folk were still keeping their silent vigil, but four others had come into sight, walking slowly up the road from the narrow place. They hauled a makeshift stretcher, and on it was a still small shape, limp and twisted as a broken doll.

A woman further down the road screamed, then, and ran to meet the stretcher. The bearers set it down, and she flung herself to her knees beside it, wailing.

For a time no one moved. Then, as the woman's cries sank into sobs and then to stillness, the others began to line up on either side of the road, with a path between them leading to the Starry Wisdom church. Owen, recognizing the rite, turned to Justin, pressed his finger to his lips, and gestured; Justin nodded. The two of them walked down to the street and took places in the lines that would receive and witness the homecoming of the dead.

The bearers lifted the makeshift stretcher again and began to carry it toward the church. The woman followed, and others—family members, Owen knew—left the lines and joined her as the stretcher and its silent burden passed. No one else moved, and no one spoke at all. Owen watched as the bearers approached, but all he could see of the one they carried was a shock of straight dark hair smeared with mud, and clothing equally mudstained.

Then the bearers went past.

The silent figure on the stretcher was Robin Hale. His head was half torn off, but no blood showed on the wound, and his face and hands were the terrible gray-brown color that olive skin turns when all the blood has drained away from it.

Owen heard Justin's sudden sharp inbreath, half turned toward him to make sure he didn't speak and disrupt the rite. Justin noticed the movement, met his gaze, and nodded. The stretcher and its burden moved past, the family followed, and only wind and shuffling feet disturbed the silence. The bearers and the family went out of sight, and a long moment later, the church's heavy back door thudded shut and the rite was done.

The others in the lines turned to go their ways. Justin blinked, and suddenly turned and stumbled up into the parking lot. In a low harsh voice: "That should have been me."

Walt Moore turned toward him. "Some of ours get taken too."

Justin gave him a long bleak hopeless look, nodded, and then headed for his room, half hunched over, stumbling as though he couldn't see the gravel beneath his feet.

* * *

"Walt Moore sent Robin to find you when the storm started brewing," Bill Downey said. "Since you don't know our weather, he figured you might get caught by it, and—" He gestured: who could have known? Around him, shadows gathered in Cicely Moore's living room, and night pressed hard against the windowpanes.

Owen nodded. "Did you let the police know?"

"We gave the county sheriff a call on the motel phone," said Cicely Moore. "Told 'em it was an accident, and they wrote that down." Her nose wrinkled. "You can live your whole life in this place and never see police here."

"They've had a lot of budget cuts," Bill reminded her.

"Thirty years ago they still never came." She shook her head. "Too good for Chorazin folks is what it is."

No one said anything for a while, but then the room was a good deal emptier than it had been the night before. The three initiates he'd met in the social hall of the Starry Temple church were there, and so was Owen; that was all. Some of the other initiates had the rites for the dead to perform, others had gone to their homes, and Justin had locked himself in his room at the motel and would only answer in monosyllables.

"I wish I knew what to say." Owen stared at the cup in his hands. "Or what to do. And it doesn't help to know that you've been facing it all these years, and it just keeps on happening."

The others nodded. "The van der Heyls kept it in check for a long while, or so I heard tell, but no one knows how any more," Cicely Moore said, "It happens more often now than when I was a girl, but it's happened since Red Eagle brought Sarah and Micah Moore here."

Owen looked up from his tea. "Ms. Eagle mentioned them," he said, "but she didn't use the name Red Eagle."

"She probably called him Mishkwapelethi," Betty Hale said suddenly. Her eyes were rimmed with red—Robin Hale was a nephew of hers, Owen had gathered. "That's Red Eagle in the Shawnee language—I looked it up. I have a cousin who works in the library up in Emeryville, and I go up there sometimes to do genealogy."

"Micah Moore was one of your ancestors, I'm guessing," said Owen.

"Oh, yes. He married Ann Eller, who'd been a slave at a farm by the Hudson River and ran away to Indian country; Sarah Moore married Red Eagle, and her children took the name Eagle; that's where you get two of the four names everyone here has. The Hales, they're from the van der Heyl family, and Brian and Patrick Downey came up from Pennsylvania, where they'd been bound over as indentured servants after the Irish troubles. There were other names back a ways, but one too many daughters somewhere along the line put paid to them." She stopped, looked embarrassed. "I'm sorry, Mr. Merrill. You didn't want to hear all that."

"I don't mind it," Owen said then. "But Ms. Eagle said something else when we where there—that the Moores brought a treasure from Roodsford, and it's been lost. Do you have any idea what that's about?"

Betty paused and then said, "I've never heard about anything like that." It was a brief pause, no more than a fraction of a second, but it told Owen what he needed to know.

"We don't know anything like as much as we ought to," Cicely Moore allowed after a moment. "As I think I said before, we've had some bad trouble here, and there were times when none of us lived anywhere near here. You know how that goes."

"Yeah," Owen said. "Innsmouth's gone now."

"So I hear." The old woman shook her head. "Things didn't quite get that bad here, but there were times we've just had to lock up the church and pray for the best. That happened last when I was young, and my mama—she was the senior initiate in those days—up and handed the keys to Miz Eagle before we drove south to West Virginia."

Owen's eyebrows went up. "Ms. Eagle was already around then?"

"Oh, yes," the old woman said. She met Owen's look squarely. "That happens sometimes, you know. Sometimes it's sorcery, sometimes it's alchemy, and sometimes the Great Old Ones decide you're going to stay around, and you stay around for as long as they want. I don't pretend to know what they've got in mind for Miz Eagle, and I don't know if she knows, but she's been in her little shack west of the hill since I don't know when."

Owen nodded slowly, finished his tea. Once again he could sense secrets within secrets hovering in the silent air, and decided to press the issue further by bringing up the most unsettling thing Sallie Eagle had said. "She told us that this business here—the Sleeper in the Hill and the rest of it—goes back to the desecration of the seven temples." He paused just long enough for the words to sink in. "To the Weird of Hali."

All three of them were staring at him by the time he'd finished. "I don't know anything about that," Cicely Moore said after a moment. "I don't think anyone here does."

Was she telling the truth? From the shocked look in her face, Owen thought so.

Something else the old witch had said occurred to him, though. "When Ms. Eagle read the cards for Justin," he said, "she told him that he needed help—that the people who were here couldn't save him, but there was someone else who might. I've racked my brains trying to think of someone to send for." He turned to Cicely and Bill. "You two are seventh degree, you've got as much knowledge as anyone in the Starry Wisdom. If you haven't figured this out, I don't know who could."

The room went silent for a long time, and then Betty Hale spoke. "There might be someone," she said diffidently. "I'm not sure you know this, but I'm a witch as well as an initiate." When Owen nodded: "Just the last year or so, there's been talk among witches about someone out New England way who's a genuine sorceress—someone who works spells out of the deepest parts of the old lore, who's been outside the world and come back to it with power, who can do things witches can't even dream of. Some of the witches out that way know her, and I can see if they can get a message to her." She shrugged. "No way of telling whether she'll answer, but that's the one thing that came to mind."

Owen, astonished at the news, began to speak, and then thought better of it and turned to Cicely. "Mrs. Moore," he said, "I know what I'd say—but it's your call."

The old woman nodded after a moment. "Please," she said to Betty. "An actual sorceress—my word. I don't think we've had sorcerer or sorceress here since Joris van der Heyl's time. If she's willing to come, well, then at least we can hope for something."

"The sky's clear tonight and the moon's up," Betty said. "I'll get a message on its way come midnight."

CHAPTER 8

THE SHRINE OF THE WINGED ELK

The next morning Owen was at loose ends. Justin came out of his room for breakfast, ate little, talked in a subdued voice, then went back and locked himself in again, begging Owen to leave him alone until dinner. "He's pretty much come to terms with his own death," Owen explained to Walt Moore, "but he wasn't prepared for someone else's—especially not when it was a kid who was just trying to help us."

Walt sighed heavily. "Yeah. If I'd had the least idea, I'd have gone myself, and let whatever it is try to take a bite out of my neck instead."

Owen nodded, said nothing. The young woman with the bottle-black hair, who was waiting out another round of morning sickness on the couch, gave them both a troubled look.

After breakfast he went out to the parking lot behind the motel, and stood there for some minutes looking up at the brown mass of Elk Hill looming up above. The morning was clear and warm, and the same line of poetry circled in his mind: *The mound was old before the white man came.* What was the rest of it? The memory would not surface.

The hill stood waiting, brown and silent, and Owen frowned. It was the height of recklessness, he told himself, to go roaming around on his own, without so much as a word to Justin.

He stood a moment longer, and then started across the parking lot toward its far end, where they'd started up the hill that first time with Robin Hale. Reckless or not, the thought of sitting in his room and doing nothing was intolerable.

He passed the twisted pine and reached the place where the trail had been, and wasn't surprised to see that it had vanished. "I'm going up to the stones," he said aloud, and waited.

Brambles rustled, but no trail opened up.

Owen pondered that. The great tangled canes shifted back and forth as if a strong wind blew past them, even though the air was still.

"You opened a path for Robin Hale," he said then, slowly. "And you've opened one for me before—but not this time. Can you tell me why?"

A sudden breeze came rushing down the slope, and the rustling and hissing seemed for a moment to be speaking words: *Follow, follow.*

"Will I come back alive if I do?" Owen asked aloud.

The breeze hissed but said nothing, leaving the question unanswered.

Owen stood there for another long moment. The practices he'd learned as a Starry Wisdom initiate focused in part on developing the pineal gland and its subtle senses, and though he still had plenty to learn, he could catch glimpses of the unseen from time to time. One such glimpse tugged at him now, pulled him forward. "Okay," he said then. "I'll follow."

Brambles rustled again, and a trail appeared a few yards away from him. He glanced back at the motel, trying to convince himself that he should do the sensible thing and turn around. The effort had no noticeable effect, and he started up the path.

For a good half of the way up the hill it followed the same route as the trail they'd taken that first afternoon, curving around the flank of the desolate hill. A short distance after the silver line of Huntey Creek came into sight, though, the path suddenly veered downwards. Where the briars to his right were low enough, which wasn't often, Owen could see the creek and, here and there, glimpses of the creekside path he and Justin had followed the day before. Then the briars grew taller still, and even the ridges on the western side of the valley became a rare sight. The breeze died away, replaced by a vast waiting hush through which nothing but Owen himself seemed to move. By the time the trail reached the southern flank of the hill, Owen walked through a tunnel made of brambles, covered densely enough that he could see nothing but occasional glimpses of sky.

Finally the path reached the foot of the hill on the southern side and went no further. There, in a hidden space surrounded by brambles, a spring bubbled out from a cleft in gray rugged rock, forming a stream that flowed out through a vast thicket of briars toward the ruins of the van der Heyl house. Owen glanced around, baffled, and then happened to step a little to his right, and saw the petroglyph.

Above the spring, a sheer wall of gray rock rose maybe twenty feet to a bramble-wrapped overhang, and reached maybe twelve feet from side to side. On that stone, high up, a shape had been chipped, and the rough lines still bore the last faint traces of the reddish pigment the people who made them had rubbed into them to make them visible. A few steps to one side or the other and the markings couldn't be seen, but when he stood in the right place they stood out clearly in the dappled sunlight.

It was a shrine, Owen guessed; he bowed, murmured words of reverence he'd learned from the *Necronomicon*, and then considered the petroglyph again. The chipped lines traced out an animal with antlers—a deer? So he thought at first, but a second look convinced him that it was an elk, with the shaggy neck and heavier body of that animal. The great antlers rose and spread, jagged as bolts of lightning. Other lines spread over the elk's shoulders and back, and after a moment Owen realized they were stylized wings.

Other markings scored the stone lower down: designs scratched in the stone, in a different style. Closest to the elk coiled something like a snake, but it had a fringe of lines splaying outward where the head should have been. Below that were two rough human figures and two others that didn't seem to be human at all. They seemed to be falling back from the snake-thing, with arms upraised as though in fear.

Minutes passed while he stared at the markings. The elk-image looked ancient beyond memory, the scratched designs less so, and faint marks lower still that looked a bit like soot from candle-smoke made him suspect that the shrine was visited and rites worked there now and then. That this place was another piece of the puzzle Owen didn't doubt, and though he had no idea how it fit together with the other bits of knowledge he'd gathered, it felt important.

He considered the faint carvings again, then turned around and tried to peer through the brambles, hoping to catch a glimpse of the ruined chimney and figure out where the petroglyphs were in relation to the buried vault. The thicket in front of the spring was too dense, though. Through a gap in the brambles, he could see some of the road south and east of the ruins, but that was all. After a moment he turned back, shaking his head.

That was when he heard the voice—if it was a voice. It might simply have been the splashing and bubbling of the spring, but through the faint sound a woman's voice seemed to whisper: *Help me. Free me.*

"Who are you?" Owen asked. "What will you do if you're freed?"

A sudden burst of wind came rushing down the hill, but there were no words in it. When it finished, the voice spoke no more.

* * *

Unnerved, he turned and climbed back up the way he'd come. Maybe halfway along the western slope of the hill, as the brambles parted above him and gave him a clear view of the sky, he paused and said aloud, "I'd like to go to the stone circle on the hilltop now." The briars around him didn't shift, and so he started walking again. As the trail curved around to the northern slopes of the hill, though, a clear path he hadn't seen on the way to the shrine turned back to the south, leading steeply uphill. He paused a moment and then went that way.

Ten minutes later, winded but elated, he stepped out of the brambles onto the barren hilltop. Daylight gleamed on the great standing stones, kindling sparks of dull green light on their sunward surfaces, and a breeze hissed to itself through the thickets all around. Owen considered going into the stone circle, but the wrongness in the voor unsettled him, and instead he walked around the edge of the hilltop until he could see the valley to the south.

The spring with the petroglyphs above it could not be seen from above, but the path of the stream was another matter. Owen traced it as close to the hill as he could, and then back out the other way to the ruins of the van der Heyl house, and stopped. It wasn't the fact that the line went straight to the location of the old vault that stopped him, though.

Whoever was digging out the vault hadn't been idle. Though it was distant enough that he had to strain to see clearly, Owen guessed that another two or three feet of dirt had been shoveled out of the old vault and lay in heaps all around. Elsewhere, the ruins seemed undisturbed.

He straightened, looked south along the valley into the distance, where Huntey Creek vanished among the folds of the land. Everything he'd seen and learned made a single pattern, he was sure of it, but what that pattern was he could not tell. The dream-voice pleading for help, the song about the Sleeper in the Hill, the voyage of Jan Martense, the hill where no birds came, the ruined house of the van der Heyls, the legends and memories of the Chorazin folk, and the hints that the Weird of Hali itself was tangled up in it all; cards in a witch's hands, stories of ghosts and snakes and thunder spirits, ancient carvings on a slab of stone, Robin Hale's corpse—all of it meant something. What?

The wind picked up and rushed past him, but no words came. He stood there for a long moment, looking at nothing in particular, trying to make it all make sense.

Time suddenly stretched and flowed, as it had done for him now and then since that terrible night in Arkham. Around him the hill rose and fell like a wave. He saw the copper-skinned people who built it, hauling earth in baskets, raising the great mound above a rounded mass of stone scarred with long straight gouges the glaciers of the ice age left behind, placing it along the ancient moon paths to tap into currents of voor that flowed through the landscape. He saw the mound as it was in its prime, rising smooth-sided to a flat top where wooden posts stood guard, replaced after centuries by standing stones, and he saw the moon paths, the hidden channels of voor in the landscape, rushing east, west, and south from the hill, harnessed by the great stones and the ceremonies performed among them. A long age passed, and then he saw the builders perish and the seasons devour their wooden longhouses. Summer rains and spring floods blurred and crannied the once-smooth flanks of the hill, brambles wrapped around its foot and climbed slowly up its sides, while medicine people from the native peoples came year after year to perform rites he could not see.

A sudden flash of light caught his attention for a moment, and after a space that must have been measured in centuries, the first campfire flickered in the place where Chorazin would one day rise. Cabins rose there, and after another interval, the tall house of the van der Heyls kept a sentinel's watch at the hill's southern foot. The house grew and so did the village, until all at once the lights of the house went dark forever, and it tumbled into ruin on a night of storm. Chorazin huddled into the lee of the old mound with its lights flickering on and off, and then—

He could see no further. Something had happened or was happening or would happen, or it had or did or would not, and possibilities he could not measure followed from the choice. Time tautened and tangled, and beyond the moment of decision everything lay hidden in a shadow that Owen's inner vision could not penetrate. He tried to push through it, and the effort sent him spinning back through the times he'd already witnessed, past the fall of the house of the van der Heyls, past the birth of Chorazin, to the flash of light and past it; he caught himself, moved with the flow of time until the light flared again.

He could see little through the light—human figures clustered at the foot of the hill, not far from where the van der Heyl house would one day stand, alongside shapes that weren't human at all; a momentary glimpse of a towering shape crowned with antlers that branched like lightning; another glimpse, just as brief, of something else even vaster, looming up with paws outstretched against night-black clouds.

Something terrible had happened then, something that shaped destinies reaching well beyond the human realm. The knowledge pressed in on him, abrupt and demanding. Cascading consequences unfolded from that act, swept out in great arcs of time, and drew back together again at the moment of choice—a moment that seemed to draw closer as he watched.

Then he was blinking in the sunlight, back in his own time. He rubbed his eyes, looked around. The wind still hissed in the brambles around the hilltop, the sun still struck dull green sparks from the standing stones; nothing had changed, or nothing he could perceive.

Just then, though, two tiny pinpoints of light on the high ground southeast of the hill caught his attention. They vanished as quickly as they appeared, but Owen recognized them at once. They'd appeared on the same part of the eastern ridge, where he'd seen identical flashes two days before. Someone was keeping watch there with binoculars. Had the watcher spotted Owen? It seemed likely, but he could not tell. He turned at once and walked away.

* * *

He headed down the way he'd come, but the path had changed direction again and wove its way down the slope to the north. When he reached the bottom, he was standing alongside the road he and Justin had followed into Chorazin the previous day. The ruined bridge was within sight; he walked up to it and stood there, watching the waters of Huntey Creek as they surged and roiled on their way to the Tonawanda River and Lake Erie.

They came here, he thought. All the way from Europe, knowing exactly where they were going, with a terrible purpose in mind. If they'd just meant to summon one of the beings of the elder world, in the ordinary way of sorcerers, they could have gone any number of places much closer. Why the long journey? Why, for that matter, the killings in Greenland?

The waters gave him no answers. He turned and headed back toward Chorazin.

He was maybe halfway there when the distant sound of a car's engine made itself heard over the hiss of the wind in the brambles. That wasn't completely out of the ordinary—some of the Chorazin folk had cars in working order, though he gathered they had to go to the next county to find a gas station that would sell them fuel—but it wasn't common, and with May Eve only a day and a half away, Owen's nerves were on edge.

The wind picked up, and for a while the hissing of the brambles and the deeper rush it made in the big oaks north of the road drowned out the engine sounds. Owen kept walking. He glanced up the slopes of Elk Hill, still trying to make some sense of his experiences.

When he looked forward, a red car had come into sight ahead, driving toward him.

Owen tensed and considered darting into the undergrowth beneath the oaks, but decided against it. The car looked familiar enough that he thought he could guess who was driving it, for that matter. He put a bland look on his face, moved toward the side of the road, kept on walking.

A few moments later the car slowed to a stop beside him, and the driver's side window rolled down. The driver was the blonde forty-something woman he'd seen two days before, driving the same car on the road back from the ruined van der Heyl house.

"Excuse me," the driver said. "Can I ask you a question?" Her voice had a trace of a midwestern accent.

"Sure," said Owen, stopping.

"My GPS says there's a bridge here that goes through to Attica, but the gas station guy says it's washed out. Do you know if he's right?"

"Sure do," said Owen. "It's been gone four years now."

"Well, isn't that special." She looked irritated. "Do you live around there?"

"Nope," said Owen. "Just visiting friends."

Her laugh had music in it. "You're better at making friends than I am, then. I tried to talk to some of the people in Chorazin a couple of days ago. If I had to guess, I'd say they don't talk to strangers much."

"Nope." Owen produced a clueless smile. "I met a guy from here when we were both in the army. We stayed in touch when we got out, and I come down here to visit sometimes."

"I suppose that'll do it." She dug in her purse, got out her phone, and then a business card. "Could you do me a favor? I'm Dr. Rowena Slater, from Partridgeville State University in New Jersey—I study American folklore. There are some old legends connected with this hill next to us I'd like to find out about. If you know anybody in Chorazin who might be willing to talk to me, would you please give me a call, or have them call me?" The card had her name and the name of the university on it, along with a cell phone number.

"I'll ask around," said Owen.

She gave him a bright smile. "Thank you. See you around, maybe." Owen said something appropriate. She rolled up the window and busied herself with her phone while Owen pocketed the card. The red compact managed to turn around without ending up in the brambles, drove back the way it had come. Owen watched it go, kept walking.

* * *

Chorazin looked as deserted as usual when he reached it. As he came in sight of the parking lot in front of the motel, he saw someone else standing there: the pregnant woman with the bottle-black hair he'd seen in the breakfast room. She glanced his way, paused, then walked toward him.

"Hi," she said, when they got within speaking distance. "Can you spare a couple of minutes? I've got some questions I need to ask. Mr. Moore says you're not from around here, and ..." Her voice trickled away into silence.

"Sure," said Owen. He considered the options. "You want to go to the lobby, or one of the picnic tables?"

They settled on a picnic table, went through the lobby and found a comfortable spot in the shade of a cluster of pines. "I'm Patty Dombrowski, by the way," she said.

"Owen Merrill."

"Pleased to meet you." Then: "You probably know why I'm here."

"If I had to guess," Owen said, "I'd say your baby has a very distinguished father."

She put a hand to her mouth, stifling a laugh. "Funny. Yeah." She considered him for a moment. "You know about Yog-Sothoth."

"I hope so. He saved my life once."

Her eyes went round. Then, with a little shy smile: "Mine too." She shook her head. "It was my own damn fault for messing around in my grandfather's book when I didn't have a clue what I was doing. Some—things—started following me, and I knew what they would do to me if they caught me, and the only thing in the book I could find that would help was a summoning of the Guardian of the Gate—and he came." Her gaze fell. "That was right around four years ago, and—things kind of happened from there."

"So you didn't grow up with people who knew this stuff."

"No. Well, my grandfather knew a lot of it, but he never taught me anything, and then he died when I was sixteen and the family put his book and all his other stuff out with the trash. I went out at three in the morning and stole the book and some other things from the trash bag."

Neither of them spoke for a time, and then Owen said, "You had some questions."

She blushed. "Yeah. I know, I talk too much." Looking up at him: "There's somebody inside the hill here."

Owen nodded after a moment. "That's what I hear."

"There is," Patty said. "I hear her in my dreams." Owen managed to keep his surprise off his face. "She wants to get out—and nobody here'll tell me who she is or how to set her free."

"I don't think they know," said Owen, after another moment. "Other people hear her, too, but as far as I can tell the Chorazin folk don't know any more than the rest of us. The Sleeper in the Hill—that's what they call her—has been there since long before they got here."

She took that in. "Okay. The thing is, I'm supposed to answer the call somehow." In response to Owen's startled look: "Somebody told me that."

Owen considered that, and began to nod. "Let me guess," he said. "Somebody very tall, who wears a black hat with a broad brim and a long black coat."

"And rings on his fingers."

"Nyarlathotep, the Crawling Chaos."

"Yeah." She paused, went on. "When I figured out I was pregnant, I knew how my family was going to react—you don't want to know—and so I called Yog-Sothoth for help, and he came to me." Her gaze fell. "He told me to go to a cross-roads south of town at midnight. That was pretty scary, but the One in Black met me there, and on the way here he told me that I was called by the Sleeper in the Hill and could answer the call if I chose. Only I don't know how."

"Neither do I," said Owen.

"He sent you."

"And the guy I'm with."

She took that in. "If you figure out anything …"

"I'll let you know right away."

That got him another shy smile. "Thanks."

They said a few more polite things, and then she went to her room to rest and he headed to Carla's for a late lunch. Some of the locals turned to look at him when he came through the door, and one headed outside a moment later, but he thought nothing of it until the door opened again maybe five minutes later, and Betty Hale came in and made a beeline for his table. She sat down in the chair facing his and said, "Mr. Merrill, you're not an easy man to find."

"I was up on the hill," he explained, "looking for—signs, I guess."

She nodded, as though that was the most natural thing in the world. "There's no harm been done. It's just that I've already heard back from the sorceress."

Owen blinked in surprise, and she went on. "I'd expected to hear at midnight—you know that's when witches talk through the moon's beams, right? But that wasn't what happened. It came through the sun." In a low voice: "I didn't know that anybody, even a sorceress, could do that." Her voice returned to its normal tone. "But the thing is, she's coming. She caught the bus this morning, and she'll be at the Emeryville stop at five minutes past eight this evening."

The thought of a powerful sorceress traveling by bus seemed absurd enough that Owen had to fight to keep a smile off his face. "That's great news," he said. "I'll talk to Justin and make sure he's ready, and we can drive up there and meet her." Then: "Do you know her name?"

"Miss Chaudronnier," Betty said. "I don't know her first name. The witches out Massachusetts way just call her Miss Chaudronnier."

Owen nodded, remembering gossip from his days in Arkham. The Chaudronniers were an old Kingsport family, rich and eccentric, the sort of people you'd expect to pup sorcerers and sorceresses on occasion. "I hope she can help sort this out," he said.

* * *

He tapped on the door of Justin's room at six o'clock sharp. A long silence followed, and then the lock clicked and the door opened.

"How are you doing?" Owen asked.

"Better than I expected." Justin looked haggard, and his disparate eyes were rimmed with red. "I've convinced myself not to walk out to the ruins tonight and get it over with—I think."

"Good," said Owen, "because a lot's happened since this morning. Let's get some dinner and talk, and then we've got someplace to go."

Justin considered him for a moment, then nodded once. "Okay."

The bar and grill was quieter than usual. Over bacon cheeseburgers and big baskets of fries, Owen sketched out the events of the day. Justin listened, and his frown faded. "A sorceress," he said finally. "That's different from a witch, then."

Owen nodded. "The way a three-masted tall ship is different from a rowboat." Then: "Well, no, that's not quite fair to witches—some of them are rowboats, some are riverboats, and some of them are in between, but none of them go out on the deep ocean."

Justin took that in. "Do witches turn into sorceresses if they get good enough, or what?"

"Not that I've ever heard. You have to be born with the ability, and what that means usually is that sorcerers and sorceresses are only part human." In response to Justin's shocked look: "The Great Old Ones mate with human beings—it happens fairly often. My wife's the daughter of one of the Great Old Ones."

"Is she a sorceress?"

"No, she's an initiate."

Justin shook his head and laughed "I'm never going to get all this straight."

"Don't worry about it. The thing that matters is that Betty Hale sent a message last night, and the sorceress caught the bus out here first thing this morning. She'll be in Emeryville in an hour and a half. We can go pick her up—I've already talked to Walt Moore, so he's got a room waiting for her—and we'll see what kind of sense she can make out of all this."

"Okay," said Justin. "That's promising."

"It's not the only thing, either." Owen passed on what Patty Dombrowsky had told him, and watched the younger man's eyes go wide. "Yeah," he said. "So we're not the only ones Nyarlathotep's sent here. He's got something planned; for all I know, he's got other people lined up to help, too. Tomorrow, if we have time, I'd like to sit down with you and Patty and try to figure out what that might be."

"I hope we can," said Justin. "May first is the day after tomorrow, you know."

Owen nodded. "I know."

They finished dinner, and Justin went to get his car while Owen walked up the street to Betty Hale's house. A few minutes later the three of them were rattling east along Chorazin Road. Owen had crammed himself into the back seat to leave the front passenger seat for Betty, and tried to make himself as comfortable as the space allowed. It didn't allow much, and the bumpy road contributed its own share of discomfort. The road north to Emeryville was even more deserted than usual. It took less than fifteen minutes to get to the bus stop, but Owen was glad when the car rolled to a halt and Betty got out, and he was able to squeeze through the narrow gap between the door frame and the passenger seat, unfold himself, and stretch.

The Emeryville bus station was a battered metal sign fastened to the side of an off-brand mini mart just off the state highway, a little north of downtown. Two other cars were parked there when Justin drove up, and another followed a few minutes later: dented and rust-spotted, all three of them, and the people inside looked as worn and battered as their vehicles. Owen thought of the show of destitution Dunwich and Chorazin put on to protect themselves, and looked around at the mostly empty strip mall, the rundown cars scattered in the parking lot, and the disused warehouse across the road with broken windows and weeds standing tall in the gutters. We're used to creating the appearance of poverty, he thought. This is the reality.

Rumble of a diesel engine announced the arrival of the bus, and a moment later it came around the far corner of the strip mall and wheezed to a stop next to the sign. The door hissed open, and the driver came clattering down the steps, walked down the side of the bus and threw open the cargo door low on the thing's flank. The people waiting in their cars hauled themselves out onto the pavement; one of them, a nervous-looking young man, clutched a ticket in his hand and moved toward the bus door. Then, the passengers: a middle-aged woman wearing a garish flower-print dress and heavy makeup, an old man with a cane who went straight to one of the cars and was hugged and greeted by the people standing beside it, and a youngish woman in a battered brown coat, short and thin, her face mostly hidden under a mop of mouse-colored hair.

The younger woman looked somehow familiar to Owen, but he scarcely noticed, because voor blazed and surged around her like a flame. He tried to focus his inner senses, but something on or near her right hand dazzled them the way a flash-bulb dazzles the eyes. Someone who's been outside the world and come back to it with power, Betty Hale had said: Owen had no difficulty believing that the words were simple fact.

The sorceress went back to the cargo hatch, waited while the woman in the garish dress got a lumpy duffel bag and hauled it back to one of the waiting cars, and then took her own suit-case from the driver. By then Betty Hale was already walking toward her. "Miss Chaudronnier?" she called out. "Thank you so much for coming."

The sorceress turned, and Owen saw her face. He'd meant to follow Betty to the side of the bus and take the suitcase, but that thought went spinning away in the sheer astonishment of the moment. His mouth fell open, and by the time he thought to close it, he'd missed whatever words the sorceress might have said in response.

Then she saw him, and it was her turn to stare with an open mouth. A moment later, she managed to speak: "Oh my God. *Owen*?"

He swallowed, nodded. "Hi, Jenny."

CHAPTER 9

THE SHAMBLER FROM THE STARS

"Miss Chaudronnier," Owen said. "Where did that come from?" He considered her, tried to wrap his thoughts around the simple fact of her presence, but the effort didn't do much good. The fact that she seemed just as astonished was some consolation.

"That was my birth name." Jenny sipped coffee. "My mom married a man named Rick Parrish when I was six. They got divorced when I was nine, but by then I'd started school as Jenny Parrish and it was a lot simpler to keep the name. I didn't change it back until after I got together with my family in Kingsport."

During the ride back to Chorazin, dinner at Cicely Moore's house, the careful courtesies with which the initiates of the Starry Wisdom welcomed a sorceress, he'd been struggling with questions too personal to ask in so public a setting. Memories of his last months in Arkham, when they'd lived in the same house, jarred with the present moment; she'd been a bookish English major doing a postgrad year in French literature, not a sorceress with voor blazing about her like a dancing star. He'd all but resigned himself to having to leave his questions for the morning, or later still, but Jenny turned to him as they crossed the street to the motel and said, "Owen, can you spare an hour or so before bed? If I don't have the chance to ask you some things I honestly think I'm going to burst."

"Me too," he said, laughing. So they'd wished Justin a good night, got coffee and tea from Walt Moore, and settled into chairs in her room at the motel as the night deepened outside.

"You've probably got more questions than I do," she said, "And I bet I can guess most of them. Dr. Akeley is fine; she's the chair of the History of Ideas department these days, and they've tried twice now to talk her into becoming dean of the College of Arts and Sciences, but she won't quit teaching. I think she had some kind of health problem last year—I don't know what it was, she wouldn't talk about it—but she seems to be doing better now."

He nodded. "You got the assistantship, then."

"No, the funds for that got cut. There have been budget cuts at Miskatonic every year since you left, big ones."

"Ouch."

"But things worked out anyway. My family has money, so I'm kind of an unpaid assistant for Miriam these days—I don't teach, I just take classes and help her with her research. That's why I was able to drop everything and catch a bus out here once I got the message; my classes are pretty easy this semester."

He nodded again, and she went on. "Let's see. Tish Martin finished med school last year and is doing a residency in New Jersey. Barry Holzer and Kenji Takamura got married—"

"Seriously? I didn't know they were an item." When he'd last seen them, as far as Owen knew, Barry and Kenji had been nothing more serious than friends and study partners.

"Seriously. I didn't know either, but they got married as soon as they graduated—they invited me, but I was going to France for the summer and couldn't make it—and then they moved to Minneapolis, where Kenji had a job offer. Let's see. Dr. Whipple and Dr. Peaslee haven't changed a bit. I think that's everyone you knew that I know about."

"Thank you," said Owen. "I've got one more question, but I think it's your turn."

She considered him, tried to find words, and then simply blurted out, "What happened?"

"When I disappeared?" She nodded, and he went on. "I found out something about—some people at Miskatonic."

"The Noology program," she said at once.

"The Radiance," he replied.

Her eyebrows went up, and then she nodded.

"They had people studying the *Necronomicon* and some of the other tomes. They didn't want anyone to know that, so they tried to kidnap me. I managed to get away. I'd already been told where to go if I got into trouble—to the white stone on the far side of Meadow Hill."

"I've been there often," Jenny said. "Shub-Ne'hurrath protected you, then."

"Yeah. The next night I followed the moon path from there to the hills north of Arkham, and Nyarlathotep was waiting for me. He took me to Innsmouth—we had some trouble getting there, and we spent part of the day with a witch at Pickman's Corners."

Jenny's face lit up. "Abby Price?

"You know her?"

"I spent last summer studying with her."

Owen gave her a blank look. "I didn't think sorceresses studied witchcraft."

Jenny laughed. "You're forgetting what Alhazred wrote. 'Not from the learned and their books did I gain this lore, but from witches and herb doctors, wandering shepherds and hermits, wizards, blacksmiths, stonemasons, and those whose trade it is to lay out the dead—it was with them that I studied, and from them that I learned the secrets of the Great Old Ones and the realms that lie beyond the world we know.'"

"Fair enough," he said. "But I got to Innsmouth, stayed there for a while, went north to Maine and met voormis and shoggoths for the first time, and then—" He regarded her for a moment. "The night that Belbury Hall burned, I was there."

"Okay," she said after a moment. "You weren't alone, I take it."

A shake of his head denied it. "Me, some guys from Innsmouth, and a lot of others. Afterwards—we had to scatter and lie low." He weighed the options, went ahead with the riskier one. "I ended up in Dunwich—you know where that is?"

"I've heard about it, but I've never been there."

"It's a pleasant little town. I basically settled down, got a job teaching school there, and married a young lady from Innsmouth—we've got a two month old daughter."

"Congratulations."

"Thank you. But that's my story. Now—"

"Mine?" A sudden smile. "Much simpler. My mom was a Chaudronnier, and two months after I came to Arkham, I wrote the family a letter. I ended up going to Kingsport for the winter holiday break right after you left. There's a festival that's held once every century, and that was the year. So I went to the festival, and when I came back I'd been given—something."

"The thing on your right hand," Owen said. "I can't see it, but I can sense it."

"You've had some training."

"Yeah. I'm a second degree initiate in the Starry Wisdom these days."

After a moment's reflection: "If you're willing, I can make you see it."

He nodded, and she got up from her chair, reached out and touched what should have been the back of her right index finger to his forehead. What he felt instead was the cold surface of a gem. She murmured a word in a language Owen didn't recognize, and drew the hand back.

A ring on her finger caught the lamplight, where no ring had been before. It was massive, made of improbably reddish gold, and set with a purple stone.

He stared at the ring, then at her, and said, "That's—"

"The Ring of Eibon."

"Seriously?"

"It's been in the family since the twelfth century."

Owen nodded after a moment, shaken. "Okay," he said. Then: "I'm glad you decided to come—for more than the obvious reason. I'm at a loss about this whole business here."

That got him a smile. "Thank you. The thing is, I was told more than a week ago that I needed to be ready to travel. These things happen." Then: "How tired are you?"

"I'm good for a while yet," he told her, guessing what she had in mind.

"Good. The message I got said that things are going to happen tomorrow night, May Eve—that's why I came out here on the first bus I could catch. I gather you've done some looking around and asked some questions. I want to know what you've found out."

He nodded. "I can do that."

* * *

The next morning he woke up later than usual—he'd fielded Jenny's questions for more than two hours, and ended up feeling as though his brain had been opened and every bit of information in it had been shaken out. He got to the breakfast room to find Justin already there, sipping coffee with a morose expression on his face. The room was otherwise empty. "What's up?" he asked the younger man, once he'd gotten a cup of hot water and a teabag steeping in it.

"Miss Chaudronnier," Justin said. "Are you sure she's some kind of magical hotshot?"

Owen started laughing, then stopped, seeing the expression on Justin's face. "Trust me," he said. "She's all of that and more." Then: "Not what you were expecting?"

He shook his head. "A drab little slip of a thing. I expected someone more impressive."

Owen smiled and said nothing. Justin considered him, and downed the last of his coffee. "I'll take your word for it that she might be able to help."

The door to Walt Moore's apartment swung open then, and Walt hauled out a square pan of scrambled eggs and got it settled into one of the steam tables. A moment later, the other door opened and Jenny came through it, looking like anything but a powerful sorceress: dressed in jeans and a Miskatonic University t-shirt, with her mouse-colored hair tied back all anyhow and a battered shoulderbag dangling from one thin shoulder.

"Hi, Owen," she said. "Mr. Martense, Mr. Moore, good morning." She turned to Justin. "Mr. Martense, when you're done with breakfast, would you mind answering some questions?"

"Not at all," Justin said, taken aback.

"Thank you." She turned to Walt. "Mr. Moore, I'd like to ask you some things a little later, and then—" She turned to Owen. "The young lady you mentioned."

"Patty Dombrowski."

"Yes. When she's feeling okay, I'd like to talk to her too."

That was how the morning went. Owen got his breakfast, and then went back to his room to wait, while Jenny and Justin went to one of the picnic benches next to the slopes of Elk Hill. An hour and a half later, when he went to get another cup of tea, she had Walt Moore sitting at the same table, and an hour after that, when he'd finished rereading "The Diary of Alonzo Typer" and the other Lovecraft stories in the anthology, Jenny and Patty Dombrowski were sitting in the same place, Jenny listening with her chin propped on her hands as Patty talked animatedly.

A little after ten, Jenny came to find him. "I've been up on the hill," she said, "and I'd like to talk to Miss Hale next. Then the senior initiate—Mrs. Moore, wasn't it?"

"Cicely Moore," Owen said.

"I'll want to have you there for that conversation."

"Do you have any idea what all this is about?"

"There are a couple of details I still need to work out," Jenny said. "Other than that, yes, it's pretty clear—and once we talk to Mrs. Moore, it'll be time to take action. There could be some real trouble when we get to that point, by the way."

He gave her a startled look but led her to Betty Hale's house, left her there, and waited for another hour before she knocked on his door. "Okay," she said. "Now to Mrs. Moore's place."

Cicely answered Jenny's knock promptly, as though she'd been waiting for it. "Please come in," she said, and brought them into the living room. "Can I get you something?"

A few minutes later cups of tea made their appearance, and Cicely Moore settled into an armchair covered with flower-print cloth. "So what can I do for you?"

"I need to ask about something I'm sure you don't want to discuss," Jenny said. "I'm sorry about that, and if there was any way around it I'd leave it alone, but there it is."

The old woman's face tensed fractionally. "Go ahead."

"When the people who founded Chorazin came here from Roodsport, they brought something with them. I'm almost certain that it was an English manuscript translation of Ludvig Prinn's *De Vermis Mysteriis*, probably one of a kind. I need to know where it is and who has access to it, because it's the key to this whole riddle."

Cicely's face had frozen into a mask as the younger woman spoke, and for a long moment she said nothing at all, staring blankly at Jenny. Finally she closed her eyes and bowed her head. "Miss Chaudronnier," she said, "you're either very good at sorcery or very clever, or both."

Owen glanced from one to the other and back. Jenny waited and said nothing.

"You'll have to pardon me. That book was Chorazin's treasure, and now it's Chorazin's shame. We had it and we lost it, and nothing's gone well for us since."

"How did you lose it?" Jenny asked.

"This land doesn't belong to us." She opened her eyes, considered Jenny. "The old van der Heyl estate was bought by a man from Buffalo named Shields, after the van der Heyls went away. His family still owns it, and leases it to the Chorazin folk. But in 1966 old Oscar Shields died and his son Curtis decided he didn't want to lease the property to us any more—he up and decided to live here, and turn the whole property into his own private estate. He built a big house up on the ridge west of here, and started breaking leases and forcing people out of their homes, just like that. It was against the law, but nobody from the county gave a damn about that.

"So all the children got sent away, with some younger folks to take care of them—I was one of those—and most of the others came after. We didn't think we'd ever come back, and the old folks, they said there was no point to passing on the lore about the Sleeper, since the rites couldn't be done and the Sleeper wasn't ever going to wake again. But some of us heard her calling, and we came back secretly twice a year and did the rites as best we could—a candle in a glass jar in place of a bonfire, that sort of thing

"It was the children who got called, the children and some of the young folk, and all we knew was the rites. You know the song Betty sang you?" Owen nodded. "The only reason we know that is that one of my cousins found an old cassette tape by some folk singer, I forget who, that had it—and then Betty found another copy of the words in the Emeryville library. That was after we came back."

"What happened to Mr. Shields?" Jenny asked.

Cicely wouldn't meet her eyes. "He took sick and died. His family, too." A few moments of silence passed, and then the old woman went on. "Once they were gone, the property went to some relative out Chicago way who leased most of it back to us on pretty close to the old terms."

"Most of it?"

"Shields sold some bits and pieces of land on the old estate to other people, friends of his or something. None of 'em were anywhere too close to here—there's only one that's in sight of the hill at all—and they didn't make trouble, so we said live and let live, like we usually do."

Jenny nodded. "And the book?"

"We left the old books in the church when we locked it up and moved away. We have to do that; there are—reasons, once a church is founded." Jenny nodded again, and the old woman went on. "When we came back and opened up the church again, most everything was still there, but the one book—the book you mentioned—that was gone. We tried everything we could to find it. We tried rituals so risky a couple of people got killed doing them, we were that serious, but nothing worked. We even went to Miz Eagle—she's a witch around here—"

"I know about her," Jenny said. "Please go on."

"All she'd say is that the book would turn up when it turned up, and it never did."

"Mrs. Moore?" said Jenny suddenly.

The old woman glanced up at her, and all at once her eyes glazed over. She stared blankly at Jenny as Jenny gazed at her, until suddenly Jenny nodded once, sharply, breaking the contact.

"I'm sorry," Jenny said. "I really am—but I had to be sure you were telling the truth."

The old woman gave her a shaken glance, but said nothing.

"I'd like to ask one more question, if I could." When Cicely motioned her to go ahead: "The people who die the way Robin Hale did, with their head half torn off and their blood gone. Did that happen back before you had to leave Chorazin?"

Cicely, gave her a puzzled look. "No," she said finally. "Not that I ever heard."

Jenny nodded slowly, and then leaned forward. "Mrs. Moore, there's almost certainly going to be serious trouble here in Chorazin before sunset. Do you think you can get the people and things you need on the hill by noon, and stay there until it's time for the rites?"

A shocked moment passed. "We can do that," the old woman said.

"Thank you. Those rites have to happen. It's very important." Then: "You'll want to get everybody else in town someplace safe—or almost everyone. If I can borrow a dozen men with guns who know how to hunt, that would be really helpful."

"You won't find a man in this town who doesn't," said Cicely, "nor many of the women, for that matter. We can surely do that."

Five minutes later Jenny and Owen crossed the street back to the motel. "Well," Jenny said. "That was easier than I expected."

Owen stared at her for a good long moment. Questions whirled in his head, but he knew better than to ask them just then. He swallowed and said, "What now?"

"Now? We get Justin and have lunch. After that, I'll talk to the dozen men, and then—"

She glanced up at him, and her expression was one he'd never seen on her face before, hard and bleak as winter. "Then we're going to pay a visit to Mr. Aubrey Keel," she said.

* * *

Thunder muttered low in the west as Owen, Justin, and Jenny turned onto the dirt road along the edge of the old van der Heyl estate. No one spoke, though Jenny glanced up at the clouds overhead and nodded once, as though they confirmed some guess of hers. The air was still and heavy, and when the thunder fell silent, their footfalls seemed unnaturally loud.

Beyond the ruins of the Hell House, the woods closed in, and the road ran for a short distance between tall oaks before Keel's house came into sight. Jenny motioned to Owen, who nodded and led the way up onto the porch and then to the front door. He looked back over his shoulder at Jenny, who nodded, and then turned back to the door and knocked.

Several minutes passed, and then Keel opened the door. Before he could say anything, Owen said, "Mr. Keel, I hope you don't mind us just coming over like this, but we didn't have your phone number or anything, and our friend Jenny— she's a grad student—she wanted to ask you some questions about the local folklore."

For a moment, something like discomfiture showed on Keel's face, and then a genial smile replaced it. "Why, of course," he said. "Please come in. Can I get you anything?"

"A glass of water would be fine, thanks," said Jenny.

"Done." To the two men: "I trust I can interest you in something a little less bland."

That got settled, and he stepped back, waved them into his living room, closed the door behind them and went to the kitchen. The three of them settled on the couch, and after a few moments Keel reappeared with glasses and set them on the table.

"Oh, I'm sorry," Jenny said then, picking up her glass. "Could I trouble you for a bit of lemon, or maybe a drop of lemon juice? I get stomach cramps otherwise."

"But of course," Keel said, and went back into the kitchen. The moment he was gone, Jenny set her glass down again and passed her right hand over the glasses, murmuring words under her breath. Owen gave her a questioning look, and she met his glance and nodded.

Keel was back a moment later with a lemon wedge on a little saucer. Jenny thanked him profusely, waited until he'd settled down on his chair, and then began to ply him with questions about the van der Heyls and the stories around their ruined house. For the first ten minutes or so, he responded with apparent enthusiasm, beaming from time to time as Justin and Owen drank their beers and Jenny sipped her water.

Thereafter, though, something seemed to unsettle him, and his discomfort grew more evident with each minute that passed.

Finally, he got to his feet and said, "I really don't wish to be inhospitable, but I'm expecting a phone call from a friend in New York City in a quarter hour."

"Of course," said Jenny. "I just have one more question, if you don't mind."

He smiled and nodded. "Of course."

"When you summoned the Shambler from the Stars on Thursday, was Robin Hale just in the wrong place at the wrong time, or did you intend to kill him?"

For a moment no one spoke. The smile on Keel's face tautened into a rictus. "You'll forgive me," he forced out, "if I question your sanity."

"No," said Jenny. "I won't forgive you."

He stepped back, eyes narrowing.

"The book you used for the summoning is in this house," she said then. "It's probably in this room, in fact. You've had it since you stole it from the Starry Wisdom church in Chorazin, and you've used that same incantation again and again to kill anyone who got too close to the secret that's hidden in the ruins of the van der Heyl house."

"You're quite mad," Keel said, backing away from her.

"No." Her thin pale face could have been carved of stone at that moment. "The soporific you slipped into our drinks was a nice touch, by the way. Pity it didn't work."

In answer he turned and sprinted for the stair up to the loft. Owen sprang to his feet and ran after him, but Keel was too quick for him. As Owen got to the foot of the stair, Keel reached the top, spun around, and shoved hard on a wooden armoire, sending it toppling down the stair. Owen flung himself back as the armoire landed halfway down the steps with a crash.

Before Owen could begin clambering past it, the old man had a great leatherbound book open in his hand and was shouting words in Latin: *"Tibi Magnum Innominandum, signa stellarum nigrarum et bufaniformis Sadoguae sigillum—"*

Owen recognized the words at once as a summoning spell, and braced himself for a leap. Jenny called out his name and made a sudden gesture, though, and he stopped. She rose to her feet then, facing Keel. Justin was already standing, and looked uneasily at the others. Keel's voice rose to a shriek as he finished the incantation: *"Veni, veni, stragitor infandus ab sideribus!"*

Silence filled the house for a moment, and the air went cold. Then a sudden wind outside made the frame of the house creak and groan. One of the big picture windows alongside the loft shattered, flinging glass into the room, as though something unseen had burst through. A moment later a new sound joined the bellowing of the wind and the sounds of rafters and walls in torment, a wild laughter that was not Keel's, nor any other human throat's. Owen's blood ran cold as he recognized it: the same laughter he'd heard in the storm the day that Robin Hale died.

Keel pointed at them. *"Istos caede!"* he screamed.

The cold wind blew toward them, but Jenny stepped forward, right hand upraised. *"Siste,"* she said, her voice low and calm. *"Consiste, monstrum aetherigenum, in nomine Sadoguae et in potestate caprae nigrae sylvarum milligenitricis. Non habes roborem nobis nocere. Tolle praedam iustum tuam."*

For a moment only the wind spoke, and Owen tensed, ready to act.

Then Keel screamed again, this time without words. The book tumbled from his hands, struck the railing of the loft, and fell past it to the living room floor below. His arms and legs flailed as he struggled with something unseen, but it lifted him and bent him back in an arc no human body could bear. The sound of snapping bones came through the wind and the wild laughter, and then the flesh of Keel's neck tore open and blood sprayed out from it.

None of the blood touched the floor.

The laughter vanished, and a rhythmic sucking sound blended with the wind. A presence became visible, hovering in midair in the loft: dimly at first, as the blood it drank began to circulate through it, and more definitely as it finished draining Keel dry and let the old man's torn and shriveled husk drop to the floor. A vague bloated mass not quite regular enough to be spherical, waving ropelike arms, dangling limbs underneath that each ended in something like a single hooked talon: that was as much as Owen saw, and more than he wanted to see.

"*Abscede, monstrum, in nomine secretissime septiplice Sadoguae,*" Jenny said then. "*In aetheribus recurre.*"

The wind howled, and the presence reared up. Owen braced himself for its onslaught, but the thing moved to the shattered window and through it, and vanished into the darkening sky. Its crazed laughter sounded once again, carried on the wind, and then faded away. A moment later, the three of them stood in a silent room with only a corpse for company.

Jenny held up another cautioning hand and moved warily forward. She picked the big leatherbound book up from the floor, opened it just long enough to glance at the title page, and then tucked it under one arm. "We should go," she said in a low uneven voice.

"No kidding," Owen said. Adrenaline surged through him; he forced his breathing to slow. "If anyone but the Chorazin folk heard that, we could be facing real trouble."

"True." She glanced up at him. "There are—other risks, too."

Justin stared at her for a moment, said nothing.

Owen motioned toward the door. "Come on," he said. "We need to get out of here."

* * *

Outside the day had turned blustery. Wind hissed in the trees surrounding Keel's house, as though in warning. Owen hurried down the steps from the porch, following Justin and Jenny, and let old reflexes assess his surroundings. Something caught his attention, coming through the trees and brush to the west of Keel's house. Adrenaline surged, but a moment later he recognized familiar shapes: Walt Moore and the others from Chorazin, carrying deer rifles.

"What the hell was that?" Walt asked as he hurried up to them. "We could hear it laughing from the creekside."

"The thing that killed Robin Hale," Jenny said.

For a moment no one spoke. "It's gone," she went on. "The one who summoned it—he died the same way Robin did." With a little shrug: "I thought it was the right thing to do."

Walt found his voice. "Thank you." Then: "What now?"

"We need to get out of here," she said. "The other side— they'll know what just happened. Every sensitive within twenty or thirty miles must have felt it."

"The river trail ought to be safe," said Walt. "Billy, Tom, you stay here for five minutes or so. Signal if there's trouble." The two men he'd named nodded, stepped aside. "Fred, Joe, you take the lead. The rest of us'll be right behind."

"Just a moment, please," said an unfamiliar voice off behind Owen.

He turned, fast, and so did the others. A young man had stepped out of the woods across the road from the house, short and brown-skinned, with an Asian cast to his face. He wore jeans and a camp shirt, but a red knotted cord was wrapped around his left arm in a curious fashion.

The moment he appeared, two of the Chorazin folk snapped their rifles up to waist level and pointed them at him. In response, the young man put a hand to his lips and let out a shrill whistle. The rest of the Chorazin folk brought their guns up, but by then it was precisely too late.

Another forty or so men had come noiselessly out of the woods across from the house. All of them had the same Asian cast of features as the young man, and wore the same kind of ordinary clothing, except that a few old men had lengths of dark red cloth tied in a sort of loose turban on their heads, and all of them had the red cords around their left arms. All of them were armed, too, with a motley assortment of guns that pointed at the Chorazin folk.

For a moment no one moved or spoke. Owen could see the faces around him tense as they measured the odds against them.

"Hold it," Walt Moore said then, breaking the silence.

Owen glanced at him. The old man had a look of astonishment on his face.

"Hold it." he repeated. Then: "You guys are Tcho-Tchos, aren't you? How the hell did you get here?"

The young man who'd appeared first looked just as astonished as he did. "How do you know about Tcho-Tchos?"

"I was in Laos during the war," Walt said. "I fought alongside 'em."

One of the old men with a red turban said, "I was in Laos."

"Around Sop Khao and Muong Hiem?"

"No. We were along the Nam Ou river."

"Never got that far north," said Walt. "I heard you guys gave the Pathet Lao a hell of a hard time up there, though."

In response, the old man smiled fractionally and lowered his pistol. The two Chorazin boys who'd pointed their guns first lowered their muzzles.

"Tcho-Tchos," Bill Downey said. "That means what?"

"Means they worship the Great Old Ones, same as we do," Walt told him.

The old man who'd been in Laos blinked in surprise. "You know Yukh Sadhadh, Khu Lhu, Tsad Thog, Shob Nekhrang?"

"We pronounce 'em a little different here," said Walt, "but yeah, we know them, and the one you don't ever call by name."

The old man broke into a broad smile, and said something in what Owen guessed was the Tcho-Tcho language. Their remaining guns pointed in less lethal directions, and so an instant later did those of the Chorazin folk.

"I live in Buffalo now," the old man said. "We came over as refugees."

"Well, damn," said Walt. "Welcome to the U.S. of A."

The old man smiled again. "Thank you."

"We need to know about something," the young man said then. "There was—an evil thing, in there." He motioned toward the house.

"A Shambler from the Stars," Jenny said.

The young man turned and said something in an unfamiliar language to another of the older men, who shook his head. He turned back to Jenny. "I don't know what that is."

"*G'nglakh U'uht'gnaa,*" Jenny said then; Owen recognized the language—Aklo, the tongue of the oldest spells in the *Necronomicon*—but not the phrase. Some of the elders seemed to know it, though, and one said, "*Thrau kharang.*" The other Tcho-Tchos gave him sudden sharp looks. "Is it—" the young man began.

"It killed the one who called it," Jenny told him, "and I sent it back where it came from."

The young man's eyes widened, and he started to say something. Just then, the distant sound of three rifle shots came echoing off the walls of the valley.

"Damn," Walt Moore said. "We all need to get out of here, fast. That's a signal—we left sentries back in town, and it means there's a whole mess of men with guns headed this way."

The young man turned to another elder, and they talked briefly in their own language. Turning back to the Chorazin folk: "We've got cars on the road back that way—" He motioned south through the woods. "—and a place up east of here that's well guarded. Will you come?"

Owen turned to Walt Moore, who turned to Jenny, who gave him a look that said, as clearly as words could, that it was his call. "Sounds like the best choice we've got," he said, "so please and thank you."

"Will your people back in the town be okay?" the young man asked.

Walt nodded. "We were expecting this—and it's not the first time we've dealt with the other side, not by a long shot."

The young man nodded. "This way, then."

CHAPTER 10

THE MYSTERIES OF THE WORM

They came out of the trees a quarter mile further south onto a long-neglected gravel road. A line of battered cars and vans were pulled up alongside it, looking for all the world as though they'd been rusting there for years.

"We ought to have enough room for everyone if we squeeze a bit," said the young man. Walt laughed and motioned to the others from Chorazin, and within a few minutes everyone, Tcho-Tchos and Chorazin folk alike, were packed into the available seats. Owen, Jenny and Justin squeezed into the middle bench seat of one of the vans; the old man who'd been in Laos got behind the wheel and started the engine. The young man plopped into the seat next to him, and four more Tcho-Tchos jammed themselves into the bench seat in back.

As the van lurched forward and turned onto the rutted gravel road, the young man turned in his seat. "I'm Shray Lharep," he said. "You can call me Larry; lots of people do. My dad's Shray Khorep." He indicated the driver with a motion of his head.

"Pleased to meet you," said Jenny. Introductions followed; Owen tried to keep track of the Tcho-Tchos' names, and failed. The adrenaline left behind by the encounter in Keel's house was finally fading, and in its place came the cold realization of just how close they'd come to a hideous death. If Jenny hadn't been there—

153

He forced the thought away. Still, it served as a harsh reminder of how little he knew about the other players in the complex game around him. That included the Tcho-Tchos, of course. The people of the Great Old Ones cooperated when they could—that was the price of survival—but that didn't guarantee that Owen and his friends were safe in Tcho-Tcho hands.

The van rattled down the gravel road, with dense woods to either side, and then started up a hill. The old man shifted into a lower gear; the roar of the engine made conversation impossible for a few minutes. Owen watched the trees rush by.

At the top of the hill the road swerved to one side and started down a low incline, and the engine quieted. "May I ask a question?" Jenny asked the young man.

"Sure," said Larry.

"The creature," she said. "You knew it was there. Would you mind telling me how?"

"We got warned this morning, by someone who's good at that sort of thing, to expect *ngam khra*—bad magic—and so we had elders with us. We were trying to find a way onto the hill when they sensed it, and we came running."

Jenny nodded. The old man in the driver's seat shook his head and muttered, "*Thrau kharang.* That's bad, very bad."

"That's your name for it?" Jenny asked him.

"That's the Tchosi name," Larry said. "*Thrau* means anything that eats people—*thrau mban* is tiger, the striped *thrau. Thrau kharang* is the *thrau* from the upper air."

"Very logical," Jenny said.

"Isn't it?" The young man grinned. "I grew up speaking both languages, and English still gives me headaches. Why on Earth do you park on a driveway and drive on a parkway?"

That got a general laugh, even from Justin, who'd barely made a sound since they'd left Aubrey Keel's house.

The road plunged beneath dark trees. On the far side, a sharp turn and a long driveway even more decrepit than the road brought them to a hollow surrounded by forest, where an old farmhouse fought a losing struggle against the pitiless wrecking crews of the weather.

As the house came into sight, Jenny said, "You've got really capable protective spells around this place. I'm impressed."

Larry turned and gave her another grin. "Grandma Pakheng's good."

The van rolled to a halt. Half a dozen cars were already parked out in front, and another came up the driveway as Owen got out. He offered Jenny a hand down, which she took. She still had the big leatherbound book tucked under her arm. The others got out of the van, and with them, he crossed the field toward the farmhouse door.

Larry pulled the door wide, and they filed in. Inside was a big living room with peeling paper on the walls and an assortment of old wooden furniture to fill it. The windows were still intact and curtained, and only a faint smell of damp touched the air. Khorep waved them toward a door, saying, "That way, please." He went off a different direction, through an open passage to what Owen guessed was probably the kitchen. Meanwhile Larry went through yet another door and headed upstairs—Owen could hear the treads creak under his feet.

Owen glanced at Jenny and Justin, and then led the way through the door. On the far side was a parlor furnished with a random assortment of chairs and a few other bits of furniture. None of the chairs were occupied; for the moment, the three of them were alone.

"The thing we saw," Justin said then. It was the first thing he'd uttered since they'd come out of Aubrey Keel's house. "Did it actually come from the stars?"

Jenny shook her head. "The Shambler? No. The Tcho-Tcho name's more accurate. Shamblers live in the upper air, and mostly eat other things that live up there, but they can dive down here the way some whales dive into the deep parts of the ocean. They're always hungry, and if you summon one, either you give it something living to eat or it eats you."

"The way it ate Keel," said Justin.

"And too many other people," said Jenny.

Just then Khorep came in through the door with a wooden tray that carried an iron teapot and a stack of little handleless cups; the red cord was no longer around his left arm. "Tea," he said, and motioned to the chairs. "Please, sit."

They pulled chairs together into a rough circle, and Owen brought over a little round table. Khorep got everyone supplied with a full teacup, then went back out of the parlor and came in again with a battery-powered camp lantern, which he set on the table and clicked on. Yellow light pooled on the waterstained ceiling above. Outside, visible through gaps in the curtains, the afternoon darkened.

The door opened again. Owen glanced up to see two figures coming in: Larry and a very old Tcho-Tcho woman in what he guessed was traditional clothing, a brocade jacket and trousers that looked black at first glance but proved to be deep red once she got close enough to the lamp.

"This is Grandma Pakheng," Larry said.

Voor gathered and swirled around the old woman. A witch? Owen guessed so. He got up, said, "Pleased to meet you, ma'am." The others stood as well; Justin seemed startled by the old woman's arrival, as though he'd been deep in thought. For her part, Jenny curtseyed, and the old woman's wrinkled face creased with a smile, and she bowed to Jenny. Larry found her a chair, Khorep poured her a cup of tea, and she sat, considered each of them in turn.

They were waiting, Owen suddenly knew. For what?

A minute later, a knock sounded at the front door. He could hear it echo through the walls: heavy and deep, as though someone had bumped the door with a fallen log or a stone.

Grandma Pakheng smiled again, and nodded at Larry, who got up at once and left the room. He came back in a moment later with two others. It took Owen a moment to recognize them: the old witch Sallie Eagle, and behind her, looking dazed, Patty Dombrowski.

He started to stand up, and so did the others, but the witch waved them to their seats. "No need for that," she said. "A chair for me if you've one to spare, and a chair for this poor thing. Chorazin's full of men with guns, so I got her away. Besides, she'll be wanted in a bit."

Owen got up then, and he and Larry found a couple of chairs that would serve. "Tea?" Khorep asked them both as they sat. The witch gave him a sharp-toothed smile and a nod, and Patty said, "Yes, thanks." Tea splashed into another pair of the little cups.

A moment of silence went by, and then Larry spoke. "Tonight is—I don't know the English word; we call it *Pakh Dau*."

"May Eve," Owen said.

"Yes. There's—Someone—inside the hill in the valley. We're here because of that."

"So am I," said Justin.

"I know." Larry grinned. "Grandma Pakheng told us this morning to look for three people and bring them back here to talk, because they know things we don't—" He gestured at Owen, Justin, and Jenny. "And there you were."

"And me?" Patty said.

Grandma Pakheng smiled at her. "I spoke to her," the old woman said, nodding to Sallie Eagle. "She told me about you. She says we come here, all same reason. We know something. You—" she nodded at each of them. "—you know something. We talk, then maybe, we know what to do."

* * *

"We got the first hints about That One not long after the first of our families settled in Buffalo in '77," Larry said. "A few of our people came here a long time before that, following up some hints in the sacred writings; not all of them came back, and not all of the ones who did came back in one piece, but that's why we chose this part of the country when we got out of the camps in Thailand. So of course the first elders who moved here tried to read the *dzau chonlep*, the signs on the land. They didn't have an easy time of it—I get the sense that elder races lived here, a lot of them, for a long time."

Owen nodded "All the way back to the serpent folk of Valusia."

"Wow," said Larry. "That's even longer than I thought. But our people figured out pretty quick that there was something really powerful in the hills east of town, something that tied together all the currents of—I don't know what you call it, the life energy."

"Voor," Owen suggested.

Larry grinned. "Not too far from our word. All the currents in the land flowed into the thing we sensed, but finding it in the hills wasn't too easy. Of course we had a lot to do, settling in and getting by, so reading the *dzau* got done a weekend here and a weekend there.

"So it wasn't until five years ago, the summer after I graduated from high school, that a couple of us drove Grandma Pakheng out this way. You know where you take the exit onto Pine Road? She had us turn there, then onto Chorazin Road, and we got our first look at Elk Hill."

"I knew," Grandma Pakheng said then. "I felt—in the hill."

"We didn't hang around, though," Larry went on. "Out here, if you're not white and you're not local, you can get in way too much trouble if you're not careful. So we took it a bit at a time. It wasn't until last year that we got this place for back taxes so we had a place to stay, and we'd probably still be watching and waiting, except—"

He stopped, turned to the other Tcho-Tchos and discussed something with them in a low voice. Grandma Pakheng nodded, and said in English, "Tell them."

"We got a visit from one of Those Ones," said Larry, obviously uncomfortable. "I don't know what you call him."

Justin leaned forward. "Let me guess," he said. "Really tall, in a black coat and a black hat, and—" He reached into a pocket, brought out something that glittered. "Rings like this one."

For a long moment no one spoke. Larry and Khorep stared at the ring with narrowed eyes, and then Khorep turned to Grandma Pakheng and said something in Tchosi.

"*Tcho Khyoron*," Grandma Pakheng said. "He speaks for Those Ones. He came to us."

"We call him Nyarlathotep," Justin said then. "He's the one who sent me here."

"Tell us," said Grandma Pakheng.

Justin told his story, then, leaning forward and clutching the bright ring in both hands: first his own part of the tale, including Owen's part in it, and then the longer tale, from Jan Maertens down. When he was done, Grandma Pakheng nodded, and turned to Patty. "And you."

"I don't have anything like so big a story," the young woman said. "I had to leave home for—" A shy smile. "Certain reasons. The One in Black met me at a crossroads and drove me to Chorazin, and on the way he told me that I'd be needed here, if I was willing to help, and it had to do with the Sleeper in the Hill. As soon as I got here I started hearing her in my dreams— but I don't know what to do."

"You know sorcery," Grandma Pakheng said.

"A little bit. My grandfather was good at it. He didn't teach me, but I've got his book."

Grandma Pakheng nodded, then turned to Sallie Eagle and said, "You we know." The old witch smiled, and the Tcho-Tcho elder turned to Jenny. "And you," she said. "You came. Why?"

"I got a phone call from one of my teachers," Jenny said. "A witch in Massachusetts. She got a message from another witch in Chorazin, but I'd already been told by the Great Old One I worship to be ready to travel. So I caught the next bus out this way."

Grandma Pakheng turned to Larry and asked something in Tchosi, and the two of them had a hurried conversation. "You are not—witch," she said to Jenny.

Jenny met her gaze. "Honored One," she said, "I think you know exactly what I am."

The old woman considered her for a moment, then smiled and nodded.

Larry said, "I think you might know more about this than the rest of us."

"Possibly," Jenny replied. "I've drawn some tentative conclusions."

"Please," he said, gesturing. The others nodded.

"The first one has to do with this." She set the big leather-bound book on the table in front of her. "I knew as soon as I heard about Robin Hale that somebody had called down a Shambler from the Stars; the way they kill and feed is unmistakable. That meant that somebody had a copy of Ludvig Prinn's *De Vermis Mysteriis*, since that's the only source for the words of summoning in any Western language. There's been talk for years about an English manuscript translation that came to this country in the seventeenth century, but it went to Roodsford, and everyone assumed that it was destroyed when the Puritans killed everyone there and burned the town. When I found out that the founders of Chorazin came from Roodsford with a treasure nobody wanted to talk about, though, that rumor came to mind.

"So I had to make sure that the Chorazin folk didn't have it, and once I'd settled that, I knew someone else had it—someone who'd been keeping a watch on the old van der Heyl house for many years, and who used the spells in the book to guard the secret that's hidden there. But there's more to the book than a means of murder."

She picked up the book and turned to Grandma Pakheng. "Would you like to examine it, Honored One?" The old woman nodded and took it, and she and Khorep bent over it for a few minutes, turning the pages and talking quietly in Tchosi. Finally, she closed it and held it out to Jenny without another word. Jenny motioned for her to pass it on to Larry, who leafed through the pages with wide eyes, and then handed it to Patty, who read several passages with an intent expression, nodding as if she'd found something she'd expected. She passed it to Justin. He quickly handed it on to Owen, who opened it and found the title page. That was handwritten in fading brown ink on heavy paper spotted with age, and it read:

Ye Mysteries of ye Worme
by yt moste redoutable sorcerour
Ludvig Prinn
late of Flanders
donne into ye Englishe tongue
by Simon Forman, gent.
MDCIII

"Sarah and Micah Moore aren't the only people involved in this business who had a copy, either," Jenny went on. "The van der Heyls had a copy of the first Latin edition from 1439."

"I thought the first edition was in 1543," said Owen.

She answered with a quick shake of her head. "That's the second. Most people don't know about the first—someone I know at the Université de Vyones told me about it." She leaned forward. "The first edition had material that's not in the second, or any of the later printings—and by all accounts Forman made his translation from the first edition."

"1439," Justin said. "So if a group of sorcerers sailed from northern Europe in 1456, they could have had a copy."

"Exactly," said Jenny. "You see where I'm heading."

"And they used something in that book to summon the Sleeper," he went on.

"No," she said.

Owen glanced at her, surprised. The others responded in much the same way, with two exceptions. One was Grandma Pakheng; her eyes had gone wide, and she nodded slowly, as though something had just made sense.

The other was Sallie Eagle. The old witch's glittering eyes gazed at Jenny with terrible intensity, and something far too ambivalent to be called a smile bent the corners of her wide mouth and twisted the wrinkles of her face.

"No," Jenny said again. "They used something in the book to imprison her."

Utter silence filled the room for a long moment.

Justin was the first to speak. "But—if she's one of the beings of the elder world—can humans even do that?"

"That depends," said Jenny. "The great powers? Of course not, but there are others who might be vulnerable to that, under certain circumstances."

"Since the holy places were desecrated," Owen said.

Jenny glanced at him, nodded. "I have a guess—it's no more than a guess—about who she is, but that'll wait. The one thing I still have to figure out is where to find the incantation that imprisoned her, so I can figure out how to break it. It'll be in the book; I'll just have to hunt for it until I find it."

"That won't be needful, child," said Sallie Eagle.

Owen glanced at her again, and wished he hadn't. The witch's not-quite-smile had cracked open into a sharp-toothed grin that reminded him uncomfortably of tigers, sharks, and other fierce and hungry things.

"You know," Jenny said: a statement, not a question.

"Oh, yes. What's more, I'll tell you." The witch turned to Grandma Pakheng. "And you." She turned the other way, toward Patty Dombrowski. "And you." She motioned at the others with a hand that, just then, seemed to end in claws rather than nails. "Leave us."

* * *

Tcho-Tchos and Chorazin folk packed the living room of the old farmhouse. The air was full of conversations, and just as full of scents from the kitchen. "Owen!" Walt Moore called out from close by. "Got some news for you—you too, Mr. Martense."

That got him a wry look. "Might as well call me Justin."

"I can do that," said Walt.

He was sitting with half a dozen elderly Tcho-Tchos, tough scarred men with ready smiles, and an open cooler full of ice and bottles of golden-brown beer that had labels in a script Owen didn't recognize at all. One of the Tcho-Tchos pulled a bottle from the ice, popped the cap off and sent it spinning into the air with a sudden motion of his thumb, and handed the bottle to Justin, who blinked, then laughed and thanked him; the Tcho-Tcho grinned, did the same trick again, and handed a bottle to Owen, who thanked him and sipped at it. It was strong and bitter, and Owen smiled and downed a larger slug.

"There you go," said Walt. "Okay, news. These folks have had sentries along the ridge for the last two weeks, watching Chorazin and the van der Heyl house. The signal we got was because a bunch of SUVs came along Chorazin Road about two o'clock, right into town. Men in military kit, twenty of 'em, fanned out, kicked in some doors, did some searching."

"The church?" Owen asked.

"Nah, they must have known better; we'd left the protections up, and the Watcher would have gotten them for sure. But all our people were already up onto the hill or in safe places out of town. They got going before the boys and I left to go to Keel's place. As far as the sentries can tell, everyone's okay."

"Well, that's something," said Owen. "Are the guys in military kit still in town?"

"Nope. They piled back onto their SUVs and headed south. Last message we got, they're on the road by the van der Heyl house."

"Who are they?" Justin asked.

Walt glanced at Owen, but it was one of the Tcho-Tchos who answered. "*Khrau Dzol*," he said in heavily accented English. "We call them that—false light, light that isn't light."

Owen nodded. "The Radiance."

The word hung in the air, an all too familiar threat. Justin glanced from the Tcho-Tcho to Owen and back, uncertain. Before he could ask the question that was written clearly on his face, though, someone called out words in Tchosi from the kitchen.

"Now that's a phrase I remember," Walt said. "Dinner's on." He glanced at Owen, a sly smile curving his lips. "Vegetarian."

Owen gave him a blank look, and then started laughing. Justin looked confused, and after a moment Walt took pity on him. "Let's just say the Tcho-Tchos have kind of a reputation."

"Cannibals," said Larry, coming to join them. "That's what they called us over in Laos and Burma." He rolled his eyes.

"Those Tcho-Tchos, very bad, they eat people," said the man who'd popped the beer caps with his thumb. "They say that, then come kill us, steal our land, take children for slaves. Pah."

"There were some times over in Laos I was just about hungry enough to take a bite out of somebody," Walt said, "and the Tcho-Tchos ate a good bit less'n I did. But they never took a bite out of anyone—not even me."

One of the old men reached out, took the flesh of Walt's forearm between thumb and forefinger, squeezed it. "Too stringy," he said. Walt laughed, and so did the Tcho-Tchos.

"Come on," Larry said to Owen and Justin. "Dinner's ready, and it's really good. Uncle Gyoreng did the cooking. He runs the best Thai restaurant in Buffalo, the place where I work— but this isn't Thai. This is Leng cooking, and you won't find anything anywhere better than that."

Dinner turned out to be big bowls of vegetables and peanuts over rice, seasoned with a red pepper sauce nearly hot enough to blister tooth enamel. Justin sat over to one side and said little, while Owen got into a conversation with some of the younger men. "You're right," he said to Larry after a few bites. "This is really good. I hope they're saving some for the women."

He motioned with one hand toward the closed door, ate another mouthful.

Larry nodded. "Oh, yes. There'll be plenty. Uncle Gyoreng's used to setting some aside for them—with us, sorcery's on the women's side, so this happens all the time."

Owen was dealing just then with a burst of pepper sauce and couldn't speak, but managed a "Hmm?" and an expression of curiosity.

"Men's side, women's side," another of the young Tcho-Tchos said. "That's our tradition. Men take care of goats, do the hunting, fighting, cooking, weaving; women own houses, spin yarn, take care of gardens, cast spells. You've seen our knives, right?" He patted the big leaf-bladed bush knife in the carved wooden sheath at his hip.

"Yeah," said Owen, finally able to talk.

"Those are men's knives. Women have their own knives, and if you ever see them get those out and they aren't chopping vegetables or something, you better pray to Tsad Thog it's gonna be over real quick."

The Tcho-Tchos laughed, and Owen nodded.

"You do things some other way, I guess," said Larry.

"Depends," said Owen. "My wife's a priestess in the Esoteric Order of Dagon, and with them, the important work is done by priestesses. I'm an initiate of the Starry Wisdom, and with us it's whoever works hard and has talent. Other people have their own ways of doing things."

"Well, there you go," said Larry. "Different for everyone. I—"

Whatever he'd meant to say went unsaid, for the door to the parlor came open then, and the four women who'd been beyond it came out. Three of them looked as though they were in shock. The fourth was Sallie Eagle, and her wide mouth curled up at the ends in a half-hidden smile, as though she was enjoying a secret. Some of the men waved them into the kitchen.

A few minutes passed before Jenny appeared again at the kitchen door, made her way across the room to where Owen was sitting. By then most of the younger Tcho-Tchos had gotten up and gone into the kitchen to help with cleanup. Jenny settled in one of the empty chairs, gave the bowl of rice and vegetables a dazed look.

"Anything I should know about?" Owen asked.

She glanced at him. "Not yet." Then: "Well, one thing. I know what we're up against. How well do you know Prinn?"

"I've read him. My Latin isn't good but it'll do."

"Do you remember the thirteenth chapter?"

Owen's gaze snapped up to her face. "Yes," he said after a pause. "But that means we're hopelessly out of our depth."

"No."

"You're talking about the Worm."

She nodded. "I know. I think we might just be able to make this work."

Owen stared at her and said nothing, and she smiled and started to eat.

* * *

The Worm.

The phrase circled around itself in the silent places of Owen's mind.

They wouldn't be able to do anything until after full dark, Jenny had explained, and so Owen found a spare corner in an upstairs room and curled up. The night ahead would be a long one, he knew, but for once he struggled with the soldier's trick of catching sleep whenever it was available. Out behind the house, the Tcho-Tchos had a fire going in an old brick barbecue and were chanting spells around it, preparing themselves for the coming night in their own way, but the muffled sound of their voices and the keening of the bamboo flute that accompanied them shouldn't have been enough to keep him awake.

The Worm.

He shifted irritably, tried to force the phrase out of his head.

The thirteenth chapter of Prinn's *De Vermis Mysteriis* talked about it, and so did a passage in the fifth book of the *Necronomicon*, half a dozen pages in the fourth chapter of von Junzt, and assorted passages in other books he'd read. Off beyond Yuggoth and Shaggai and the thousand cold worlds of the Ghooric zone, they claimed, it coiled in the endless night. Owen remembered headlines from five years back, when two space probes flung out beyond the solar system vanished, one after the other, with no discernible cause. He'd wondered what had happened to them, but in those days he hadn't yet turned the pages of ancient tomes and knew nothing of the Great Old Ones and their children. It hadn't occurred to him then that there might be something vast and hungry out there, lurking with open jaws in the void places beyond the turning worlds.

The Worm.

Owen closed his eyes, sighed in frustration, and gave up trying to push the thought away.

Prinn had the most to say about the Worm. *De Vermis Mysteriis* recounted a jumbled heap of lore the old sorcerer had learned from mages in the hills of Syria, some of it garbled beyond recognition but some uncomfortably precise. Under certain circumstances, Prinn had written, one portion of the Worm—whatever exactly that meant—could be bound into an earthly place. Tormented by the crushing force of gravity and the agonizing heat of the planet's surface, it would rage and devour until it was freed to return to its home in the cold silent void of space. The age-old city of Sarkomand in central Asia had been destroyed by such a working, or so Prinn claimed, but how the thing had been done or undone—of that *De Vermis Mysteriis* said nothing. Nor did that book, or any other tome known to Owen, give the words and signs of power that might summon and release the Worm, or breathe the least hint of its true name.

The Worm.

The phrase turned into a long twisting circling shape that grasped its tail in its mouth. It turned and writhed, and all at once the darkness filled with countless vast jawless mouths gaping open, fringed with searching tentacles miles in length, ringed with jagged hooked teeth the size of mountains. Behind each mouth stretched a serpentine body, writhing across hundreds of miles through the cold darkness, with distant stars shining through its unearthly substance. There were hundreds of them, maybe thousands. Yet Owen sensed obscurely that all these were one Worm, one vast many-bodied entity coiling around the edges of the solar system, feeding on comets, meteorites, and the occasional stray and tasty space probe, and now and then contending or mating with kindred beings when another star swung close enough to bring them into contact. For a moment Owen thought he glimpsed an entire galaxy of Worms, each surrounding its native star, hatched from some monstrous egg when that star kindled to thermonuclear life, thriving until the star met whatever fate its mass and composition decreed, concerning itself wholly with its own affairs and those of its kind, and utterly indifferent to whatever infinitesimal life forms might happen to spring up on the wet film around one or another planet in the hideously hot and cramped inner reaches of its solar system.

The glimpse shattered after a moment, because one of the mouths was moving toward Owen. Some unknown sense seemed to alert it to his presence, and it groped toward him with its tentacles, feeling its way through the cold void. Each tentacle, Owen saw, was itself a smaller Worm with mouth and tentacles of its own, and each subtentacle had a mouth and tentacles in turn. He tried to back away from the closest of the sub-sub-tentacles and found that he could not move; he tried to speak a protective incantation but his lips would not stir. Closer and closer the thing came to him, until finally the tentacle brushed his arm and then wrapped tight around it.

Owen woke with a jolt. The grip on his arm was Justin's, shaking him gently. The curtained window next to him showed blackness, lit with distant flickering lightning. "They're ready," Justin said, as Owen sat up. "And there's more news. It's not good."

The living room of the old farmhouse seemed empty when Owen followed Justin into it. Jenny, Walt Moore, Larry, and Khorep stood near the kitchen door, and Patty Dombrowski sat in a chair against one wall with her eyes closed. Grandma Pakheng's voice came in from the porch, chanting something in Tchosi. "What's up?" Owen said.

"Our people have been watching the men in the ruins, the *Khrau Dzol*," said Larry. "They took up positions around the trench that's been dug there, northwest of the old chimney, and two others joined them about half an hour ago. They've got paramilitary gear—camo uniforms, AR-15s, that sort of stuff."

"And that's a problem," Jenny said. "We need to have people at three places by midnight at the very latest, and that trench is one of them."

"We can take them out if we have to," said Walt, "but it's going to cost."

Owen frowned, considering the options. "They'll probably have night vision gear, too. That's going to make this really tough."

"No worry," said Khorep, "*Dzha* Pakheng casts a spell so those don't work."

Owen gave him a surprised look, then stopped, put a hand to his chin. "Could she do that for the Chorazin folk too?"

"Of course." Khorep gave him an assessing look. "You have a plan?"

"Maybe," said Owen. To Khorep and Walt: "You guys know this business better than I do. Tell me if you think this will work." Quickly, he explained his idea.

The two old men looked at each other. "That could do it," said Walt. He turned to Owen. "You'll be taking a hell of a risk, though."

"I'll be taking it with him," said Justin.

Owen turned to him. "You're sure?"

"Yeah. I need to go there anyway, so—" He shrugged. "Might as well."

"Okay," said Walt. "Unless you want to try something else instead," he said to Khorep, who shook his head and said, "No. If it fails—we take them."

Walt glanced out the window, gauged the dark sky. "Let's do it."

They turned toward the door. Jenny gave Owen a worried look, but said nothing. "I can give you a ride to the top of the ridge," Larry said.

Out on the porch, sheet lightning provided most of the light. The rest came from a big bronze cauldron full of glowing coals. Grandma Pakheng stood beside it with knotted red cords draped over one arm. The acrid scent of unfamiliar herbs hung thick in the air. She tied cords around Khorep's arm, then Larry's, then motioned to Owen, Justin, and Walt. "You too," she said. "If you like. It protects."

"I'd be honored," said Owen, and held out his left arm. Grandma Pakheng took one of the cords and wrapped it around his forearm with practiced ease, tying it in place while murmuring words in Tchosi. Owen could feel voor surging through the cord, blending with his own life force and flowing out to surround him with a shell of subtle influence. He gave Justin what he hoped was an encouraging smile as the old woman repeated the spell, and then the two of them followed Larry across the yard to a waiting car.

CHAPTER 11

THE SLEEPER IN THE HILL

The drive that followed reminded Owen of nightmares he'd had, long journeys rushing through landscapes of shadows that rose up tall and threatening against the stars. He knew the towering shapes were trees, but the knowledge didn't help much. Sheet lightning flared across the sky; off in the middle distance, the clouds over Elk Hill had begun to glow with a fitful greenish light. All in all, the road was sufficiently well-lit that Larry turned off the headlights, the better to escape whatever watchers the Radiance might have set on the countryside. Sensible as that was, it made the journey more spectral, the tall shapes of the trees more unnerving.

Finally the car pulled off the road just before the crest of the ridge. "Here you go," said Larry. "Straight ahead, then follow the road to the right as it goes downhill. At the bottom you'll be on the road that goes past the ruins to Chorazin." Owen and Justin both thanked him, and he grinned. "Sure thing. See you soon, Tsad Thog willing."

They got out of the car and started up the road. Behind them, Larry backed up, turned, and headed back the way they'd come. Once the noise of his car faded past hearing, a tense hush filled the night. No wind stirred. The trees huddled together, waiting.

From the crest the valley spread open before them, a chasm beneath the lightning-tinged sky. The lights of Attica burnt in the distance like murky stars, but the landscape closer by lay wrapped in blackness, and the great silent mass of Elk Hill stood black against the flickering greenish light like a hole cut in reality.

"The day we got here," Justin said as they walked, "when you mentioned the other side, I wanted to ask you who they were. After that, not so much." He made a rough noise in his throat that passed for a laugh. "Was Keel one of them? If he was, I've tangled with them already."

"I don't know," Owen admitted. "He might have been with them, or he might have been on his own. You get people like that, who learn a little sorcery and use it for their own purposes."

"Like Mad Dan Morris," said Justin; it took Owen a moment to place the name, and recall the stone figures in the Museum of Mystery outside of Lefferts Corners. "But I'm about to face a whole bunch of them, if they don't just open fire the moment they see us." He glanced at Owen. In the flickering light, his face looked pale but composed. "The Radiance—is that what they're called? What do I need to know about them?"

Owen considered that. "They're the enemies of the Great Old Ones," he said after a moment. "A long time ago they desecrated seven temples in the Middle East, bound the Great Old Ones so that they couldn't use more than a tiny fraction of their strength, and stole some powers our species was never supposed to have. They've got lots of money, lots of influence, lots of people with guns, agents in most of the world's governments. They think human beings are the masters of the cosmos, or ought to be—and they're the reason why so many people think that acting like the masters of the cosmos is a good idea."

"And the Great Old Ones are the masters of the cosmos?"

"No," said Owen. "The cosmos doesn't have masters. It's nobody's property. It just does what it wants."

Justin took that in, and nodded after a while.

"The Great Old Ones aren't even the most powerful beings in the cosmos," Owen said then. "The *Necronomicon* says that Cthulhu is their high priest."

"So there are things as far above them as they are above us."

"And things above those, and so on."

Justin gave him a startled look, said nothing.

They walked on for a while, and the crunching of broken pavement beneath their feet blended with the mutter of distant thunder and the first sighings of wind in the branches of the trees that lined the road.

"Are they our masters?" Justin asked then. "The Great Old Ones, I mean."

"Depends on what you mean by that," Owen said. "Some of them have humans who serve them. Some of them are willing to do things for us if we return the favor. Some of them won't have anything to do with us at all. The thing is, we're just not that important to them. They've seen plenty of species come and go."

"And we're just one more passing by."

"Basically."

Justin made the same rough sound in his throat. "That's comforting, in an odd way."

"I know," said Owen. Another silence passed, broken only by their footfalls.

"So what are we facing?" Justin asked then.

"A Radiance negation team," Owen told him. "A paramilitary force led by an initiate of theirs. They'll have assault rifles, and they might also have ways to mess with your mind."

"Like on the way back from Miz Eagle's place."

"Yeah. The Tcho-Tcho cord might protect you from that, but it might not."

They walked on. Elk Hill loomed ahead, blotting out more and more of the sky. The muttering of the thunder grew louder, and the greenish glow spread through the clouds above the hilltop, joined by a red glow from beneath; the fire had been lit atop the hill. The road ran straight between tall trees for a time. Then the trees failed, a dirt road went off to the left, and great heaped masses of bramble loomed up beyond, spectral in the unsteady light.

Justin turned to Owen then. "Before we go in, I just want to say—thank you. You could have sent me on from Dunwich with some advice, and I'd have been happy with that. If we both get out of this in one piece, I owe you one, big time."

Owen nodded. "You're welcome. I may take you up on that one of these days."

A bright flash of lightning seared the sky to the west. Seconds passed, and then thunder shook the air around them. As the last echoes muttered into silence, a rifle shot sounded in the distance, and then another: the signal they'd arranged.

Owen and Justin looked at each other, and then crossed the dirt road. The wind was rising, hissing in the brambles, and it seemed to form words: *the hour falls.*

This time nobody had to ask the brambles to open a path. A broad trail led straight in toward the broken chimney, wide enough that Owen and Justin could walk side by side. The flickering glow in the sky, up over the crest of Elk Hill, had become bright enough that they could see their way easily. Owen, falling back into habits from his army days, glanced from side to side as he went, listening intently with his ears and his intuition alike. He could feel the presence of danger all around him, but nothing stirred and no unexpected shapes or shadows could be seen in the tangled briars around him. Then—

Then he realized that something was following them.

Owen felt it clearly, though he heard no footsteps and saw nothing when he glanced back over his shoulder. He couldn't sense anything but the raw fact of presence, for it seemed to change with every step: now an animal, now a human being, now a shape vaster than Elk Hill. It took an effort to pay attention to anything else, but he wrenched his awareness back to the task at hand. Whatever it was, the thing that followed was no soldier of the Radiance.

They passed the wrecked chimney, struck out for the brick mass and the trench before it. Lightning blazed again, flooding the ruins with harsh unforgiving light, and the wind hissed its message more loudly, in tones that might have come out of the cold heart of space: *THE HOUR FALLS*. The lightning gave them their bearings, and they picked their way past masses of bramble and broad patches of bare ground until the low mounds of soil came into sight.

Another bolt of lightning, off to the south of them, poured blue-white light straight down the trench. It was more than ten feet deep at the northern end, where it ended at a wall of brick—a wall pierced by a great circular opening that led into darkness.

Justin glanced at Owen, and started toward the trench.

All at once light flared again—but it was not lightning. Half a dozen beams of brilliant light converged on each of their faces, blinding them.

A musical laugh Owen recognized at once sounded above the muttering thunder. "And here they are," said the voice of Rowena Slater. "If you're going to dabble in these matters, you really have to be more careful about talking to strangers, Mr. Owen Merrill."

* * *

It took an effort for Owen to keep his reaction off his face. "No comment?" she said then. "Pity. Maybe you'd like to know that a negation team's been sent to Dunwich. Yes, we knew you were there. It just wasn't worth our while to act."

"Slater," a man's voice said, warning her: a deep voice with a rough edge to it.

She laughed again. "Humor me. It's not often I get the chance to enjoy a victory like tonight's. In another twenty minutes, this whole business will be over once and for all, and the Sleeper in the Hill will never whisper in anyone's dreams again."

Justin's breath caught. "You hear her," he said.

A silence, and then she spoke again, her voice sharper. "That's irrelevant."

"Slater," he went on. "Of course. You had an ancestor named Pieter Slaader, didn't you?"

Thunder, rumbling in the middle distance, filled the stillness that followed.

"Fortunately," she said, then, "that's irrelevant too. It's all over—do you understand me? Not just the thing that's bound in the hill, the Weird of Hali itself."

The words struck Owen like a physical blow, though he managed not to show it. Memories surged: the voice of Nyarlathotep, the story of the destruction of the Moon Temple of Irem and the doom invoked by its martyred priest, verses penned by a poet the rest of the world called mad. He forced his attention back to the present moment.

"Enough, Slater," the man's voice snapped. "Malkin, Jespersen, get these two—wrist and ankle ties, belly down."

"Before you do that," Owen said, and then raised his voice until it was loud enough to carry over the distant thunder: "Red Eagle."

In response, from the surrounding darkness, came the unmistakable sound of rounds being chambered in dozens of deer rifles.

The negation team members were professionals. They scrambled for cover at once, switching off the flashlights, preparing to return fire. As Owen's eyes cleared, he saw two people maybe ten feet from him, crouched in the trench for shelter. One was Rowena Slater, still in her expensive outdoor clothing, staring at him with a shocked look. The other was a man in his forties he was sure he hadn't seen before, dressed in military camo. Lightning flared, showing an angular clean-shaven face, harsh blue eyes.

"Sir," someone said a few yards away. "No IR trace at all."

"Pity about your night vision gear," Owen said at once. "I hope it's still under warranty."

The man's eyes narrowed, and without a word he straightened up, pulled a pistol from his belt and pointed it straight at Owen's face.

"Kill either of us and you and all your men are going to be dead in a few minutes," Owen told him. "You're surrounded, you're outnumbered, and the light over the hill is bright enough to make you really good targets. There's an alternative."

The man said nothing.

"You've already lost this round," said Owen. "The ritual's going to happen with me or without me, but you and your people can still leave. Go now and nobody's going to stop you."

"No!" Rowena Slater said. "Dyson, we can't. This is our one chance."

"I have operational command," he replied, without looking at her. He paused, his eyes still fixed on Owen, and then said, "Allen?"

"Sir," said one of the men crouching in the trench.

"Team to staging area. Secure and report."

"Yessir." He came up out of the trench, and five others rose and joined him. They left at a trot, crouched and wary as wolves.

"Dyson!" Slater snapped, furious. He ignored her, kept the pistol pointed at Owen's face.

Sheet lightning flared across half the sky. Against it, a looming shape rose high up above the ruins of the van der Heyl mansion, reaching out black paws. Owen did his best to keep his concentration on the negation team officer in front of him, the gamble he could still lose.

Finally an earpiece the officer wore hissed and muttered something, and he said, "Cody? Team to staging area. Report."

Six more men scrambled to their feet and headed off into the darkness. The pistol did not waver. Thunder rumbled, and the glow over the hilltop flickered and brightened. At last the earpiece hissed and muttered again, and the officer said, "Beckman, we're out of here. Slater—"

Lightning struck the ruined chimney behind Owen, flooding the scene with light. The thunder broke a moment later with stunning force. Only when it had died away to muttering echoes did Owen realize that someone was sitting on the top of the rough brick wall at the far end of the trench—someone wrapped in rough shapeless garments, whose eyes gleamed fierce and intent out of the wreckage of an ancient face.

"No," said Sallie Eagle. "She'll stay right here."

Slater screamed.

The officer turned, gun lowered to hip level, ready to shoot. He gestured with his left hand, and the other negation team members got to their feet and moved warily back from the trench. Beyond them, the thing with black paws stood half-visible against the flickering sky.

"She can't leave," the old witch said. "Let her try to step in any direction she likes, it'll take her straight toward the door."

"Dyson," Slater shouted. "Get me out of here."

The officer glanced at her, the witch, and Owen, and did not move.

"No, child," said the witch. "He can't help you. You drugged your dreams to silence and told yourself you came here of your own will, and all the while you were answering the call." She glanced up at the officer. "Time for you to go," she told him. Her smile showed sharp teeth. "You and your men. Go and don't come back, or you won't leave ever again."

"Dyson!" Slater shrieked.

"You don't have much time," the witch said to Dyson. "Go."

He started backing away. His men were already most of the way to the chimney. Owen turned to face him. Their eyes met. The officer nodded once, slowly, and went after his men.

"No," Slater's voice rose unsteadily. "No."

"It's too late for that," the witch replied. "Much, much too late. You've come, willing or otherwise, to undo what your ancestor did." Justin's sudden gasp was drowned out by rumbling thunder. "Do it." The witch's voice was a hiss. "Open the door."

All at once Slater clawed at her jacket, pulled out a handgun.

Faster than thought, one of the black paws plunged down. Owen saw only a blur of motion as long snakelike things tangled around Rowena Slater and dragged her shrieking up into the sky. The shriek ended abruptly. A moment later, something tumbled down from above and landed hard on the ground beside the trench: the pistol she'd drawn.

A moment of thunder-edged silence passed, and then Justin said aloud, "Ms. Eagle."

The old witch regarded him, said nothing.

"I don't know what Jan Maertens did—but I'm here to try to make it right." He drew in a ragged breath. "Tell me what I have to do."

"Good," she said. Black eyes gleamed in the flare of distant lightning. "Willing, that's stronger than unwilling, and might just get you through." Her voice rose, harsh and shrill. "The door, child. You've seen it in your dreams. It's older than the hill, older than the land itself, but your ancestor helped close it. It binds the guardian to this place, and so long as it stays closed the wrong can't be set right." She motioned toward the dark opening in the brick wall below her. "Open it. Open it if you can."

* * *

Justin nodded, slowly, and began to walk into the trench. Above him, the black paws loomed, growing more solid as the light strengthened. For the first time Owen saw the writhing shapes that splayed out from them. Lacking any other option, he began to chant the Vach-Viraj incantation: "*Ya na kadishtu nilgh'ri stell-bna—*" It felt useless, worse than useless, against the vast twisting form that towered above them, but it heartened him to hear Justin join in, repeat the ancient words in an unsteady voice.

Then one black pawlike shape plunged down, as it had for Rowena Slater.

A few feet above Justin's head, no more, it flinched back. It rose up, plunged again, and the same thing happened. Whether it was the incantation, the Tcho-Tcho cord, or another protection—Owen suddenly recalled Sallie Eagle handing cups of potion and saying, "It'll protect you from worse than colds"—he didn't know, but something kept the Worm from reaching its prey.

Lightning blazed, and Justin stumbled forward toward the circular opening ahead of him. His voice shook as he repeated the chant, and so did he, but he kept going. Owen watched him reach the black circle and disappear within it.

Silence crouched over the valley like a beast of prey prepared to spring. Justin's muffled voice, still repeating the Vach-Viraj incantation, sounded with uncanny clarity in the night. Owen kept his attention on the chant, barely heard the sounds of the rattle of an ancient latch, the shrill despairing cry of the hinges as they turned for the first time in centuries.

Then the sky above him exploded into light.

High above, lightning surged down from the cloud to strike each of the standing stones atop the hill—but these were no ordinary bolts, blazing for a moment and then gone. They remained, incandescent and writhing, joining the hill and the billowing clouds above it in branching lines of light. Thunder shook the hill like the roar of a furious beast, and a sudden sharp wind came rushing down from the hilltop, taut with the scent of ozone.

In that same moment, something changed in the voor upon the hill. Owen sensed the change at once, though it took him a moment to be sure what it was and another to guess what it meant. The wrongness knotted into the voor of the hill surged and strained, and then all at once came undone, and voor flowed out all at once through the moon paths, east, west, south, shattering and torrential. For a moment vertigo seized Owen, and he felt the earth tumbling away beneath him as he tore himself free from intolerable heat and pressure. The moment passed, and he realized that he'd sensed the liberation of the Worm.

As he struggled to keep his balance, the old witch sprang to her feet with a terrible cry of longing, faced the dark mass of Elk Hill. Great masses of brambles flowed away to either side like water as the ground bared itself to her, revealing the stream that flowed from the hill, the stone slab above the spring, and three figures who stood there with their arms raised, tracing strange arabesques of gesture together. If they were chanting, the thunder drowned their voices.

The witch cried out again, but her voice had changed. Deeper, more resonant, it rang above the thunder in a torrent of sounds that no human throat could have uttered. She flung her arms toward the sky and strained, and all at once the shapeless clothes and the body that had been Sallie Eagle's broke apart like dried leaves and tumbled away in the wind.

In their place was something vast and dark that rose towering into the sky. In the flaring light, Owen could make out only glimpses—the coarse rank pelt that covered a mighty hip, the dark curve of an abundant breast, the arc of a great curved horn silhouetted against the lightning—but that was enough, and he fell to his knees. The voice called out again, triumphant.

Then the world dissolved into light. An instant later, darkness swallowed everything, and a moment after that, rain came down hard in a blinding, drenching torrent. Owen choked and spluttered, and by the time he could perceive anything around him but darkness and streaming water, the vast presence was gone.

Between the light and the downpour, though, he'd heard the one thing that mattered:

Another unhuman voice raised in answer, trembling, uncertain, but alive.

The rain streamed down. Owen clambered unsteadily to his feet, tried to get his bearings. The trench was somewhere nearby, he knew. The trench—and Justin.

He moved in what he thought was the right direction, stumbled and nearly fell when one foot lodged in what had been a heap of dirt and was now a mass of sticky mud. Another few steps, and the ground sloped away before him. Ahead, something splashed in a black pool.

"Justin!" Owen shouted.

Justin's voice cried out something unintelligible in answer. Owen scrambled ahead. He was knee-deep in the pool before his outstretched hand touched a bedraggled sleeve. He could see nothing, but another hand seized his and nearly pulled him forward into the water. He fought for balance, nearly lost it twice more, then finally got his feet under him and hauled on Justin's hand. Step by step they clambered, and finally made it to level ground.

"Owen," Justin said, "Owen, I saw—" His voice trailed off. Making a renewed effort: "I—I saw—" He gave up. "There aren't words."

"It's okay," said Owen. "I know."

The rain began to slacken as they stood there. Elk Hill loomed over them, black against the lesser darkness of the clouds. Minutes passed, and off to the west, a first sprinkling of stars appeared at the horizon.

"Owen?" Walt Moore's voice, calling from a distance. "Justin?"

"Over here," Owen shouted back.

Mud splashed, and all at once a flashlight played over the sodden ground off to the east. A short time later the old man came up out of the darkness. "You two okay?"

"I think so," Owen said.

"Good to hear. We're still making sure everyone's accounted for, but it looks good."

"What about the other side?"

"Piled into their SUVs and drove off in a hurry. They must be halfway to Buffalo by now." He motioned toward the old road, and they followed. "Come on—there'll be something to eat at the church. We always have a party after the ceremony, and this time—" He laughed. "This time, we've got even more to celebrate. The Tcho-Tchos brought some cars down if either of you need a ride back to town."

"Justin might," Owen said.

"No." Justin shook himself. "No, I'm fine." A slow lopsided grin creased his face. "I'm still breathing, and the Sleeper's free at last. It doesn't get much better than that."

* * *

The walk back to Chorazin was dream rather than nightmare. The last of the clouds blew past, letting stars blaze down, and though everyone was dazed and stumbling there was always an outflung arm to catch those who lost their balance. Somewhere in the process he'd given the red Tcho-Tcho cord to one of the old men, but he couldn't remember when, or which one.

When they passed the rock where he and Justin had met Robin Hale the last time, Owen murmured a prayer for the boy's sake, but that was the one coherent moment in a long journey in darkness. Worries pressed against him, about Laura, Asenath, and the people in Dunwich, but he knew there was nothing he could do. They'd stand or fall by their own strength and that of the Great Old Ones they served, and he'd have to wait for news of their fate, the way that Laura and the others waited for news of his.

Back at the motel, a hot shower and dry clothes did much to jolt him out of his daze, and once those necessities were taken care of, he and Justin crossed the street to the Starry Wisdom church and went around back. The door was wide open and light spilled out of it. That was allowed on special occasions, and this May Eve, Owen knew, would be remembered as a special occasion as long as Chorazin endured.

They went down the stairs and through the hallway. As they came into the social hall, some of the Chorazin folk at the nearest table spotted them and started clapping. A moment later everyone else in the hall was applauding, and some of them were on their feet. Justin turned bright pink. As the noise died down, Cicely Moore came over to them, took Justin's hand and said, "Mr. Martense, bless you. You did it."

"Seems to me," Justin said, "that a lot of other people did plenty, too."

"I won't argue," said the old woman. "We had our work to do up on the hilltop, so did the ladies down at the spring, and I know Mr. Merrill and our boys and the Tcho-Tchos had to be there and do their part, too, for you to do yours." An expression too ambivalent to be a smile bent her lips. "But if the door hadn't opened, none of the rest would have mattered a bit."

The expression passed, and she waved them to the tables. "Sit yourselves down, both of you, and someone'll get you something to eat and drink."

The social hall was crowded enough that it took them a while to find empty seats. Finally they found places to sit near the end of a table. Owen slumped gratefully into his chair and let his eyes drift shut for a moment, only to be roused by a familiar voice.

"I'm glad it worked out," Jenny said. She'd come up to the table's end and stood there, considering him. "It would have been pretty wretched if—" She let the sentence trail off.

"I won't argue," said Owen

She glanced at Justin, then at Owen again. "We could see the road from where we were—Patty, *Dzha* Pakheng, and me. Watching the two of you walk right up there into the gunsights of a negation team taught me something about courage."

Justin mumbled something inaudible. "It seemed like the best thing to do," Owen said.

That got them both a broad smile. "We'll talk sometime soon," she said then, and headed back to wherever in the crowd she'd been sitting. Owen glanced at Justin. He was watching Jenny, and for one unguarded moment a tremendous longing showed in his face. It was only a moment, and then he put on his lopsided smile as though he was shrugging on a coat.

Food and drink arrived promptly, carried by a bevy of middle-aged women in aprons—one of the church guilds, Owen guessed—and kept on arriving thereafter, in impressive volume and variety. Uncle Gyoreng had apparently joined the kitchen crew and brought fixings with him, for a steady stream of rice and noodle dishes heated to incandescence with pepper sauces and curries found their way out of the kitchen along with plenty of down home Chorazin cooking. Bottles of the golden-brown Asian beer the Tcho-Tchos preferred shared space on the tables with big glasses of mahogany-colored beer brewed in Chorazin cellars.

Maybe half an hour later, when food and beer had taken the sharp edge off the day, there came one of those moments when everyone happens to stop talking at once. In the stillness, Owen heard a rhythmic sound overhead. It took him a moment to recognize it:

Footfalls.

They paced down the length of the worship hall from the sanctuary to the stair. Well before they reached the latter, Owen recognized the long swinging stride. He wasn't the only one to do so. Tcho-Tchos around the room got to their feet nearly as quickly as Owen did, and Patty Dombrowski, three tables away, let out a little low cry and stood, staring upwards. Justin, jarred awake from a doze, blinked and pulled himself out of his chair. By the time the footfalls sounded on the stair, everyone stood waiting, and the Tcho-Tchos were bowing with hands folded.

The footfalls finished their descent, and shadows stirred in the doorway. A long black coat swirled, dark eyes in a lean dark face regarded the room from beneath a broad-brimmed black hat: the soul and mighty messenger of the Great Old Ones was among them.

He waved them to their seats. "You've earned your rest and your celebration," he said, his deep voice ringing through the silence. "Tonight's work was well done."

"Lord Nyarlathotep," said Cicely Moore, still standing. "Welcome."

"Thank you," he said. "I'm glad to say the reasons for my long absence no longer apply, and you'll see rather more of me in the years to come. Tonight, though, I'm here entirely in my capacity as messenger, to bear a message of thanks from the Great Old Ones.

"Justin Martense." Justin sat bolt upright. "You took my advice and followed it despite everything, all the way from Paris to the door you opened tonight. Owen Merrill, you understood the hint I sent your way and made sure, in the teeth of no small danger, that Justin got to the place he needed to be. Jenny Chaudronnier, you hurried here on no notice to do the work my masters asked of you. Patty Dombrowski, you freely offered to do the same thing. *Dzha* Pakheng, *dzhalabeen* Tcho-Tcho'*ya*—" A motion of his head included all the Tcho-Tchos in the room. "—you took another hint, and made sure that there would be enough sorcery and armed force on hand to stop the Radiance if it came to a fight.

"And the people of Chorazin—yours was the hardest road of all. Since Mishkwapelethi brought Sarah and Micah Moore to this place, you kept the promise they made; you performed the rites on Elk Hill, endured prejudice, exile, the death of friends and children, and never knew why—because your part, a part no one could be allowed to know, was to keep the Sleeper alive."

Utter silence filled the hall. "The men who bound her with their spells hoped that she would die as Great Cthulhu did, without the strength to dream herself back into life as he will. The rites kept her from perishing. The medicine people of the Seneca did those for many years, until the smallpox came through. That was why Mishkwapelethi made his journey and the Moores came here—because I asked them, and they consented.

"And all through the years that followed, we moved each of you, silently, like pieces on a gaming board, and you did everything we hoped. The Sleeper in the Hill is awake and free."

"Old One," Bill Downey said, "who is the Sleeper?"

Nyarlathotep considered him. "I wonder if any of you have guessed that."

A silence passed, and then Jenny Chaudronnier spoke. "I think I have, Old One."

His glance called her to go on.

"Yhoundeh the elk goddess," said Jenny.

A slow smile spread across his lean dark face. "Excellent," he said. "Yes. Someday I'll want to hear how you figured that out. But you're quite correct: the Lady of the Beasts is awake at long last, and the woods and fields will no longer be safe for those who despise her."

Silence coiled in the room for a moment, and then Justin spoke. "Old One," he said, "what happened to Sallie Eagle?"

"There never was any such person," said Nyarlathotep. "The hands that brewed tea and shuffled cards for you, that healed colic and sore throats in this town across the years— those hands belonged to the Black Goat of the Woods herself. I don't imagine she'll take the form of Sallie Eagle again, but invoke her and she'll answer. You've all earned her gratitude."

"Old One," Cicely Moore said then. She had risen to her feet again, but her head bent as though the weight of more than her own years pressed down on it. "I'm glad, gladder than I can say, that we've done what we did—but what will we do now? The rites on the hill were our life. We lost the lore, we lost our songs, and now the rites—" Her voice trickled away.

"You kept faith with Yhoundeh in her time of need," Nyarlathotep told her. "Don't think she will abandon you now. There will be new ceremonies upon the hill, new lore to teach, new songs to sing. And for the time being—" A broad smile creased his face. "Celebrate."

Then, in the blink of an eye, he was gone.

* * *

Another half hour or so slipped by. Justin, blinking and rubbing his eyes, said his goodnights and headed for the motel. Others had already gone, leaving the social hall less crowded. Owen considered following them out the door, but something whispered a caution in the deep places of his mind: not yet.

Then, in another moment of silence, he heard the wordless summons.

He got to his feet. Others stood as well: Patty Dombrowski, Jenny Chaudronnier, Cicely Moore, Bill Downey, Grandma Pakheng. Six, Owen thought, counting himself. He knew well enough who the seventh would be.

They gathered at the foot of the stair. Cicely went up first, to perform the necessary rites, and Bill murmured to those who weren't Starry Wisdom initiates the word and sign for the use of honored guests. They climbed the stair in single file, entered the worship hall with appropriate words and signs, went down the hall's length, and passed between black pylons into the sanctuary beyond. There seven chairs of Gothic design stood in a circle around a curiously angled pillar four feet high, atop which a dark crystal in a complex metal fitting rayed out what faint light filled the room. Behind each chair rose an abstract figure carved of dark wood, barely visible in the dim glow, resembling nothing so much as the famous statues of Easter Island. The rest of the sanctuary was drowned in shadow.

Two of the places were already filled. The chair just to the right of the empty eastern point was the place of the senior adept, and there Cicely Moore sat, her face serene as the statue high above it. The chair in the west was traditionally left empty for the messenger of the Great Old Ones, but it was not empty now. A familiar dark figure sat there, and his onyx eyes regarded each of the others as they filed in and took their seats.

"I have certain messages for each of you," Nyarlathotep said. "Mrs. Moore has already received hers. Mr. Downey, a year from now you will become senior adept of this church, so you will need to make the necessary preparations."

Bill stared at the Great Old One for a moment, then closed his eyes and nodded.

"Mrs. Moore will not be dying quite yet," the Crawling Chaos said then. "She has certain tasks to perform—among them, the founding and consecration of a new church where one existed many years ago—and someone else will need to attend to the work of the church here. You'll need to be ready to accept converts. It has been a while, I know."

Bill gave him an astonished look, said nothing. Nyarlathotep turned to Grandma Pakheng. "*Dzha* Pakheng," he said, "you and your people have been very patient. I know how hard it's been to stay in the cities, when so many of you long for farms and pastures like the ones you had across the sea. It was necessary that you stay in hiding—but it's necessary no longer. There are farms and fields waiting for you, here and in other places where the worshippers of the Great Old Ones dwell. Seek them; you'll find them."

The old woman beamed. "*Dzha yanh, Tcho Khyoron*," she said. "Thank you."

He turned to Jenny. "Miss Chaudronnier, to you I have only this to say. You may know that there was once a great quarrel between Yhoundeh and—shall we say, another Great Old One. Yhoundeh knows who sent you here and whose wisdom guided you, and she wishes me to say that the old quarrel is ended, once and for all. She feels herself to be deeply in his debt."

"I'll tell him, Old One," Jenny said.

"He knows," said Nyarlathotep. "But it's important that you know, too." He turned to Patty. "You have a journey ahead of you," he said, "and friends and family waiting at its end to replace those you left behind."

"That's what I was told, Old One," she replied.

"Good. The father of your child has made—certain arrangements. Be patient, and those will become clear to you."

"Thank you, Old One." Her eyes shone in the dim light.

He turned to Owen, and a slow smile creased his lean dark face. "You're worried about your wife and child, and about the people of Dunwich. They were warned in time, and reached safety well before the Radiance arrived. There are still certain risks, but—" The smile turned hard and dangerous. "Certain powers the Radiance has not measured are at work. I don't think the people of Dunwich will be in danger much longer."

"Thank you, Old One," said Owen. Then: "One of the Radiant initiates said something I need to tell you about."

"Please do so."

"Rowena Slater said this when she thought she'd won: 'It's all over—do you understand me? Not just the thing that's bound in the hill, the Weird of Hali itself.'"

Nyarlathotep regarded him for a moment, and then nodded. "We've long suspected that the Radiance knows much more about the Weird than we do. Thank you; it's useful to have that confirmed."

"To stop the Weird, to bind a Great Old One," Owen said, baffled. "I didn't think human beings had the power to do anything like that—not by themselves."

"They don't," said Nyarlathotep.

Silence filled the sanctuary. "There are deeper magics and older troubles at work here than you know of," the Crawling Chaos told him. "If you're fortunate—if this world is fortunate—you'll never have to learn about them."

CHAPTER 12

THE MAN OF STONE

That night, Owen dreamed that he was climbing Elk Hill, following a path through brambles that had turned green with new spring leaves. Birds fluttered everywhere. Someone walked beside him, though for a reason he did not know, he was forbidden to look at her. All he could see of her was the shadow she cast on the trail before them, as they crossed the southern face of the hill and the sun rose out of morning mists behind them: slight curves of a slender body, lean as a runner's; long straight hair sweeping out like a pennon in the wind; and above her head, branching like summer lightning, the great spreading antlers of an elk.

"Not everyone I called heard me," she was saying, in a voice light and quick as water splashing over rocks. "Not everyone who heard came in answer, and not everyone who came took part in setting me free. You did all three, and so I am minded to give you three gifts. You may choose them, or you may ask me to choose them for you."

Owen laughed. "Great Lady," he said, "I know the answer to that riddle. You have the wisdom to choose the right things. I don't."

Her laughter joined his. "It is well. One gift I give you now. Your wife, your child, others you care for—they are pursued by their enemies and yours, who are also mine. Is it not so?"

"Yes, Great Lady," Owen said.

"They are safe. By the time the sun rises over Dunwich, the ones who pursue them will be no more. Do not ask me how. You will learn soon enough."

"Thank you, Great Lady."

"It is a little thing," she said.

They reached the top of the hill. The standing stones stood golden in the sunlight; the dull green flecks had turned bright, like tiny emeralds, and the voorish dome above the hilltop rose clean and rejoicing to the skies. "This was a place for my worship," Yhoundeh said. "They turned it into a trap. I was caught, and others of the Great Old Ones might have been caught, too, had they been unwary as I." Her voice went low and cold, so that Owen shuddered at it. "For that, there will be a reckoning." Then, turning to him: "I may ask your help in that."

"Great Lady," he said, "I chose my side in that war two and a half years ago. Of course I'll help, in any way I can."

"It is well," she said again. She turned to face west, then, across the dim morning landscape toward the low bleak shapes of the Attica prison and the lands beyond. "This poor half-ruined world," she said then. "My fish that thronged the deep, my herds that filled the plains, my flocks that darkened the skies—so much wasted and killed, and so little, so very little left." Her voice dropped low again, into a harsh whisper: "There will indeed be a reckoning."

With those words, Owen blinked awake.

He was lying in bed in his room at the Elk Hill Motor Inn, with morning light filtering through the curtains. A glance at the clock showed that he couldn't have had more than four hours of sleep, but that and the two hours or so he'd gotten at the Tcho-Tchos' house felt like enough. He blinked again, rubbed his eyes, and got out of bed.

All through his morning routine—Starry Wisdom meditations, workout, shower, and the rest of it—he felt something obscure but forceful tugging on him, pulling him toward the door and the world outside. In the shower, he prodded the feeling, tried to figure out what it might be. It reminded him, absurdly enough, of memories from his childhood: the last day of school, when he and his classmates sat fidgeting at their desks in a gray windowless room, waiting for the bell that would send them spilling out into summer's warmth and freedom.

He toweled off, pulled on his clothes, left the room.

One part of his dream stood before him in the clear morning light. The brambles on Elk Hill had burst overnight into leaf, and birds, scores of them, wheeled about the hill and perched on the tangled green canes. Amazed, he crossed the parking lot to the edge of the briars. Little furtive shapes scurried under the cover of the brambles, and flower buds had sprung up amid the thorns. There would be flowers soon, he guessed, and berries come late summer, and he guessed the berries would be like none other in the world.

Movement caught his attention, and he turned. Someone had come down from the hill onto the parking lot, out past the twisted pine at the lot's far end. Owen waited, and presently saw that it was Justin. He crossed the parking lot, noticed as he did so that the younger man looked dazed. "Justin," he called out. "Are you okay?"

"Yeah," he said as Owen came up to him. "I'm fine." He blinked, tried to focus. "Apparently," he said then, "I'm going to be a father."

It took Owen another moment to process that. "Shub-Ne'hurrath?"

"After the storm," Justin said, "when I asked for her help, I offered to do something for her if I could. She took me at my word."

"Not the first time that's happened," said Owen. "She's a fertility goddess, after all."

"No kidding." He met Owen's gaze then. "My child's going to be named Robin."

Owen took that in, and nodded "I'm glad to hear that."

"I'm not sure what I'm going to do, but ..." He shrugged.

"I've got a suggestion." In response to his questioning look: "Your Aunt Beast talked about how much she wanted babies to spoil."

Justin's face broke into his lopsided grin. "You're right, of course. I'll probably be staying with her for a while anyway, while I figure out what I'm going to do."

He stopped, then, reached into a pocket, and pulled out a packet wrapped in a frayed silk cloth. Owen recognized them at once: the cards Sallie Eagle had read for Justin in the little shack west of Elk Hill. "She gave me something else," Justin said. "I don't know how to read them, but she said they'd teach me."

"Have you tried that?" Owen told him.

Justin gave him a bleary look. "Not until I get some sleep."

"You do that," said Owen. Justin put the cards back in his pocket, and crossed the parking lot to the door of his room. Owen stood looking after him until the door closed.

* * *

He went to the unnumbered door, found his way to the breakfast room, got a cup of tea steeping and waited until it was nearly black before squeezing out the bag and taking a sip. Walt Moore was doing something in the kitchen that involved crackling sounds and the scent of hot butter, and Patty Dombrowski had apparently managed to sleep past dawn for once. Owen sat back, sipped his tea, and tried to let the events of the days just past settle into an order that made some kind of sense to him.

He was still at it a quarter hour later, and Walt had put one tray of hotcakes and another of sausages into the steam tables, when the door opened and Jenny came in, looking bright-eyed and cheerful. They said the usual things, and Owen unfolded himself from the chair and followed her over to the counter to get some breakfast. That occupied the following minutes, but when his plate was empty and she'd finished fixing a cup of coffee with milk and sugar and curled up in a chair across the table to enjoy it, he said, "Do you mind if I ask you a question or two?"

"Go ahead."

"How did you figure out that Keel had the lost Prinn translation?"

That got a sudden smile. "I didn't actually know for sure until he started conjuring from it." She sipped her coffee. "I knew that whoever had it had to live close to Elk Hill, close enough to find out right away when somebody started poking around the van der Heyl house. I also knew that whoever it was had to know a fair amount about the old lore. Keel was the logical person on both counts, since he lived in sight of the ruins and knew enough about Hyperborea to identify a pottery shard from the Uzuldaroum period. That was reason enough to go talk to him, and it took less than five minutes for him to convince me that he almost certainly had the book."

"Okay," Owen said. "I must have missed something."

"Did you see how he reacted when he saw me? He sensed the Ring of Eibon the way you did—people who don't practice sorcery or spend time with the Great Old Ones are oblivious to it, the way Justin is. The drug he put in our drinks confirmed my guess, and since I already knew what he would summon, and had a spell ready to banish it, I took the risk of confronting him." She gestured with her cup. "But I knew as soon as you and I talked that he might not be acting alone, and that there was a pretty good chance the Radiance knew all about the Sleeper."

Owen gave her a puzzled look. "How so?"

"Justin said that one of his relatives got called here in each generation—say, once every twenty or twenty-five years. Mr. Moore said that they got someone coming here from outside every ten years or so, and at least two of them were convinced that something evil slept under the hill and they could get rid of it—which isn't something that any of Justin's people were likely to think. That meant that someone else knew about the Sleeper."

"It actually meant that someone else was being called," Owen said, and described Rowena Slater's words and Justin's response to them.

"That makes sense," said Jenny. "I thought that was possible, but I wasn't sure."

He nodded after a moment. "And when did you guess who the Sleeper was?"

"Before we finished talking the night I got here." In response to his startled look: "Elk Hill, Huntey Creek, the winged elk of copper Keel had and the one you saw above the spring. The winged elk was Yhoundeh's symbol in Hyperborean times—and that got me thinking." She drank more of her coffee. "Before 1457, you didn't just kill animals for fun. All over the world there were traditions, ceremonies, taboos, and everyone knew that if you got stupid and greedy and killed more than you needed, you'd go out hunting one day and never come back. After 1457, it took a while for memories to fade, but it wasn't that long before whole buffalo herds were being killed and left to rot on the prairies, and whales were being harpooned by the thousands to make corset stays and dog food. So it wasn't too hard to guess what happened."

Owen was nodding by the time she finished. "All very straightforward," he said. Then, with a smile: "And I'm feeling more than a little stupid for missing it."

"Don't," she said, giving him a distressed look. "The only reason I was able to figure things out so quickly is that you asked all the right questions and went looking in all the right places. That's a talent, too. Besides, I had an unfair advantage."

He gave her a questioning glance, and she laughed. "It's kind of silly, actually. I'm doing a paper right now on the poet

Justin Geoffrey, and he wrote a sonnet that gave me one of the clues I needed. I'm pretty sure he must have come here himself. Do you know it?"

Recognition dawned. "'The mound was old before the white man came.' I've had that line stuck in my head since the day we got here, and I couldn't remember the rest."

"That's the one," she said, and recited:

> "The mound was old before the white man came.
> The crown of ancient stones upon its crest
> Stood long before the first sail ventured west
> From Europe's crowded shores. What secret name
> It might have had in those far distant years
> No legend tells. It stands against the sky
> Forgotten, while strange clouds go drifting by
> And breezes hint at vanished hopes and fears.
> Yet those who dwell beneath it murmur low
> That deep within the mound, with vast wings furled,
> Some mighty presence from the elder world
> Lies bound in sleep. How long? They do not know.
> They wait and watch, and chant their ancient lore,
> Until the hour the Sleeper sleeps no more."

When she was finished, Owen nodded slowly. "One way or another," he said, "I'm glad it all worked out the way it did."

"So am I." Jenny considered her coffee for a moment, then: "The business with Aubrey Keel—in a way, it's really sad. He was a young man when he got the book, you know. My guess is he happened to walk past Chorazin, got the urge to explore the abandoned town, forced open a door or a window in the church building, and found what was obviously a rare old manuscript, just left there to rot. He took it home with him and started dabbling in what was in it, and that drew the attention of the Radiance. Then an unexpected visitor showed up, making precisely calculated offers and veiled threats, and before long he was just a cog in their machine. No wonder he stopped writing poems."

She shook her head. "But he made his choice, and he's gone. Rowena Slater made hers, and she's gone too." Glancing up at Owen: "And now we know something about the Weird of Hali that nobody outside the Radiance knew until last night—that it has something to do with Yhoundeh's imprisonment and release."

"True enough. Was there anything about the Weird in the copy of Prinn?"

"No, but there are amazing things in it. I took some time to read through it when you were asleep yesterday evening. Some of what got left out of the later editions is dangerous stuff; there's a potion that's supposed to turn a living body into stone, and some other—what is it?"

Owen's eyes had gone wide. "Can you wait a moment?" he said. "There's a booklet I want to show you."

* * *

"The kids and the old folks are going," said Walt Moore. "Just for a little while, until we're sure the Radiance isn't about to come back shooting. If they do, we'll be ready for them."

"I bet," said Owen. Around them, the lobby radiated a familiar aura of discomfort and foreboding. The clock on the wall ticked loudly; the hands showed a few minutes past ten.

The old man grinned. "Me and some of the others have been talking with the Tcho-Tchos," he said. "They're good people. We're going to be seeing a lot of each other from here on. But some of our folk are going with them to Buffalo, and the others to a couple of towns down in Pennsylvania and Ohio—we heard back from them this morning and they're glad to help." His smile went away. "We haven't heard from Dunwich yet. I'm sorry."

Owen nodded, said nothing.

Just then the lobby door creaked open and Patty Dubrowski came in. "My ride's about to go," she said. To Walt: "Mr. Moore, thank you for taking such good care of me. I'll see you soon, I hope." She turned to Owen, and suddenly flung her arms around him. He returned the hug. "Keep in touch if you can, okay?" she said when she drew back. "And stay safe."

"I'll do that," Owen promised. "Where are you headed?"

"Buffalo for now. I'll be back here once everything's okay." She glanced back over her shoulder at the glass door and apparently saw a signal. "Gotta go—take care, both of you." A moment later the door swung shut behind her.

"You know where you're headed?" Walt asked then.

"I'll settle that with Justin once he's up," Owen said. "Probably back to his aunt's place in the Catskills for now. After that—" He shrugged. "Depends on what news I get."

The old man nodded. "If it's really bad news, you'll be welcome here, you know."

"Thank you," Owen said.

"Sure thing. And if things turn out better'n that—why, don't be a stranger. Next time Ben and Cassie come out here for deer season, why don't you and Laura come along?"

"That sounds like a plan," Owen said. Then, thinking of the dream he'd had: "I wonder if that's even going to be an option now, though."

"I talked to Bill Downey about that," said Walt. "He's pretty sure we can ask the goddess to teach us the right way to do things—and of course we never did take more than we needed, and you can bet your butt we're not going to start now."

The lobby door opened again, and this time Jenny came in. She had a stack of paper under one arm. "Well, that's taken care of," she said. "Any idea yet, Owen?"

He shook his head. "Still waiting on Justin." In response to the question she hadn't asked: "No word from Dunwich yet."

She gave him a worried look, sat down on one of the ugly chairs. "Let's hear it for old photocopiers," she said, setting the stack of paper on her lap. "We got all of it."

"The translation?"

She nodded. "Once I get this home to Kingsport there'll be more copies made. There are dozens of spells in here I'm sure I've never seen anywhere else."

The door to the lobby creaked open a third time, and Justin came in. He stopped dead in his tracks, staring at Jenny, then blinked and said, "Good morning. Where's everyone going?"

"Off to safe places for a couple of weeks," said Walt Moore. "Just to make sure the other side doesn't make trouble. Some of us and some of the Tcho-Tchos are staying here in case they do. You three probably ought to get clear of here before long—though I'll say to you two what I already said to Owen: don't be strangers. Any time you want to come this way, why, you've got friends and a place to stay."

"I'll do that," said Justin. "Thank you—and if you or anybody from Chorazin is minded to visit the Catskills, just let me know."

The phone rang back in the office, and Walt excused himself and went to answer it. "Any word from Dunwich?" Justin asked Owen.

"Nothing yet. I had something that might have been a message from the Great Old Ones in my dreams this morning, but—" Owen shrugged. "It might just be a dream."

"I get that," Justin said. "If if was my family I'd be worried sick. You know you can stay with Aunt Beast as long as you need to." Jenny gave him a startled look, and he laughed. "Josephine Hasbrouck, my aunt. An old lady who looks a little odd—she's got a hereditary disease—but you won't find anybody nicer." He drew in a breath. "Miss Chaudronnier—"

"Please," she said. "Jenny."

He turned pink, but nodded. "Jenny, then. If you want to take the bus back home, that's okay, but if you'd like a ride, there's room in the car and I'd be happy to drive."

"I can take the back seat," Owen said.

"No you don't," Jenny told him. "On the way here from the bus stop you looked like a pretzel back there." She turned to Justin. "Please and thank you—and there's actually a reason why I'd like to go to Lefferts Corners. Owen told me about Slater's Museum of Mysteries. Do you think they can handle losing their prize exhibit?"

Justin looked blank for a moment, and then realized what she was saying. "The Petrified People," he said. "So they're real after all."

"I'm pretty sure of it," she said, "and that means two people and a dog deserve a better fate than the one they've had."

"You can undo the spell?"

"It's all in here." She patted the stack of paper in her lap. "We'll need to stop on the way and get a few things—some chemicals and an old perfume atomizer if we can find one— and then stop again for a little while so I can get everything properly mixed. The spell's easier to reverse than it is to cast, and I've got an advantage Dan Morris didn't—but we'll have to find a phone book or someplace with internet access, so I can find what I need."

"You always used to carry a smartphone, didn't you?" Owen asked her.

She nodded, laughed. "I had to give that up. They kept going dead after a few weeks—sorcery and electronics just don't mix."

"I can call around once we get someplace that has cell phone service," Justin said. "After I call Aunt Josephine. She deserves my first call."

* * *

A long day of driving later, gravel crunched beneath tires as Justin's car turned into the parking lot of Slater's Museum of Mysteries. The old building looked even more deserted than it had the first time that Owen had seen it. Beneath the cloudy evening sky, the last of the red seemed to have trickled out of the paint on the cinderblock walls, and the flags hung limp in the still air. Owen wondered if the museum was still in business.

Justin shut off the engine and turned half around in his seat. "Is there anything I can do?" he asked Jenny.

She considered that. "Maybe. We'll see what happens."

They got out of the car. Jenny pulled out a shopping bag from the seat beside her. Justin took it from her and carried it as they crossed the parking lot to the door. The neon OPEN sign was off, but a piece of cardboard with the same thing written on it in red marker stood propped on a window next to the main door. Justin pulled the door open, and Jenny went in first, with Owen following close behind.

Behind the ticket window, the same gray-haired woman looked up from what might as well have been the same crossword puzzle. "Can I help you?"

"Yes, you can," said Jenny. She pointed her left thumb toward the woman and said a word in a language Owen didn't know, and the woman's face went slack. "You can let us into the museum when I tell you to," said Jenny, "and then you can fall asleep, stay that way until it's time to close the musem for the night, and forget that you ever saw us."

The woman stared with blank eyes, said nothing in response.

Jenny turned to the others, put one finger to her lips, and then locked the front door, took down the makeshift OPEN sign, and set it on the floor as though it had fallen. She went to the turnstile, motioned for Owen and Justin to follow her, and said aloud, "Let us into the museum."

As though sleepwalking, the woman reached for the button on the wall. The turnstile buzzed as Jenny went through, then Justin, and Owen last of all. "That's good," Jenny called back through the doorway. "Now sleep, and feel much better when you wake up."

The woman slumped forward on the counter, nestling her head on her arms, and closed her eyes. After a moment her soft snoring whispered through the still air.

Jenny gestured then—which way?—and Justin led them through the rambling museum. When they were a couple of rooms away from the entrance, Jenny whispered, "Once we're out of earshot it'll be safe to talk." Owen and Justin both nodded.

They passed the murals made of thumbtacks and postage stamps, the room full of optical illusions, and the Skull of Mystery. Beyond it was the room of the Petrified People. Jenny stopped in the doorway, drawing in a sudden sharp breath, and then went to the glass wall, which was nearly chin high on her. "Is there a door?"

"Over here," Justin said.

The door was over in a corner, the same height as the wall, and half hidden in shadow. Justin reached over it and fumbled with the latch for a moment, and then pulled it open. The three of them went through. "Okay," Jenny said. "The dog first."

"To make sure it works?" said Justin.

Jenny glanced up at him, amused. "No, it'll work. I just need to be sure of the dose."

She knelt in front of the dog and took the sign saying "Petri-Fido" off its neck. One hand fished a secondhand atomizer full of pale golden fluid out of her shoulderbag. She murmured something over it, and then squeezed two puffs of the fluid into each of the animal's nostrils.

For a moment nothing happened, and then the nose began to change color. It darkened and moistened, and the fur behind it turned brown. Moment by moment the change spread. As the very tip of its tail turned back to fur, the dog trembled, and let out a low unsteady whine.

Jenny chanted something under her breath, and patted its head. The bristling fur on the dog's back sank down and its tail essayed a tentative wag. Jenny scratched its ears, then stood up. "The woman next," she said. "Rose. It would help if the two of you could turn your backs."

She got clothing out of the shopping bag as Owen and Justin dutifully looked away. Owen heard Jenny's voice mutter again, then the faint hiss of the atomizer four times, and then a long silence, a sudden ragged breath, and a faint cry.

"Shhh," Jenny said quietly. "It's okay."

"Oh my God—" said a woman's voice, shaking with fear.

"It's okay," Jenny said again. "I gave you the antidote. Let's get some clothes on you."

Cloth rustled. "Owen, Justin," Jenny said then, "you can turn around now."

Owen turned. Rose Morris, very much alive, was sitting on the floor, dressed in the garish orange muu-muu Jenny found in a dollar store on the way, touching her face with her hands and staring at nothing. A moment later she had something to look at, for the dog came bounding over to her with its tail wagging frantically, and licked her face. She gasped, cried out "Rex!" and flung her arms around it, then buried her face in its fur and let out a muffled sob.

Meanwhile, Jenny took the atomizer and went to the man who was lying on his side. She murmured the words again, and then two squirts of the solution went into each nostril. Once again, time passed, and then the terrible gray color of the stone faded into the brown of a well-tanned nose. The color spread as Owen watched, until the statue had become a living man who blinked, drew in a sudden hard breath, and grabbed Jenny's arm in a frantic grip.

"It's okay," Jenny said yet again. "I've just given you the antidote for the thing Dan Morris dosed you with. You should be fine now."

Arthur Wheeler stared at her for a long moment, then sagged. "Thank you," he said. Then: "But—where—poor Rose—"

"Oh my God," said Rose. "Arthur?"

Jenny got out of the way. A few minutes later, Justin carried the shopping bag of clothing over to the two of them and said, "Mr. Wheeler, you might find these useful."

Arthur blushed, thanked him, and pulled on a tee shirt and sweat pants. While he was busy, Rose Morris turned to Jenny and said, "Ma'am, can I ask a really big favor of you?"

"What do you have in mind?"

"That antidote—don't use it on him." She indicated the gray stiff shape of Mad Dan Morris. "For the love of God, please, just leave him as he is."

"That's what I intended," Jenny said.

Rose stared at her for a moment, and then started to cry. Arthur took her in his arms, and she crumpled against him and sobbed while Rex, tail wagging, pressed up against her and made whimpering noises down in his throat.

* * *

Jenny walked to the other end of the exhibit. Owen followed and, after a moment, so did Justin. "The one thing I hadn't thought of," Jenny said in a low voice, "is what to do with them now. It's going to be a tremendous shock, dealing with everything that's changed since 1930."

"I've got a thought," Justin said. "Aunt Beast. She loves house guests and dogs."

"That could work," Owen said.

"I can give her a call," Justin said, and when the other two agreed, he went into the room of two-headed calves, got out his cell phone and started dialing.

"Forgive me, but—" said Arthur Wheeler then. "What the hell is this place?"

Owen and Jenny both turned to face him. "Are you sure you want to know?" Owen asked point-blank. When Arthur nodded firmly: "What it looks like. You've been on display."

Arthur winced. "How long has it been?"

Owen glanced at Jenny, who nodded. "Most of a century," he said, and told him the year.

Arthur flinched as though he'd been struck. Rose took his hand and squeezed it in both of hers, though, and his face softened; he raised her hands to his lips and kissed them, and then said, "Well." Then: "I suppose I'll just have to cope with that."

"We're finding the two of you a place to stay," Jenny said then. "Three, counting Rex." The dog, recognizing its name, wagged its tail enthusiastically. "Someplace where you can get used to everything that's changed since—" She gestured, at a loss for words.

Justin came back into the room again. "I've talked to Miss Hasbrouck, and she'd be delighted to have house guests." He turned to Rose and Arthur. "Miss Josephine Hasbrouck is an aunt of mine, a lady in her sixties. She looks a little odd—she's got porphyria, so she's got hair all over her face—but you won't meet a nicer person."

"Hasbrouck," said Arthur. "Are we by any chance in Ulster County?"

Justin's eyebrows went up. "Yeah. How'd you know?"

"I used to get stone from a couple of quarries up this way." His voice faltered. "I don't think I'll ever be able to carve again, not after—" He stopped, mastered himself. "But I knew a man named George Hasbrouck who had that same ailment. Furry as a bear, and couldn't go out in sunlight at all."

"Kin of mine, then," Justin said. He glanced at Owen and Jenny, then at Rose and Arthur. "We should probably get going," he said then. "There'll be tourists sooner or later. Besides, I don't know how soon you two will want a meal, but Miss Hasbrouck sets a fine table."

"That," said Arthur, "sounds very promising."

They filed past the two-headed calves, the Native American artifacts, and the Dutch colonial relics to the gift shop. "I'll need a few minutes," Jenny said then. "Justin, can you bring the car up to the door? I didn't think of shoes, and I don't imagine these two will want to walk over gravel with bare feet."

"Sure," said Justin, and left. Jenny went to the door behind the cash register and slipped through it. Owen turned to the others and said, "Care to step outside? It's a pretty nice day."

"Please," said Rose.

Outside the evening sun slanted down between great masses of white cloud, glowed on the green slopes of the Catskills. A hawk circled high above. Below, the distant rushing of traffic on the highway blended with the whisper of wind in the leaves. Arthur flung his arms wide and drew in a full breath, let it out in a rush. Rose looked around wide-eyed, as though trees and gravel and cloud-dotted sky were wonders never before displayed to human sight. Rex stayed close to his mistress, sniffed the air and everything else within reach, and wagged his tail.

Out in the parking lot, Justin's car rumbled to life, and drove slowly over the gravel to the exit door. Arthur turned at the sound, and considered the car with a quizzical look on his face, until it rolled to a stop in front of him. "With all due respect," he said to Owen then, "that has got to be the ugliest thing I've ever seen."

"I won't argue," said Owen.

Just then the door opened behind them, and Jenny came out. "I've left a note for the woman at the desk," she said. "I apologized for making off with you two and Rex, told her what happened—in general terms, at least—and asked her, when the museum finally closes for good, to have someone toss Dan Morris overboard into a lake, so he'll stay as he is forever."

Rose stared at her for a moment, and then said, "Thank you." A moment later, turning suddenly pale. "But—you—you must know about—"

"Sorcery?" said Jenny. "Yes, but there's much more to it than the kind of thing Dan Morris did. I'm just glad I could be of help."

"You're glad," said Arthur, and suddenly laughed, a great ringing laugh that came echoing back from the hillsides and sent Rex capering and barking around them with his tail wagging briskly. "You're glad? If you're half as glad as I am, you must be wondering why you're not carrying on like Rex here." Abruptly serious: "You saved my life; you saved the life of someone who deserved it much more than I ever will—" He smiled at Rose, who blushed. "—and you even took the trouble to save poor Rex. If that's what—sorcery—is supposed to be about, then frankly, I'm for it."

Jenny glanced up at him, a faint smile on her thin pale face. "Thank you," she said.

CHAPTER 13

THE GIFT OF YHOUNDEH

It took some work to get everyone into Justin's car. Jenny, Rose, and Arthur managed to squeeze into the back seat together, and Rex bounded up and lay across them, with his head and forepaws in Jenny's lap and his tail beating an enthusiastic rhythm on Arthur's chest and the back of the driver's seat. Finally, Owen got into the passenger's seat, Justin climbed behind the wheel, and the engine grumbled to life. "We don't have too far to go," Justin said encouragingly as he turned the wheel and headed for the exit.

"I think I'll manage," Arthur said. "I certainly can't complain about the company."

The highway wound past forest and farmland and tall pale cliffs. Out of the corner of his eye, Owen could see Arthur staring out the window, nodding as familiar landmarks went by, blinking in surprise as something unexpected came into sight. Rose nestled her head against his shoulder and closed her eyes. That reminded Owen of Laura, and he closed his own eyes for a moment, until the stab of loneliness and longing had passed.

Finally the car came to a stop on the street next to Aunt Beast's driveway. "Here we are," said Justin as he yanked up the parking brake. They managed to coax Rex out of the back seat—he seemed content to play lapdog to the end of his days—and then piled out of the car. Justin led the way around back to the kitchen door, knocked loudly twice, and then opened it and went in. The others followed, Owen last of all.

By the time he closed the door behind him, Aunt Beast had already come in from the living room. She made a beeline for Justin, flung her arms around him and murmured something Owen couldn't make out, and then let go of him and turned to Rose and Arthur. "You poor dears. Justin told me what happened to you. How horrible!" She smiled at Owen, and then turned to Jenny and stopped still for a moment, staring at her right hand.

"This is Jenny Chaudronnier," Justin said. "A friend of Owen's from Massachusetts."

"Very pleased to meet you," Aunt Beast said, recovering. She waved them all into the living room. "Make yourself comfortable. And you," she said to the dog. "What's your name?"

"Rex," said Rose.

"Why, that's a grand name for a big pup like you," she went on, as though the dog had answered. "Let's get you some water and something to eat."

She went back into the kitchen; dishes clattered, water splashed, something edible landed in a bowl, and then she came into the living room again, pursued by an assortment of lapping and crunching sounds. "I'll get him a soup bone once he's eaten," she said, as though the dog's welfare was obviously the first concern of them all. "Can I get you coffee or tea?"

They got that settled, cups made their appearance, and for a moment no one said anything at all. Aunt Beast glanced around the room and effortlessly filled the gap with harmless talk about the Adirondacks, directed at Rose and Arthur, and about Massachusetts, aimed at Jenny, and before long the six of them were chatting companionably enough.

After a second round of coffee and tea, though, Aunt Beast excused herself and went into the kitchen to get dinner going.

Rose murmured something to Arthur and went after her, and though the old woman made a pro forma protest, a few minutes later the two of them were talking cheerfully while pots clattered and something began to sizzle on the stove.

In the living room, the conversation faltered. After a few moments of silence, Arthur said, "I certainly don't want to pry, but—well, I was in France in the Great War, and I remember the way men looked when they'd just come out of one fight and were about to go into another. I'm more grateful than I can say that you rescued Rose and me, but—" He fell silent.

"You're wondering what you might get dragged into," Jenny said.

A quick unwilling smile touched the sculptor's face. "Partly, yes."

Jenny shook her head. "You're right that we've come from one set of troubles and we might be heading into another, but that's not something you have to worry about."

"Is it something I can help with?" he asked.

Jenny glanced at Owen, who said, "No. Right now your place is here with Rose."

Arthur nodded, after a moment, and said, "If there's another time—"

"There might be, someday," said Owen. "If there is, you'll hear from us."

"And in the meantime," Justin told him, "I'd be grateful if the two of you would stay with Aunt Josephine. She's getting on in years, and things aren't as safe around here as they used to be. If everything goes well, I'll be back in a couple of days, but—" He shrugged.

"I can do that," said Arthur. "I'm—I was—an amateur boxer, and a pretty good one, if I might say so." He looked at his hands. "It still feels like yesterday."

"It was," said Jenny. "For you, Rose, and Rex. It's just the rest of the world that did something else."

The sculptor glanced at her and nodded, but said nothing. Out in the kitchen, Rose and Aunt Beast laughed together.

* * *

Dawn showed gray through the windows when Owen picked his way down the stairs the next morning. He'd made an early night of it, pleading tiredness, and slept hard. If any dreams came to him, they vanished before he woke.

He half expected Aunt Beast to be busy in the kitchen, but the only light downstairs was in the living room, and the only person there was Jenny, who was perched on the edge of the sofa, concentrating on a set of round stone disks the size of coins, which she'd laid out in a strange pattern on the coffee table in front of her. She glanced up as he stopped in the doorway, said, "Good morning, Owen."

"Good morning," he replied. "If you need me to go somewhere else—"

"Not at all."

He sat down in an armchair facing her, watched as she moved the stones one at a time, her lips moving as though repeating some silent chant. Finally she sat back, looked up at him again. "Do they teach the Mao games in the Starry Wisdom church?"

"No," Owen admitted. "I don't think I've ever heard of them."

"My family's from Poseidonis," said Jenny. "All the old Kingsport families are. The Mao games are one of the things we brought with us."

"Do the Kingsport families have much to do with the Deep Ones?"

"No, and we probably should." She started picking up the stone disks, putting them in a pouch of silk brocade. "The Atlanteans had dealings with the Deep Ones, or so I've read, but when the rest of Atlantis went under—" She glanced up at him, grinned. "I'll risk the pun: we got really insular. Since Poseidonis drowned, especially, we've kept to ourselves. There were some raised eyebrows in Kingsport when I started studying with Abby Price, but I'd like to talk to the Deep Ones someday."

"That won't be hard to arrange," said Owen. "All the Innsmouth folk have Deep One relatives, you know, and my wife Laura's a priestess in the Esoteric Order of Dagon."

Jenny's eyebrows went up. "I really look forward to meeting her, then." When Owen said nothing: "For what it's worth, three voolas of the Mao games tell the future, and three more tell what's hidden in the present. I've played all six this morning, and they all told me that your family's safe. They're not infallible, but it's a good sign."

Owen nodded, and neither of them spoke for a short time. Jenny yawned, then, and blushed. "I'm sorry," she said. "I was up late last night talking to Josephine."

"I saw the way she reacted to your ring," he said. "I'm guessing she knows more about the old lore than she admitted to me."

"She's got a partial copy of the *Book of Eibon*," Jenny told him. "Probably the only thing that survived when the Starry Wisdom church here in Lefferts Corners was burned. From the time Justin left here until the time he called her, she was doing rituals of protection for him, dawn, noon, dusk, and midnight. She was terrified—she'd hardly touched the book before then, and she broke down and started crying, just talking about it— but she did it."

"I wonder if that's why the Worm couldn't touch him," said Owen.

"A good part of it, probably." She settled back in the couch. "I'll see if I can find a witch nearby who can give her some training in exchange for the chance to copy the book. One way or another, though, she'll be fine."

Owen gave her a questioning look, and she went on. "Sorcery deals with the unhuman. If you stay stuck in human fears, human jealousies, human passions, it'll drag you down, the way it dragged down Dan Morris, or Aubrey Keel. If you can step outside the human, and do what you've chosen to do just because it needs to be done—the way the Great Old Ones do things—then you can practice sorcery and not be torn apart by it. Josephine had to step outside her fears, and that's a really good start."

"Outside the human," Owen said, turning the idea over in his mind.

"Not everyone can manage it." She looked away, then, and her face tensed. Owen watched her for a moment and guessed what she was thinking. "Justin?"

She glanced back toward him. "You've probably noticed how he looks at me when he doesn't think anybody is watching."

Owen nodded. "Yeah. Not your style, I gather."

Jenny looked away again, and was silent long enough that Owen wondered if he'd accidentally said something hurtful. "It's not just that," she said at last. "The whole business—love, romance, sex—isn't my style. It just isn't."

He took that in, and nodded after a moment. "I knew a guy like that in the Army," he said. "Not straight, not gay, not anything, and he took a lot of crap for it he didn't deserve."

"I bet."

"Asexual—is that the right word?"

Her expression said "thank you" more clearly than words could. "Yes."

"With any luck it's a passing crush," he said.

"I hope so. I'd like to have his friendship."

Neither spoke for a few minutes. Outside, catbirds announced the morning.

"There's something you should probably know," Jenny said then. "When it comes to getting outside the human, I have a certain advantage."

"I thought you might be a child of the Great Old Ones," Owen said at once.

That got him a startled look. "Is it that obvious?"

"Well, to me, yes. Laura's a daughter of Shub-Ne'hurrath."

"Then I really *really* look forward to meeting her," said Jenny. "My father's Tsathoggua, and I've never had the chance to spend time with anyone else who's only half human."

Owen blinked in surprise. "You haven't?"

"They're not all over the place—" She saw his expression and stopped. "Are they?"

"If you look in the right places, yes," Owen told her. "There are something like eleven of them in Dunwich right now— that's partly because a lot of the people from Innsmouth are living there, but the Dunwich folk have their own. Wherever you find people who invoke the Great Old Ones, you'll find their children." With a sudden smile: "As Patty Dombrowski said, things kind of happen."

She considered that. "I had no idea." Then: "The Kingsport families have kept to themselves too long, I think. Maybe it's time—"

Stairs creaked as someone came down from the upper story, one slow step at a time—Aunt Beast, Owen guessed. Jenny stopped in midsentence and glanced at him with a smile; Owen nodded in response, and they waited for their hostess to arrive.

* * *

After a breakfast hearty enough to put the previous night's dinner to shame, Owen, Justin and Jenny said their goodbyes and climbed into Justin's car. Owen glanced back over his shoulder as Justin pulled out of the driveway. Aunt Beast was nowhere to be seen—the morning sun was already too bright for her— but Arthur Wheeler and Rose Morris had come out to see them off, and stood there hand in hand watching until Owen could no longer see them.

From there on it was the earlier journey in reverse. Narrow crumbling roads that wound among the Catskills gave way to a good two-lane road, then to the easy curves of a state highway, and then to the great gray line of US 87, sweeping north alongside the Hudson River past long-abandoned factories and fading river towns. They talked much of the way. Justin told stories from his time in Europe and the strange things he'd seen there, Owen shared some tales of the Starry Wisdom, and Jenny had the others silent and listening as she recounted legends of her ancestors and their flight from sinking Poseidonis.

By the time the car was climbing up into the Taconic Mountains, though, the conversation lagged. Owen tensed, though he knew that they wouldn't reach the first of the signs he hoped to see for hours more. In his mind, the hints offered by Nyarlathotep, the words of a goddess heard in a dream, and the equivocal assurance Jenny had given him balanced against everything he knew about the Radiance and their negation teams: efficient, experienced men like the ones he'd faced below Elk Hill, dedicated to the destruction of everything that mattered to him.

The miles dragged on. The Taconics gave way to the Berkshires; the car left New York for Massachusetts west of Pittsfield and crossed the Connecticut River east of Turners Falls, and followed the state highway east to Aylesbury. There Justin turned off the highway, followed Owen's directions into the middle of the old mill town, and finally turned up an undistinguished street that led through mostly abandoned storefronts to the edge of town.

One of those storefronts had been a print shop once, and still did a little desultory trade now and then for the sake of appearances. The thing that mattered, though, was a certain window in the second story, which had curtains of a peculiar design. By old custom, those curtains were closed in the daytime whenever the people of Dunwich had to flee their homes to escape the Radiance or any of the other perils they occasionally faced, and open otherwise.

They stood open. Owen stared at them, and let himself begin to hope.

Other signs of the same sort met them as Justin found his way to the old Aylesbury Pike and then away from it again, onto a narrow road that led across level country toward tall hills wrapped in forest and topped, here and there, with standing stones that were old millennia before the Pilgrims arrived. Jenny stared out the car windows at the hills, her eyes wide; Owen guessed she was seeing, as he did, the great voorish domes that rose above them, surging billows of the life force channeled through the ancient stones for purposes long since forgotten.

The road came to the feet of the hills, with Round Mountain a stark presence not far beyond them. Justin slowed the car to a halt, and turned to Owen. "Forward or back?"

"All the signs say they're okay," Owen told him. "Forward."

Justin nodded, and sped up again.

The road snaked among the feet of the hills, crossing steep ravines now and then on narrow wooden bridges, and the trees loomed huge and silent to either side. On they went, and suddenly the car rounded a curve and there, parked just off the road, stood four gray SUVs.

For one frozen instant Owen thought that the signs had misled him, and he'd gambled and lost everything. Then he realized that two of the SUVs had doors hanging open, and all of them had spring pollen from the trees dusted over them, at least a full day's worth of it. "Keep going," he said, before Justin could slam on the brakes. Justin gave him a startled glance but said, "Okay," and drove on.

Low scattered shapes lay in the weeds and tangled grass around the SUVs. Owen glanced at them and then wished he hadn't. He heard Jenny's breath catch, but none of them spoke until the road curved again and the SUVs were out of sight.

"Those were people," Justin said then, as though hoping he was wrong.

"What's left of them," said Owen. "Yeah."

One more great sweeping curve around the foot of Round Mountain, and a cluster of gambrel roofs came into sight, huddled between a steep-sided creek and the sheer wall of the mountainside. The thin line of smoke that rose unsteadily into the sky from a chimney here and there did nothing to chase off the look of desolation and abandonment that filled the town. The tumbledown houses seemed to exude the odor of decay, and the few half-seen faces that glanced out of windows at the passing car vanished at once as soon as they were glimpsed. As the road turned into Dunwich's main street and Justin slowed, the Starry Wisdom church, the humble public library, and the Standing Stone tavern looked empty and lifeless as rifled tombs.

Owen, seeing all this, let himself sink back into the seat and let out a sigh of relief. "Everything's okay," he said aloud. "The general store's another block—that's our first stop."

Justin grinned, and pulled over in front of the battered sign. "Give me a moment," said Owen then, unfastening his seatbelt. "I'll be right back."

A few moments later he pulled open the general store's front door and went in. Ken Whateley, who was leaning on the counter talking with the storekeeper Jemmy Coles, straightened up and broke into a broad smile. "Owen!" he said. "Welcome back. We heard from Chorazin last night that you were on your way, but it's good to see you."

"It's good to be seen," said Owen. "Everyone's okay? I heard you had some trouble."

The storekeeper laughed. "Everyone meaning Laura and the little one, first of all. They're fine, and so are the rest of us. Yeah, we had a bit of trouble, but it ended real fast."

"I saw the mess out just past Round Mountain," said Owen.

Jemmy nodded. "It was somethin' to watch."

"Laura and Asenath are up at her folks'," Ken said then. He turned to look out the window. "Who're the people with you?"

"The driver's Justin Martense, the guy I left with, and I can vouch for him. The woman in the back is Jenny Chaudronnier. She's a sorceress from Kingsport, out on the coast."

Two pairs of eyebrows went up. "I've heard of the Chaudronniers," said Ken, "and some rumors about a daughter of theirs."

"That's the one," said Owen. "Can I leave them with you for a few minutes? I want to let Laura know we're going to have company."

It was more than that, and all three of them knew it, but Jemmy Coles just nodded. "Sure thing. I bet I can even find somethin' for 'em to drink, if I look real hard."

They laughed, and Owen went back out to the car. A few minutes later Jenny and Justin were inside the store, and Owen left and headed up the street toward Jeff and Annabelle Marsh's house, a place big and comfortable enough that they'd had to put extra effort into making it look desolate. Two blocks uphill toward the steep slopes of Round Mountain, a right turn onto the nameless side street that ended half a block away in a fence and a goat pasture: the route was utterly familiar to him, but it seemed to stretch on for half of forever.

As he left the sidewalk and passed the crazily boarded-up front door, the kitchen door in back slammed open, and a moment later he heard the soft rushing sound Laura's tentacles made in grass, in place of footfalls. Then all at once she was in his arms, and the dear salt smell of her skin filled his lungs as they clung to each other.

"Owen," she said. "Father Dagon, I missed you."

He kissed her by way of answer. "You're well? And Asenath—"

"She's fine. I'm not sure if you heard, but we had some trouble." He nodded, and she went on. "Nothing serious, though it could have been." Then, looking up at him:

"The message we got from Chorazin last night had some very strange news."

"I have some stories to tell," Owen said.

"I bet," she answered. "So do I."

* * *

Introductions, tea splashing into cups, yellow light from the oil lamps: the living room of the Marsh house surrounded Owen with familiar sights and sounds, helped him convince himself that the world really had come around right again. He let himself sink back into the couch, felt Laura nestle against him and Asenath shift in restless sleep in his lap. Laura's father Jeff and her stepmother Annabelle sat on a second couch at right angles to the first; Jenny was curled up in the big armchair, and Justin leaned back comfortably in a ladderback chair that could have been the twin of one in his Aunt Josephine's house. Outside, evening drew on, and the first bats danced against a clear sky.

"We got word from the watchers, what would it have been, three nights ago," Jeff was saying. "The other side's sneaky but there are tricks we know that they don't, and so we had about eight hours' warning. We got the children, the old folks, everyone else vulnerable out first, to the old road on the far side of Sentinel Mountain—Laura and Asenath went with them, of course—and most of the others followed as soon as the folks from Stillwater arrived to pick them up. Some of the Dunwich folks and some of our young men stayed behind."

"With guns, I'd guess," Justin said with a smile.

"Among other things," said Jeff, with an answering smile. "We've got a few things the Deep Ones make that the Radiance really doesn't like."

Justin laughed, gestured for him to go on.

"So the negation team came into town and, when they didn't find anyone here, they sent patrols up into the hills. Our people fell back to just this side of the Devil's Hop Yard—they figured the other side had night vision gear, so they laid some traps and some false trails to hold them until dawn, and got ready for a fight come morning.

"And about five in the morning yesterday, just before first light, they heard shots and shouting, and then screams—the way they told it, screams like nothing anybody'd ever heard before. Of course they figured it was probably a trap, so they waited a while, then sent some scouts by a roundabout way to take a look, and what they found was pretty much what you saw by the roadside coming into town.

"As near as anyone can tell, what happened was this." He leaned forward. "Everything living in the forest—badgers and weasels, feral cats and those coyote-dog hybrids that're getting so common around here these days, deer, wood rats, snakes, not to mention bats and owls and nightjars—they all jumped the negation teams at once. They found some dead animals, but not that many. The Dunwich boys are good at tracking, and they said they all came in a swarm, the flying things clawing at faces and the others biting and scratching and kicking and goring whatever they could reach. They said—" He bit his lip, went on. "There were still animals feeding what was left when they got there."

For a little while nobody spoke. "Nyarlathotep talked about that," Jenny said then.

"True enough," said Owen, and quoted: "'The Lady of the Beasts is awake at long last, and the woods and fields will no longer be safe for those who despise her.'"

"I can well believe that," said Annabelle. "I've read some of her legends, though it's been a while. I don't know that it's accurate to call any of the Great Old Ones hot-tempered, but she's supposed to be as close to that as eternal beings get." She shook her head. "I wonder if the Radiance has any idea what it's facing."

Justin gave her a puzzled look. "Is she more dangerous than the other Great Old Ones?"

"More dangerous? No," said Annabelle. "But a good deal less patient."

Later, after dinner, Owen came back into the living room with Asenath in his arms—it had been his turn to change her diaper—to find Laura and Jenny talking like old friends. Justin was out in the kitchen, discussing something in low earnest tones with Jeff and Annabelle; the name of Shub-Ne'hurrath reached Owen's ears as he passed the kitchen door, letting him know what the conversation was about. As he settled onto the couch next to Laura, she turned to him and said, "Jenny's invited us to visit her in Kingsport. Do you think we can—"

"Of course." He didn't need to see the sea-longing in Laura's eyes just then to know how difficult it had been for her to spend so long this far inland. He turned to Jenny. "When school lets out for summer, maybe? For us, that's about half-way through June."

"That would work," Jenny said. "Miriam's headed for France this summer, reading dusty old tomes at the Université de Vyones, and I was planning on spending the summer at home for a change, reading dusty old tomes from the family library." She laughed. "Some sun and salt water would probably do me good—and the family's got shares in a private beach club, south of the old Wavecrest resort at Martin's Beach."

"That sounds wonderful," said Owen, "so yes, please, and thank you." He glanced down at the infant in his lap. "Asenath needs to get to know the sea," he said then, "and she has relatives she's never seen."

Asenath gurgled and made vague motions with her hands and feet. "She has the most remarkable eyes," said Jenny.

"The violet color runs in Dad's family," Laura replied. "Most of us have it for a few months after we're born, and then it turns brown—but now and again it stays. I hope Asenath's eyes keep the color."

"They might," said Jenny, considering the little face. "They just might."

"Jenny and I were talking," Laura said then, "about Yhoundeh, and how she was imprisoned and freed, and it occurred to us that there's another Great Old One who's in something like the same situation."

Owen took that in. "You're talking about Great Cthulhu."

"I don't know if it's even possible," said Jenny. "Not even the Great Old Ones know when the stars will come round right again, and to break the spells that bind him before that happens—" She made a little helpless gesture. "But I want to find out."

"To awaken the Dreaming Lord—" The possibilities dazzled him.

"I'm going to talk to the elders of the Esoteric Order of Dagon and the Starry Wisdom church," Laura said then, "and see if they know of anything relevant. Jenny's going to see what she can find in the old tomes. It may be a waste of time, but I want to try and so does she."

"If there's anything I can do," said Owen, "I'll do it."

"Thank you," said Jenny. "There may well be."

ACKNOWLEDGMENTS

Like the first two novels in this series, this fantasia on a theme by H.P. Lovecraft depends even more than most fiction on the labors of earlier writers. Lovecraft himself was the most important source of raw material for my tale, but his collaborations with other writers—in particular, William Lumley, the coauthor of "The Diary of Alonzo Typer," and Hazel Heald, the coauthor of "The Man of Stone"—were also valuable quarries in which many gems turned up. Robert Bloch, the doyen of modern American horror writers, wrote several Lovecraftian stories in his youth that also contributed mightily to my story; "The Shambler from the Stars" and "Servants of Satan" were particularly helpful, as of course was Lovecraft's elegant riposte to the former, "The Lurker in Darkness." The Hyperborean stories of Clark Ashton Smith and the Silver John tales of Manly Wade Wellman both contributed a detail here and there, as did tales by Robert W. Chambers, Arthur Machen, and August Derleth.

Several nonfiction sources also provided raw material for *The Weird of Hali: Chorazin*. The people of Chorazin, described by Lovecraft and Lumley (in typically insulting terms) as multiracial, are partly modeled on the Melungeons of Appalachia, the largest of America's multiracial minorities. I am especially indebted to Lisa Alther's lively memoir of her search for her own Melungeon ancestors, *Kinfolks: Falling Off The Family Tree*, for my introduction to the history of this proud and fascinating people. A different branch of Americana gave me Sallie Eagle's deck of divination cards—students of American occult folklore will recognize them as a variant of the Gypsy Witch cards, a traditional American cartomancy deck.

The spells used by Aubrey Keel and Jenny Chaudronnier in their magical conflict are in medieval Latin. The first was composed by Lovecraft for Robert Bloch's "The Shambler from the Stars;" the others are my inventions, copying the language of medieval grimoires. In order of appearance, they mean:

"Unto Thee, Great Unnameable One, by the sign of the black stars and of the sigil of toad-shaped Tsathoggua ..."

"Come, come, unhallowed Shambler of the Stars!"

"Slay them!"

"Stand. Stand back, aether-born monster, in the name of Tsathoggua and by the power of the Black Goat of the Woods with a Thousand Young. You have no power to harm us. Take up your lawful prey."

"Depart, monster, in the secret sevenfold name of Tsathoggua. Return to the upper air."

I also owe, once again, debts to Sara Greer and Dana Driscoll, who read and critiqued the manuscript. I hope it is unnecessary to remind the reader that none of the above are responsible in any way for the use I have made of their work.